DEATH IN THE WALLED CITY

Also by
Aditya Banerjee

Broken Dreams: A Callipur Murder Mystery
Stolen Legacies

DEATH IN THE WALLED CITY

An Old Delhi Mystery

Aditya Banerjee

This is a work of fiction. Names, characters, businesses, events, and incidents are the products of the author's imagination. Any resemblance to actual persons, living or dead, or actual events is purely coincidental.

Copyright © 2021 Aditya Banerjee

All rights reserved. This book or any portion thereof may not be reproduced or used in any manner whatsoever without the express written permission of the publisher except for the use of brief quotations in a book review.

ISBN: 978-1-7773578-4-9 (paperback)
ISBN: 978-1-7773578-5-6 (Electronic book)

To the few who travel but are unsure of their destination.

Table of Contents

Introduction · ix

Promotion · 1
Riots · 46
Aftermath · 85
Stranger · 114
Old Delhi · 148
Faith · 189
True Colors · 224
Spectacle · 270
Journey · 312
Revelation · 352

About the Author · 405

Introduction

Old Delhi, a walled city, was founded by the Mughals in the seventeenth century. They filled it with palaces, gardens, and mansions. Over the years, the grandeur and the character of the city have changed dramatically. By the time India became independent in 1947, it had become a crowded part of the expanding metropolis of Delhi. Post-independence, the demographic of the area changed with migrants from all parts of British India settling there. Only a few mansions or *havelis* now remain, and most of them have not been able to retain their past glory. Many of the crumbling buildings and neglected gardens have been replaced by modern buildings stacked against one another.

The population of Old Delhi is a mix of many ethnicities from different parts of India. It is a melting pot of different cultures and religions, and a mix of Hindi and Urdu are spoken in equal measure. Despite becoming extremely crowded with newer structures, it still boasts of national monuments. It is also well-known for its street food and bazaars. As the demographic of this part of the city changed, so did its economic status, with most of the power and wealth moving to New Delhi. Old Delhi also became a riot-prone area with constant skirmishes and communal fights. These disturbances led to several police outposts being created in an effort to maintain law and order.

Our story takes place in the winter of 1983. In January that year, Old Delhi was witness to a riot in which there were several victims. This story follows the exploits of a police officer and some journalists trying to get to the bottom of what happened to one of them.

Promotion

The New India Courier did not have many days like this. It had been lauded in the national media and the foreign press for its articles exposing corruption and archaic laws, which had made it difficult for whistleblowers to come forward. A series of articles and editorials had also uncovered systemic government bureaucracy that was stifling well-meaning attempts to bring about any change. In addition, anyone who tried to speak up from within the system was either being threatened with lawsuits or being muzzled by superiors. However, due to the spate of well-written and well-researched pieces in the newspaper, the general public had reached the consensus that things had to change. Even the slow-moving government machinery had grudgingly acknowledged that long-standing issues needed to be addressed. The politicians had seen a change in the public mood and had decided to follow suit. Across the political spectrum, many decided to ride the popular wave and bring forth laws supporting transparency and protecting whistleblowers. For some time at least, especially with the elections around the corner, they did not want to draw the ire of an increasingly politically conscious public by stifling change.

At *The New India Courier*, the task of putting together some of these important articles and making them public had fallen on Nitya Chaturvedi, a relatively young journalist who had joined the paper a little less than four years ago. Initially, there was a lot of skepticism, not only because of the topics she was trying to tackle but also because the senior management was co-opted by an exclusive old boys' club. Thankfully, for Nitya, that changed when some of them retired. The new people who replaced them were open to giving her a chance. Nitya knew that although the new folks were less chauvinistic, they still had their biases, and she would have to perform much better to make her mark. She had not disappointed and had spent almost a year and a half researching every aspect of each article. Initially, she worked on her own, but when her bosses realized that she could be onto something, they decided to give her a few new hires and interns who could help her. She managed them well and the results were nothing short of exemplary. In fact, most of the accolades that the paper received were due to Nitya and her team's efforts.

The senior management was delighted with the results. The circulation had increased dramatically, and *The New India Courier* had become one of the three top national dailies in urban India. By continuing on their current trajectory, they could be at the top in a year. Nitya managed to keep her team focused on research and insulated them from any distractions. She also made it a point to include the names of the researchers and give them their due credit on each article and editorial piece. Usually, the junior reporters did not get much airtime, so their names being published in the articles they had worked on was unheard of. This earned Nitya a lot of respect from her young team. Any misgivings that the male journalists might have had about reporting to her were short-lived. They knew that she was demanding but fair. Although some of them did not like her right away, they grew to respect her, and once the accolades started pouring in, they were more than happy to be associated with her. The owners and senior management decided to give her a promotion and move her to a coveted managerial position in the current affairs department. This was the most sought-after division in the paper. Nitya knew it was going to be a high-profile and stressful job, but she was ready for it. No one at the paper, male or female, had made it to this position till their forties, and Nitya was only in her early thirties.

When Nitya walked into *The New India Courier*'s main office on that beautiful January morning in 1983, the only thing on her mind was the meeting that she had been summoned to with one of the owners and the managing editor. She was looking forward to the meeting as it would cement her role as one of the main journalists of the paper. The day seemed brighter than usual to Nitya, and anyone who saw her would have noticed the bounce in her step.

The offices of *The New India Courier* were in Connaught Place, a prime location in New Delhi. The owners had bought the building nearly a decade ago, and now it had become one of the most coveted and expensive locations in the city. Having an office in Connaught Place enhanced the reputation and exclusiveness of the paper, or at least that was how it was perceived in the news business, and that's all that mattered.

The three-story building was entirely dedicated to the journalists and the management team. The paper itself was printed in a press in the outskirts of the city. This was partly because of zoning regulations that did not allow a factory with heavy machinery to operate in that part of town. It suited the employees just fine. Most of them did not want to share their offices with the blue-collar folks of the printing press. The paper and its journalists had a reputation of being snobbish and highbrow. Dissent was tolerated but only to a point. The senior management was well-connected to the upper echelons of the civil service and across the political spectrum. In their articles, they were careful to distribute the accolades and censure in equal measure across all the different parties.

When Nitya had moved from her previous role in a small regional paper to her current employer, it had been a dramatic change in many ways. *The New India Courier* was bigger and different in every respect. Nitya had been on a steep learning curve but had excelled beyond her own expectations. She was lucky, but she knew that she had worked harder than all her peers to get where she was. She had grown to like Delhi too. She especially enjoyed her office's central location, the hype that went with it, and with its surroundings. Most of her friends were either colleagues from work or neighbors from the building where she rented an apartment.

As she walked into the office building, she was greeted with friendly glances and gentle nods. Almost everyone had come to know of her after her recent editorials. She climbed the stairs of the majestic building to the second floor to reach her office. This was where most of the junior and mid-level reporters and journalists had their offices. The ground floor was reserved for the administrative staff, interns, new employees, and the support staff who helped in the maintenance of the building. When she entered her closed office, she realized that her days in it were numbered. She would soon be moving to the third floor where all the senior journalists, the management, and the owners had their offices. If there was one thing she missed about her previous employer, it was the lack of hierarchy. *The New India Courier* had a management structure so hierarchal that it could have given the famed Indian bureaucracy a run for its money.

Once she was inside her office, she quickly glanced at her watch. Since there was half an hour until the meeting, she could quickly review the files on her desk. She kept her purse in one of the tall cabinets in the office and locked it. As soon as she settled down to read the files, Swati, one of the junior reporters on her team, burst in with a big smile on her face. Nitya had repeatedly warned Swati to knock before entering, but to no avail. Today she was happy and didn't want to admonish anyone. Swati had joined the paper six months ago, right out of school. She was hardworking and eager to please. She followed orders, didn't ask too many questions but, by the same token, didn't show much initiative when taking on new tasks. Since Swati was still new, Nitya gave her some time to flourish. In her bright orange dress, Swati seemed even more cheerful than her usual talkative self.

"Good morning, ma'am," Swati said, with a giggle.

"Good morning, Swati," Nitya replied, with a smile on her face.

"I guess today's the day. I am so excited for you, ma'am. Do you know which office you will be getting upstairs? Who will be reporting to you? What will be your first story?" Swati rambled on as Nitya kept shaking her head. There was no way for her to get a word in. Finally, when Swati paused, Nitya took a deep breath and asked her to sit in one of the chairs across her desk.

"I don't know the answers to any of those just yet. Let's not get ahead of ourselves. I will get to know after the meeting, and I will certainly let everyone know then."

"Oh, you mean they haven't told you anything yet?" Swati asked, clearly disappointed.

"Not yet. Now I want you to go back to your desk and read up on the story you are working on."

"Sure, ma'am," Swati replied softly.

"As soon as I come to know, I will let all of you know. I promise."

"Thank you," Swati responded with a half-smile.

When Swati left the room, Nitya thought of how she had become a role model for many of the young women who had joined the paper. The only other woman in a senior position was a senior editor, but she was related to the owner. There were some women in their thirties and forties who were in mid-level positions, but they were usually never given the stories that could propel their careers. Most women at the newspaper were younger and in junior roles. That reflected contemporary India, where more women were joining the workforce. Although Nitya did not feel that she had an obligation to be a role model or mentor, she knew that her success could be a stepping-stone for many toward a rewarding career.

There was a gentle knock on the door. Through the large glass window beside the door, Nitya saw that it was Suresh, her trusted deputy and one she was closest to at work. Suresh and Nitya were about the same age, but he had been at the paper longer than her. He had helped Nitya the most at work, and she trusted him above everyone else. Shy and reserved, he was perceived as someone who lacked ambition, so while many of his peers were considered for senior roles, he wasn't. The senior management felt that he wasn't interested, though that was simply not the case. Suresh was happy to be working with Nitya. It had given him the visibility that he desperately needed. He was also hopeful that it would boost his stagnant career. Seeing the worried look on his face, Nitya thought to herself what a contrast he was to her previous visitor. Suresh was conservative in every sense—in demeanor, in outlook, and even in attire.

"Suresh, how are you?"

"I am fine, ma'am," Suresh replied.

Although of the same age, the strict hierarchy meant that he would need to address her as "ma'am," though Nitya had repeatedly insisted that he call her by her name.

"Something on your mind?"

"Yes."

"What is it?"

"It's about your promotion. Does it mean that we won't be reporting to you anymore?"

"I don't know. They haven't told me anything yet."

"We would still like to report to you. At least I would."

"Honestly, I don't know what their plans are, but I will know soon enough. I really must go to my meeting now. I wouldn't be too worried. You are very good at what you do. If I am given a choice in the matter, I will retain my entire team. Though, I am not sure if they will give me any say in what happens next."

"Understood, ma'am," Suresh replied, sounding a bit relieved.

"Don't worry," Nitya tried to reassure Suresh as she got up to leave.

"Congratulations on your promotion."

"Thank you," Nitya replied as she followed Suresh out of the room.

Nitya made her way toward the end of the hall toward the stairs. As she walked across the hall, she could see the desks of all the journalists. The closed cabins of the managers were lined up against the walls with windows. The journalists reporting to them had cubicles and desks in the middle of the floor. The giant hall with high ceilings could have resembled an indoor gym had it not been for all the desks, chairs, typewriters, cabinets, phones, and photocopiers. The chaos was compounded by the sound of the workers barking into their phones, some simultaneously smoking. Although the hall had ample lighting, the smoke emanating from the cigarettes made it seem dark and dingy. Nitya could sense their eyes on her as she walked across the hall. She smiled and nodded at them and on reaching the stairs, quickened her pace. She was partly excited and partly worried about what was in store for her.

On the third floor, she walked past a long corridor of closed cabins. Unlike the second floor, there were no open offices or cubicles on this floor. Here, hierarchy was maintained through the size of the offices. The senior editors, around thirty of them across different areas, had larger offices. In addition to the senior editors, there were around twelve directors across different departments like marketing, advertising, and sales. These directors headed the departments on the ground floor and the printing press outside of town. All the directors and senior editors reported to the managing editor, Manoj Vij.

Manoj had been at the paper for more than two decades. He had started in a managerial role and had slowly risen through the ranks to become an effective leader. He reported to the editor-in-chief, Prakash Jain, who was the owner of the newspaper, and its largest shareholder. Manoj and Prakash ran the daily operations. While Manoj focused on the content, Prakash focused on the business itself.

Prakash Jain was well-known and well-liked in the business community. In a country with well-established family businesses dating back decades, Prakash was a bit of an anomaly. He had started a small regional newspaper in Delhi in the late 40s and had slowly grown its circulation. He then bought out some small papers and consolidated them under a single banner. He had risked his family's wealth and personal reputation on the paper, and it had paid off. His fortunes were tied to the paper's growth. In a little more than three decades, Prakash had personally amassed a lot of wealth and created a name for the paper and himself.

Prakash and Manoj had met at university and had been close friends ever since. Initially, Prakash was unsure about hiring Manoj, since he already worked for a well-established national newspaper. Manoj, too, was uncertain of how things would work out when he applied for the managerial role. But Prakash was impressed with Manoj's work ethic, and when the senior staff started retiring, Prakash quickly decided to promote Manoj to a senior position. Their friendship had weathered the storms that came with running the paper.

It was Manoj's idea to hire Nitya. Manoj knew Nitya would be a good addition to their organization. He had read some of her articles in her previous paper. One article had caught his eye. Nitya had even received an award for it. When he had first contacted her, she had been unsure about joining, and this had surprised Manoj. He had assumed that she would jump at the opportunity to join a coveted paper like *The New India Courier*. He sensed that being a woman, she probably faced other pressures from her family. After a few months, she had suddenly called and asked him if the position was still open. He discussed it with Prakash, and they decided to hire her. Whatever their initial misgivings might have been, the decision to hire Nitya was one of the best that they had made. Not only had she excelled at her job, but her writing had improved the standard of the editorials. Even their competitors agreed that the quality of articles had vastly improved. People had started inquiring about the new additions at the paper that had brought about this change. Both Prakash and Manoj were aware of it. It was all the more reason why they wanted to make sure that Nitya stayed with the paper.

The only thing that bothered Prakash and Manoj were the rumors about Nitya's brief affair with Vijay Jha, one of the senior editors in the current affairs division. Since it was a personal matter, they didn't have the right to confront her about it. Their relationship would typically not have been frowned upon had Vijay not been married. Nitya and Vijay had been discreet and tight-lipped, but their co-workers had seen them together at clubs, parties, at the theaters, and other places. The sightings were enough to make them a subject of juicy gossip. Then suddenly, a few months back, things subsided. It almost seemed that there had been nothing going on. Whatever had happened seemed to be in the past, and the office folks moved on to new interests. With many young, unmarried, and unattached people joining the growing newspaper, budding relationships were common. Manoj and Prakash's urban mindset and upbringing had conditioned them to assume that these were bound to happen and it did not deviate them from their focus of growing the paper and hiring the best talent possible.

Manoj's office was at the end of the corridor. It was one of the two largest offices in the building; the other belonged to Prakash. Manoj's secretary, who had a desk right outside his office, stopped typing, greeted Nitya with a smile, and asked her to take a seat at the lavish sitting area usually reserved for guests. Nitya made herself comfortable in one of the sofas and leafed through one of the many magazines. As she waited, pretending to read, she couldn't help but wonder how far she had come in the last ten years. Now in her thirties, she had established herself as a well-known, sought-after journalist. Sometimes it had meant making choices that went against the norm. Although there were invariably some regrets, she had mostly enjoyed the journey. When Manoj had first hired her, she had insisted that she be given investigative assignments in the current affairs division. She could sense that her request had put Manoj in a difficult situation in the organization. But he had taken the risk of assigning her to high-profile stories that would have ordinarily been given to those who had been at the paper for a while. This had caused some friction among her peers, though they gradually realized that she was up to the task. Soon, even her most ardent detractors grudgingly admitted that her writing and research were well above par. Nitya also ensured that any accolades that came her way were shared with her team and this gave her a loyal following.

Nitya's only regret was her brief fling with Vijay. She couldn't quite reason with herself why it had happened. In her initial days at the paper, she was assigned to different senior editors on various stories that she had to work on until she had her own team. Vijay was the friendliest of the lot and easy to work with. He had also helped her adjust to the new job and the new city. They had gotten close while working on a story together, and that had led to a brief affair. She knew he was married, and they both knew that their affair wouldn't last. They had decided to end it amicably a few weeks after it had begun. She was happy that Vijay had never discussed it with anyone. Any gossip or rumor was just that. However, she knew that colleagues had seen them together and that had let their imagination run wild. Since her affair with Vijay, there had been no serious relationships. Nitya had gone out on a few dates that her friends had set up for her, but none of them had led to anything. Her mom had also "arranged" a few meetings with acquaintances, but those hadn't materialized either much to Nitya's delight and her mother's disappointment.

Just as Nitya was about to put down the magazine and pick up another one, Manoj came out of his office. A few senior journalists were filing out and once they had left, he walked up to her and smiled. Manoj's tall, lanky figure seemed out of place among those leaving the room. His six-and-a-half-foot frame was quite uncommon in India and Nitya thought he could have been mistaken for a retired cricket player, had it not been for the generous proportion of white hair and the thick spectacles.

"Nitya, good morning."

"Good morning, sir."

"I am sorry to have kept you waiting. The meeting lasted longer than I'd imagined. It seems that journalists like to not only write but also talk," Manoj said with a smile.

"We do," Nitya replied, returning the smile.

"Well, let's get to it then. Let's chat in my office. Prakash and Anand are there too."

Manoj's office looked like the office of a senior partner in a law firm rather than the editor of a newspaper. His office was just above Nitya's so they had the same view of the main road from their windows. Though, of course, Manoj's office was bigger and more impressive. His large, mahogany custom-made desk was at the opposite end of the window. There was a large comfortable chair for him and a set of four chairs across the desk for visitors. On the other side, opposite the door, was a sofa set and coffee table for when he would entertain visitors and colleagues. Along the walls in frames were famous newspaper headlines from all over the world. Nitya could spot front-page headlines on the end of the Second World War, India's Independence, the moon landing, Kennedy's assassination, and the declaration of emergency in India. She sensed that Manoj not only valued current events for their immediate impact but also viewed them in their historical context. This is what made him a good journalist.

Anand was already in Manoj's office. Although many senior editors helmed the current affairs department and directly reported to Manoj, it was well-known that Anand was the most experienced, and that both Prakash and Manoj highly valued his opinion. It was also common knowledge that if Manoj were to either retire or leave, Anand would take over as managing editor. Nitya had briefly worked with Anand and had been very impressed. He was a good leader, valued research, had a good command of the English language, and didn't mind collaborating on stories with other senior editors—all of which were required skills for running a national newspaper. Prakash and Anand were engaged in conversation, but when Nitya walked in they paused, walked over to her, and shook her hand.

Prakash motioned Nitya to sit on the sofa. Manoj and Anand sat on the other sofa on the other side of the coffee table.

"Do you want some tea, Nitya?" Manoj asked.

"I am fine, sir."

"Alright, let's get to it then," Manoj continued, "as you might have guessed, we have called you here today for two things. One, to tell you that we are extremely pleased with the work you have done so far. It has meant a lot to the paper and to us personally. Second, and more importantly, we want to give you a bigger role in the paper and make you one of the senior editors in the current affairs division."

"Thank you, sir."

It was Prakash's turn to speak. Unlike Manoj, Prakash was short, bald, and had a round, bulging figure. Had they not been her bosses, within the confines of a professional work environment, they would seem like quite the comical pair. Prakash was also the extrovert and the more talkative one. Although they had been classmates in university, Prakash looked much older than Manoj. The stress of starting, growing, and running the paper had taken its toll on him. He had built the paper ground up. He drank and smoked heavily, which made his lips dark and the lines on his face more pronounced. He had a habit of speaking quickly and often interrupted people midway. He was a success story. He worked harder than anyone else and it showed. For Prakash, the paper was both a blessing and a curse. A couple of years ago, he had had a mild heart attack that had kept him in the hospital and at home for a few weeks. The doctor had advised him to rest and take time off. But this seemed impossible to him. His wife and daughter had been driven up the wall and finally pleaded and begged his doctor to allow him to go back to work for his own sanity and theirs.

Prakash had been impressed with Nitya. He liked people with ambition. He also knew that if she were given the right environment, she could improve the reputation of the paper. The foremost thing in his mind was to ensure that she stayed at *The New India Courier*.

"Nitya, I want to congratulate you on your success. You are certainly deserving of all the accolades and awards. Manoj and I have decided to give you a bigger team and a larger role."

"Thank you, Prakash-ji. It means a lot to me, sir," Nitya replied, gratefully.

"You already have a team of your own, and you can retain them. Manoj and Anand will be giving you a few more reporters, and you will be managing and driving their stories as well," Prakash said, quickly getting up. Nitya was about to do the same, but he gestured for her to keep sitting.

"Thank you, sir."

"You are most welcome. Unfortunately, I must leave for an important meeting with one of the ministers, but I wanted to be here in person to congratulate you. We are lucky to have you on the team, and I am sure you will do well in your new role," Prakash said with a smile. He then turned and headed toward the door.

Once he left the room, Nitya observed that both Manoj and Anand's demeanors became more relaxed.

"I don't know how he does it. If he continues like this, he will have another attack," Anand said.

"Yes, and I have told him many times. He doesn't know how to slow down or relax. Well, let's talk about what we are here for," Manoj said, as he handed one of the files on the coffee table to Nitya.

She started reading it, and after a moment's silence, Anand said, "Nitya, this file has the stories that your team will be working on."

"Yes, sir," Nitya replied, wondering if she had to continue calling Anand "sir" given that they were going to be peers and reporting to Manoj directly. But she guessed that the office etiquette demanded that she do so since Anand was the most senior editor and since his other peers also addressed him as sir. Since he was to take over from Manoj, it wouldn't be prudent for her to disrespect him. And anyhow, Nitya had great respect for him, and she knew that she could learn a lot from his experience. Anand had a good fifteen years on Nitya and was known to be fair in assigning stories to the rest of the teams. Nitya shifted her gaze toward Manoj again, who handed her another file.

"Nitya, this is another file for you to look at. It has the names of all the new people who you will be managing. You have four people in your team now. You will get three more. As you know, most senior reporters manage anywhere between six and ten junior reporters and interns. In your case, you will have four junior reporters and three interns."

"I will go through the files, sir."

"Yes, I'm sure your current team will be happy to be continuing with you. The two junior reporters and the intern joining your team have been working with various senior editors," Anand said. This wasn't surprising, as there was a constant movement of junior reporters and staff depending on the stories they were assigned.

"Apart from what is on my plate at the moment, is there something specific that you want me to prioritize?" Nitya asked.

"Well, I think I will let you decide, but from the list that has been given to you, I think the one that is probably most important is the one on government tenders," Manoj replied. Nitya and Anand both nodded in agreement. They briefly discussed how government tenders were being awarded for public works projects in Delhi. The capital had a unique arrangement with the central government. The departments at the central level were directly in charge of floating tenders and accepting bids. What raised eyebrows was that in the past two years the same three business houses had ended up bagging most of the lucrative contracts. Although everything seemed above board, something didn't sit right. It was almost as if the three companies had carved out the same amount of funds while bidding on different contracts. Of course, proving that would require a lot of investigative work. The businesses were always careful not to make any missteps that would lead them to be accused of collusion. From *The New India Courier*'s standpoint, this was a good story to work on, and if any wrongdoings were uncovered, it would cause quite an uproar and scandal.

"I will take a look at it right away, sir," Nitya said, as she closed both the files.

Anand was just about to say something when there was a knock on the door. Charu, Manoj's secretary, walked in.

Addressing Anand, she said, "sir, there is someone here to meet you. He says he is an insurance agent and has a meeting scheduled with you."

"Oh yes, thank you, Charu. Manoj, Nitya, I need to go to this meeting. It's for a story that I am working on about insurance brokers."

"It's alright, Anand. We are almost done here anyway. I will speak with Nitya for a few more minutes and then we can go back to what we do best," Manoj said with a smile as Anand got up and followed Charu out of the room.

Before leaving, he turned to Nitya and said, "congratulations again. You will be a great addition to the senior editorial team, and I look forward to working with you. Oh, and by the way, we didn't talk to you about Shiv Kumar. Be careful with him. He has already been given a warning. If he gives you any trouble, come to us right away and we will toss him out. Manoj will fill you in."

"Thank you again, sir," Nitya said, wondering what this was all about.

Shiv was a junior reporter and had been at the paper for a year and a half. She knew him because his desk was on the same floor as her office, but they had never worked on anything together. She had heard some fleeting gossip about his heated arguments with some senior editors, but she didn't know the details. Now Shiv would be reporting to her. He was one of the three people joining her team.

Charu and Anand had forgotten to close the door behind them. Manoj got up, walked over, and closed the door gently. He then sat across from Nitya and said, "before you go, there are a couple of things I want to talk to you about." Nitya could sense that Manoj was being cautious as always and choosing his words carefully.

"Certainly, sir."

"First off, it is probably not lost on you that you will be our youngest senior journalist. If you had faced any professional jealousy or competition before, please be forewarned things might get personal."

Nitya knew Manoj was right.

"Yes, sir. I am aware of it."

"What I want to tell you is that although I want you to tread carefully, I don't want you to take any undue or unfair comments from anyone. The senior team has been, for the most part, an old boys' club, and they are not used to someone in their thirties challenging them. You got your promotion on your own merit. You deserve to be where you are, and if you feel anything is unfair, I don't want you to hesitate in bringing it to my attention. I know it will be difficult to maintain the balance, but from what I have seen in the last few years, you have a good, mature head on your shoulders and you are up to the challenge."

"Thank you, sir. I can't even begin to tell you how much that means to me. What's the other thing, sir?"

"I am sorry?"

"You said there were two things, sir. What's the other thing?"

"Ah, yes. You will be moving to this floor. We have assigned you an office. It's down the same corridor that you came through. Charu will show it to you. I hope you don't mind that it will take a few days for it to get ready. From what I understand, it needs another coat of paint."

"I really don't mind my current office. It has a nice view."

"Yes, but now you need a bigger office to match your role. It's all about perception. It's not the office itself. It's what it says about you," Manoj said with a smile.

"Thank you."

"One last thing," Manoj said, handing over a piece of typewritten paper.

"What's this, sir?"

"It's your official promotion letter, which has your new salary and benefits. You can go over it. You will get access to a car and a driver like most senior editors. Most of your meetings will be outside the building from now on, so it's best to have your own transport. It will also drive you to and from work."

Nitya nodded with a smile. This was one perk she was looking forward to. Having a paid-for car and driver in Delhi was a godsend. She hated taking public transport. She found most of the taxi and auto drivers rather uncouth. Most of them could easily make out that she wasn't from the city and would take advantage by taking longer routes so they could charge more. Although she had been in the city for a few years, taking public transport made her feel like an outsider. Then there was the issue of safety. Having her own car and driver would certainly be safer in a city that was notoriously unsafe for single women, especially at night.

Manoj gave her some time to read through the letter. After reading it, she placed it neatly on top of the two files she had been given.

"Will that be all, sir?"

"Yes, I think so. Unless you have any questions for me."

"Yes. Anand mentioned something about Shiv."

"Oh yes," Manoj replied with a sigh. Nitya could see that he really didn't want to talk about it.

"What's that all about, sir?"

"Do you know Shiv Kumar?"

"I know who he is."

"Well, it seems that he has a habit of getting into spats with senior journalists. Some of them have been complaining to me about him. Even though he has been with us for less than two years, he tends to do things on his own, get into arguments, and challenge decisions made by the senior staff. I have assigned him to many senior journalists and most have complained about his attitude."

"Anand said something about him being given a warning."

"Ah yes, that. Well, we are giving him one last chance. He has been given two warnings already. Prakash and I spoke to him last week. All you need to know is that if he doesn't do well or doesn't behave properly, it's not good for the team and we will have to let him go."

"Right, sir."

"Well, he is reporting to you now. You will get to decide what he will be working on. Let us know what you think of him."

"Yes, sir."

"The three journalists joining your team have already been told by their current managers that they will now be reporting to you. I think that's about it really. Good luck on your new role," Manoj said slowly getting up.

"I will get a move on these right away," Nitya said, pointing to the folders.

"Yes, thank you. Take the day to get to know the new stories that you have been assigned and the new members of your team. It's perfectly alright to take in all the accolades and bask in the moment, but tomorrow, it's business as usual. Please remember what we talked about before. All your actions and decisions will be scrutinized and challenged even more. But I am confident you will do well," Manoj said, opening the door for Nitya. Nitya nodded and left Manoj's office with the folders and papers that she had been given.

Charu got up from her desk and walked toward her.

"I will show you to your new office, ma'am."

"You can just call me Nitya."

Charu smiled. Nitya could sense that she was happy there was a woman senior journalist now. She remembered how, when she had first joined, Charu had gone out of her way to ensure that she got a good office. She had also ordered new furniture for it. Charu had tried in many little ways to help Nitya adjust to her new surroundings. Occasionally, she would come down to Nitya's office and check if she needed anything. Initially, Nitya had thought that Manoj had asked Charu to check on her. But later she realized that it wasn't the case. Charu was in her late forties and had been Manoj's secretary for more than a decade. Most of the senior journalists didn't really interact much with her. Charu led Nitya to the end of the corridor near the staircase. There was a hallway across the landing and another corridor leading to the side of the building that overlooked a park. The offices were at the very end. Most of the doors were closed and they could hear murmurs from meetings. Through the few open doors, they could see the large offices of other senior journalists. Many were empty, which wasn't unusual. They were probably on the road following up on stories. Charu stopped in front of one of the doors and opened it. Nitya could smell the fresh paint on the walls. The room was mostly empty except for a big filing cabinet in one corner. Nitya walked over slowly to the large window to take a peek and saw people in the park enjoying the sun. The view was as majestic as the one from her small office downstairs, but she liked the spacious room. She looked around to get a feel of her new office.

"We have ordered some new furniture. It will be arriving in a day or two. The phone should be here in a few days as well. The painters are coming back tomorrow to finish the job. It should all be ready in a couple of days," Charu said.

"Thank you," Nitya said with a smile. Just as they were about to step back outside, they heard a booming voice.

"Hello, Ms. Chaturvedi. Welcome to the elite club and to the floor that matters. It's good to see that you have rid yourself of the lesser mortals downstairs."

The voice was unmistakable. It was Colonel Harry Singh, though he was neither a colonel nor was his name Harry. He had been in the army a while back but had taken early retirement following an injury. His name was Harjinder Singh. He had shortened it to Harry for his friends and Colonel for everyone else. Harry Singh had been at the paper for nearly a decade. He was pompous, loud, and colorful. For someone who had been in the army for almost twenty years, he was in terrible shape. To match his booming voice, he had a large belly and a mighty mustache. It was quite evident that although he took little care of his belly, he took enormous pains to ensure that his mustache looked proper and wavy at all the right places. Nitya had heard that he was close to Prakash and had been hired for his connections in the government and the military. He had been resourceful in getting many interviews with high-ranking officials and was known to enjoy a good cigar and a drink.

"Good morning, sir," Nitya said while Charu nodded.

"So you will be my new neighbor. Finally, we will have some young blood on this floor. I don't know if you have noticed Nitya, there are two things that people lack on this floor. One is a sense of humor and the other is good looks. Pity they can't do anything about either. You have to be born with it. Now both of us will make up for it."

"Yes, sir," Nitya said with a smile as the phone in Harry Singh's room started ringing.

"Duty calls, or maybe it's the wife. Either way, I will have to take that," Harry said, pointing to his room.

"Right."

When he left, Charu and Nitya made their way through the corridor toward the staircase.

"You should pay no attention to him. His language is brutish, but he is otherwise alright," Charu said with a sigh.

"I know. I have seen him at parties and at the club. That's just how Harry is," Nitya agreed.

Once they reached the staircase and were about to go their separate ways, Charu touched Nitya's arm and said to her softly, "I am so glad that you have made it to the senior staff and this floor. I hope you do well."

"Thank you for all your help, as always," Nitya said with a smile.

As Nitya climbed down the stairs, she could see some people on her floor huddled around the desks listening to the radio. She wondered if there was a cricket match. As she made her way back to her office, she smiled and nodded at the few folks she met along the way. Once inside, she opened her desk drawers and kept all the files and papers safely. Through her door, she could see the huddle growing. She didn't want a radio in her room since it was a distraction, and she didn't like listening to it anyway. But now she started to wonder what the hullabaloo was about. She didn't have to wait long. Swati burst into her office with Suresh quietly following behind.

"Did you hear what happened?" Swati asked frantically.

"What happened?" Nitya asked.

"Communal riots, ma'am. It's all over the radio. It started in Old Delhi last night and it looks really bad."

"Any trouble here?"

"No, it doesn't seem that way," Suresh replied.

Old Delhi seemed like a world away from New Delhi. Unlike New Delhi with its grand boulevards, majestic buildings, and leafy neighborhoods, Old Delhi was crowded, noisy, and a tinderbox when it came to communal tensions. It also had more character, history, food, color, and diversity. Riots weren't uncommon in that part of the city whose inhabitants were poorer than in other parts of the sprawling metropolis. However, the riots usually started and died down quickly, and over the decades the police had been quite successful in managing tensions between the various communities. They had smartened up, and each time something started, they were quick to engage local leaders on both sides and force them to reach an amicable solution. Sometimes that meant a few nights of curfew and a strong and visible police presence.

"What happened upstairs, ma'am?" Swati asked, changing topics.

"They have made me a senior journalist and our team will have three new members. And yes, before you ask, I get to keep my current team."

"Yes!" Suresh and Swati said almost in unison. Nitya smiled at them.

"It also means more work and sometimes long hours. Now, I want all of you to be nice and welcoming to our new team members."

"We are nice," Swati replied.

"Yes, I know."

"Who are the people joining our team? Do they know?" Suresh asked.

"Yes, they were informed yesterday by their managers," Nitya said, and gave them the names of their new team members.

"Oh no, not Shiv," Suresh sighed.

"I have heard he is bad news," Swati nodded in agreement.

"Why is that?" Nitya asked.

"I don't know for sure, ma'am. I once heard him arguing with two senior journalists. They were scolding him for something he had done. Instead of apologizing, he was arguing with them. It became a big shouting match in the cafeteria," Suresh said.

"Do you know what prompted it?"

"No, ma'am. I don't know all the details," Suresh replied.

"I once saw him in the parking lot with Mr. Vijay. He was giving Shiv an earful. Again, the argument quickly descended into a shouting match for everyone to hear," Swati said.

"Well, we don't always get to pick and choose who we work with. So, let's give him a fair shake, and since we don't know what happened, let's start with a clean slate," Nitya said.

"Yes, ma'am," Swati replied unconvincingly, and Suresh nodded.

"Alright, first order of business is that I want to meet everyone. Can both of you book one of the conference rooms and let everyone know that we will be meeting in half an hour?"

"Sure, ma'am," Suresh replied.

After they left the room, Nitya looked through the files and checked out the stories that her team had been assigned and the new members who would be joining her team. There was Rakesh, an intern who had started only a few weeks ago. There wasn't much on him except his CV. He had graduated with good grades and was working on a story about the state electricity board overbilling some residents. Then there was Moina, who had been with the paper for five years. Nitya had worked with Moina on a short story and really liked her. She was a familiar face around the office. Finally, there was Shiv Kumar. He had been with the paper for eighteen months. He had also graduated from one of the best schools and his CV was great. This was his first job and though he had worked for such a short period, he had been shunted from one story to another.

His latest assignment was on a string of thefts at jewelry stores all over Delhi. Nitya had read about it in the papers that the police were having a hard time apprehending the suspects.

Nitya reread her promotion letter and then filed it away. She looked at her watch; it was time to head to the conference room to meet her team. The team had already assembled, and she was happy to see them interacting with one another. But there was no sign of Shiv.

"Please take a seat," Nitya told them.

Moina spoke first. "Shiv called earlier today and informed one of the receptionists downstairs that he will be late."

"Thank you, Moina. Do we know why?" Nitya asked, placing her files on the big conference table.

"I don't know, ma'am. It could be because of the riots in Old Delhi. That's where he lives," Moina replied.

"Alright. Well, I hope everything is fine. We will know more when he gets here. Let's get started then," Nitya continued, opening the first file, which contained all the stories and articles that they were currently working on. They spent the next two hours discussing these. She was happy to see that Moina and Rakesh were interacting well with the rest of the team. They seemed nice, and everyone appeared to be in a good mood. Nitya told them what she expected of them. She did not micromanage but liked to be kept informed of what was going on. She also wanted to make sure that the stories they were working on were moving forward. If that meant pairing her team up with other journalists, she would facilitate it. She wanted her team to travel, to meet the subjects of their stories, and most importantly, interview as many people as possible to understand the various angles of the articles they were working on. She asked her team to attend the training sessions on soft skills, a new initiative underway at the paper for junior reporters.

Toward the end, she gave everyone a chance to talk about themselves, what they did outside of work, their hobbies, and their interests. They shared a few laughs when everyone let their guard down and talked about music, chess, cooking, gardening, and reading. Finally, right before closing the meeting, Nitya reiterated their priorities and the work structure. Nitya's strategy was to pair up an old team member with a new one. She knew that the article on government contracts was their top priority. She asked Suresh and Moina to work together on it and pull in other members of the team as needed. Rakesh was asked to help Swati with her story. She still didn't know what to do with Shiv. She decided that she would use him as needed to help one of the other team members on articles they were working on.

As Nitya walked back to her room after the meeting, she saw that everyone had returned to their desks and not huddled around radios any longer. That was probably a good sign. *Maybe the riots in Old Delhi are now under control,* she thought to herself. She could hear the phone in her room ringing from afar so she quickened her pace. She picked up the receiver just in time. It was her mother.

"Hello, Nitya, how are you?" Mrs. Chaturvedi asked in her usual loud voice.

"I am fine, mom," Nitya replied, stretching the receiver cord just enough to reach the door so that she could close it.

"On the radio, we heard about the riots in Old Delhi. You know how your father gets when these things happen. He has been trying to reach you for an hour now. But your phone kept ringing and it got us really worried."

"Don't worry, mom. I am fine," Nitya said, sitting on her chair. "Whatever is happening is far from where I am. There's nothing to worry about."

"Okay, speak to him first, and then I want to talk to you about something."

Nitya sighed. She knew what that "something" was going to be. It was always the same thing—when would she find the time to meet someone and get married? The distance between Callipur and Delhi had made things a bit better. Keeping her mom at bay had been easier. There was only as much that could be said over the phone. Mrs. Chaturvedi no longer had the luxury of pestering her daughter every day about marriage. These conversations were now confined to annual vacations and whenever her parents came to visit, which was usually once every six to nine months. But Nitya knew that her mom possessed an enormous talent of making her feel guilty and low even through a set of copper wires. What had made matters worse was that both her elder and younger sisters were now married. In her mom's circle of friends in small-town Callipur that made Nitya "the unmarried one." Nitya didn't mind the reference, but it irked her mom who made sure that her daughter got a dose of her "uncomfortable" life because she was unmarried.

When Nitya moved to Delhi, it was general knowledge that she would be marrying Raj, her family friend from childhood. In the end, though, she had decided against it. Nitya hoped that today's conversation would be different; perhaps it could be about her promotion. She was happy to hear her father's voice, though. He was much easier to talk to and never brought up anything about her past relationships. She enjoyed her conversations with him on various topics and they were full of longing and affection for one another. She spoke to him for a few minutes, assured him that she was fine, and then informed him about her promotion. She could sense that he was ecstatic. She could hear him relaying it to her mom but couldn't gauge her reaction. After a few minutes, he handed the phone over to her.

"Nitya, what's this I hear? You got a promotion. Congratulations!"

"Thank you, mom."

"When did this happen?"

"They told me this morning."

"What does this mean?"

"A bigger team, more responsibilities, and a bigger office," Nitya said knowing really well that her mom would be weighing all of this against what she would say next.

"I am so happy for you. Your dad is already getting ready to go to the club to share the news with his friends. How is your health? Are you eating properly?"

"Yes, mom, I am doing fine."

"I have to tell your sisters about your promotion. Kavita just called a little while ago. She may be coming over next month for a short visit. Can you come too?"

"No, mom. Not so soon. I was just there a couple of months ago for Kavita's wedding. I have a lot on my plate," Nitya said, as she sensed the momentary silence on the other end and dreaded the inevitable conversation that would follow.

"Have you thought about what we talked about last time? Are you seeing someone?"

"No, mom, I am not."

"It seems that you don't like any of the boys we arrange for you to meet. I was discussing this with your father yesterday. I think we will be fine with you selecting someone yourself."

Nitya couldn't imagine her father getting a word in during this "discussion". In her family, her mom made the decisions and everyone else just had to go along with it.

"Fine, mom. If you want to leave it up to me, then just leave it up to me."

"Yes, but time is running out, you know. You are already well into your thirties."

"I am well aware of my age."

"Now you will become busier and have less time to meet people."

"I have to go, mom."

"Even Raj is married and has a daughter now. We met them, his parents, and his in-laws at the club. If you had stayed in Callipur, you could have married him and had a more normal life."

"My life is quite normal now."

"But you are not settled. What's worse is that I don't get a sense that you are interested in anyone at all. It is very stressful for us as parents. Your dad may not say it openly, but he is worried too."

"I didn't want a 'normal' life in Callipur. I am happy for Raj, but I am also happy with my decision to leave and come to Delhi."

"What exactly has that resulted in? You are still single, and all these promotions are getting you nowhere. You are getting older and soon, even if you want to marry, there will be no one left to marry. Boys are not waiting around for you to be ready."

"Alright, mom. We are just going around in circles. I thought today was going to be about me and my promotion. But you managed to talk about the same thing. You really have a unique ability to make me feel sad on a day I should be really happy."

"Nitya, please think about what I am saying. You need someone with whom you can share your life. You are getting older, and you will get lonely."

"I am alone, mom, but not lonely. They are two different things."

"I don't know why you have to be so stubborn and headstrong. It is completely pointless talking to you. You just don't understand."

"Fine. I have to go now," Nitya said, raising her voice slightly.

"Fine," said Mrs. Chaturvedi, in a shrill voice as she banged down the phone.

They had been having the same conversation for years now. It had become more pointed since the weddings of both Kavita, Nitya's younger sister, and Raj. Kavita had married someone from Bombay and Raj had married one of Nitya's school friends from Callipur. To her mother, that meant that they were both settled and happy and she yearned for Nitya to have the same. Nitya's decision to not marry Raj had been a shock and embarrassment for her mother. It had taken her a few months to come to terms with it. Raj's parents were family friends and that had made things awkward. But since then, Nitya had moved to Delhi and Raj had gotten married. With time, everyone had moved on, except Nitya's mom.

After the conversation with her mom, Nitya kept staring at the phone. Usually, her mother would call back after a few minutes to soothe things over. However, if the self-righteous Mrs. Chaturvedi was really upset, it could take her a couple of days to call back, and even then, she would talk about mundane things pretending that nothing had happened. That was her way of apologizing. As Nitya stared at the phone, she couldn't gauge whether her mother would call in a few minutes or take a day or two. Nitya was angry and fuming. Her mother had managed to upset her and make her feel low on a day that was so important to her. Then the phone rang. Nitya decided to give it back to her mother.

She picked up and said in a loud voice, "enough mom. I have had it with your guilt trips. I don't want to talk to you about this anymore."

There was a momentary silence on the other end. She could hear a faint noise in the background but couldn't make out what it was. Then someone spoke in a clear, soft voice.

"I may have got the wrong number. Is this Nitya Chaturvedi?"

Nitya immediately realized her mistake and regained her composure.

"Yes, this is Nitya. I am sorry, I thought it was someone else."

"That's alright, ma'am. I'm Shiv Kumar. I understand you will be my new boss. I have been trying to reach you for the last hour and a half."

"Oh yes. We were at a meeting. Moina told me that you had called to say that you will be late."

"Yes. I am in Old Delhi now and the police have cordoned off a lot of streets. We are not being allowed to leave, and I'm told there will be a curfew soon. I am calling you from a public phone booth near my apartment."

"Oh. Are you alright?"

"Yes, ma'am. I am fine. Luckily, nothing happened on the street where I live. But some houses and cars have been burned a few streets over. I heard on the radio that there have been a few casualties, but I am not sure what to believe."

"Is there anything we can do to help?"

"I am not sure. I think we must follow police orders and stay indoors till they get the situation under control. I don't think I will be able to make it to the office."

"That's alright, Shiv. I want you to be safe and at home. Please call me if you think there is anything I can do. If you want to get out of your neighborhood for a while and live with someone else, maybe some relatives in other parts of Delhi, please do let me know. As soon as the curfew is over, I can send over a car to pick you up."

"Thank you for the offer, ma'am."

"From what I have been told, the riots are confined only to Old Delhi."

"I am not sure that's the case. That's another reason I have been trying to reach you. I heard from my neighbors that a large rowdy crowd is making its way to Connaught Place. I think it would be a good idea to close the office for today and send everyone home."

"I have been here since morning, and everything seems fine here. This is a relatively safe area, and there's a lot of police presence all around. I am sure we are fine," Nitya replied. She was amused at Shiv's assumption that the offices would be closed simply on the basis of his message.

"I spoke to the receptionists and some of my colleagues on the ground floor and told them what was happening. They wouldn't connect me to any senior staff members," Shiv said, sounding a bit disappointed.

"It's alright, Shiv," Nitya said confidently. "You take care of yourself and stay safe. We are fine here. Once things have died down and the police have lifted the curfew, you can come to work."

"Right, ma'am. I will keep you informed of what's going on here, and as soon as I am able to make it to the office, I will."

"Thank you, Shiv," Nitya replied and hung up.

She could imagine Shiv trying to reach the senior journalists on the third floor to warn them about the riots and not managing to get through. She smiled, imagining what their reaction would be if the offices considered closing because of Shiv's advice, especially after his recent run-ins with them. Soon after hanging up, Nitya heard a growing ambient noise outside. Through the glass partition, she could see the journalists on her floor looking out the windows. Just as she was about to turn and look outside her office window, a large, fiery rock came crashing through the glass pane and landed on her desk, missing her only by a few inches.

Riots

The next few days were tense all around the old city. The police and the security forces were successful in quickly bringing things under control. In just a few days, normalcy had returned in most places, except for where the riots had first started. Although the initial reports and pictures from the old part of town were bad, most of the damage was concentrated on old, run-down buildings, cars, motorbikes, and shops. The initial fires had spread quickly through some neighborhoods, but, thankfully, the residents of those areas had been evacuated quickly. Slowly the number of casualties started to trickle in. Most of New Delhi and the outlying areas were largely unaffected by what had happened. The police had cordoned off the affected areas and curtailed the movement of people in and out of the old part of town. Only security forces, government vehicles, and emergency staff had permission to be on the roads.

The crowds in Connaught Place were mostly troublemakers trying to take advantage of the riots to rob high-end stores in and around central Delhi. Their activities did not last more than a couple of hours, but even in that limited time, they had managed to break windows of shops and offices and steal merchandise from multiple jewelry and electronic stores in the area. They knew that most of the police force was diverted to Old Delhi, and by the time other security forces could reach, most of the looters had dispersed.

The security guards at *The New India Courier* offices were successful in locking the premises so that no one could enter. The miscreants were anyway not interested in attacking the offices. Their main target was the stores. They only threw rocks at the windows of the offices to instill fear among the workers and prevent them from clicking any pictures or taking any action against their criminal activities. Yet, many journalists decided to go to the roof and take pictures. In the next few days, this would aid the police in nabbing some of the suspects. They had also managed to call nearby offices to caution them to be safe and police stations to inform them about the unruly crowd. This had somewhat minimized the damage.

Yet, those two hours seemed harrowing to the staff at the newspaper. Nitya had been completely shaken by the rock piercing the window in her office and landing on her desk. She had never thought that something like this could happen in such a picturesque neighborhood. Some other windows in the building had been smashed too. Thankfully, no one inside was injured. The only damage was the shattered glass that was quickly cleaned up. When Suresh and Moina heard the window crashing in Nitya's office, they were right outside and quickly came in to check on her. Seeing that Nitya was visibly shaken, Moina gripped her hand and quickly took her to a conference room while Suresh removed papers and anything flammable from near the window and the desk. Meanwhile, the security guards had locked down the building and had asked everyone whose office was next to a window to leave their offices, close their doors, and congregate at the center of each floor.

The threat from the rowdy mob passed as quickly as it had started. Suddenly, the surrounding areas had become eerily quiet. The predominant emotion inside the building had changed from fear to anger. People were upset about the day's events and wanted to go home, but they had to wait for almost three hours for the senior management and security to ensure that it was safe to step outside. There was a heavy police presence in the area. The security guards informed everyone that Manoj and Prakash had increased the number of guards inside and outside the building. It seemed that apart from the events in Old Delhi and the rowdy mob in Connaught Place, the rest of the city had been peaceful. The employees were all escorted out in batches and driven home in company cars.

Nitya had her company-provided car too. She sent off those employees who lived further away while she stayed behind with Moina and Suresh who lived closer to the office and her home.

While waiting for the driver to return, she thought of Shiv and how he had been right about the mob heading toward Connaught Place. She had heard on the radio that a two-day curfew had been imposed in Old Delhi. There was no way to get in touch with Shiv now. She recalled that he had called from a public pay phone. The paper had provided phones to most of the senior journalists and mid-level managers at their residences. But Shiv was not part of that group. While waiting in the conference room with her team, she asked Moina if there was any way to contact Shiv. Moina knew where he lived, but since he didn't have a phone, there was nothing much that could be done till the curfew was lifted.

On their way home, they could see the damage that had been done. Connaught Place was a sprawling locality with a circular array of majestic colonial buildings and lined with large avenues crisscrossing blocks with massive gardens at the center. There were also post-colonial, modern buildings, mainly offices, restaurants, and shops. They noticed how empty the streets were. The hustle and bustle of their noisy neighborhood had been replaced by an eerie silence. Usually, the late afternoon traffic would jam up all the streets and the honks from the slow-moving cars would drown out the voices of people shifting in and out of the posh stores and offices. This had been replaced by police sirens in the background and people quietly leaving their offices to make their way home. Many buildings had been damaged. Fire trucks were dousing a fire on a building across the park. Before getting into the car, they turned back to take stock of the damage on their building. Several windows had been smashed. A small fire had started on the ground floor, but it had quickly been brought under control. When Nitya looked up, she could see her broken office window. The sight unnerved her, and she quickly made her way into the car and sat next to Moina. Suresh sat next to the driver in the front. After dropping them off, Nitya picked up some food from a nearby restaurant and headed home.

For Nitya, home in Delhi was a two-bedroom apartment in central Delhi, not far from the office. The paper had arranged the accommodation for her, a service they offered senior journalists and those employees who were from out of town. Her apartment building was in a relatively greener neighborhood and was surrounded by the streets where politicians and bureaucrats had their official residences. That meant that it was in a part of town that was relatively safe. Till then,

Connaught Place had seemed safe too, and yet the unruly mob managed to wreak havoc in just two hours. When the car had turned onto the avenue that led to her building, Nitya could see police checkpoints and security vehicles stationed at the main crossings. That didn't provide her with any comfort. She was still shaken up from what had happened earlier. She could not get the sound of the rock smashing the window out of her head. Tilak Singh, the new driver who was assigned to her, was a calming presence. He seemed well-versed with the roads in Delhi and was able to navigate the streets quite deftly. Although she couldn't have a long conversation with him, somehow his assurance that things would get better soon calmed her down.

As she got off and slowly headed toward the stairs that led to her first-floor apartment, she could hear the police sirens in the background. At home, she changed, ate, and was about to go to bed when the phone rang. It was her father. She could sense that he was worried. Thankfully, most of the reports on the radio had downplayed the incident. With the airwaves being controlled by the government, they wanted to make sure that there was no large-scale panic. Nitya was able to quickly allay her parents' fears about her safety although she still couldn't get over the events of the day. Though she was both physically and mentally tired, she couldn't sleep. She read through some of the files that she had brought home with her. Then she picked up a book and suddenly remembered to check her mailbox. She was glad to find a letter from her younger sister, Kavita. This letter was shorter than her usual ones. There was no complaining and whining followed by phrases of affection. This one seemed more direct and less detailed and that made Nitya worry that something was wrong. But the letter carried some happy news: Kavita had written that she would be visiting Delhi soon and that made Nitya smile after a long and stressful day.

The next day Nitya woke up to a phone call from Manoj who was calling to say that the situation around the office was calm. Yet, he insisted, that for the next couple of days, unless anyone was working on a story that absolutely required them to be in the office, they shouldn't come in. Nitya knew that she had nothing urgent going on now. Some senior journalists had been assigned to the riots and were needed at work. The rest could stay home until Thursday. Not everyone on Nitya's team had a phone. Manoj had sent notes to their residences through the office drivers. Nitya was glad and disappointed in equal measure when Manoj informed her that her team wouldn't be tackling the riots. He sensed her disappointment and assured her that she would be assigned something connected to it. Nitya could sense that there was something on his mind and he was in a hurry to call the other journalists. He hung up after instructing that her team and her to be at the office on Thursday for a new project.

Nitya was glad that she had brought home all her files from work. She could spend time reading them, something she never seemed to have time for under ordinary circumstances. She also decided to check on her team members. Many of the younger members lived with their parents who had phones. She could reach them all except Moina, who was out for a jog. For the ones who did not have a phone, she thought of sending notes through Tilak and asking them to call her from a phone booth. She wanted to make sure that everyone was fine.

The morning paper made Nitya realize how different Delhi was from Callipur. There were multiple reports on the events that had happened, interviews with folks in the affected areas, articles trying to explain why it had happened, and comments from the police. If something like this happened in a small town like Callipur, the whole town would be shut down completely. In Delhi however, people went about their daily lives completely oblivious to how the riots had affected some areas. It was a city that was almost competing with itself to regain normalcy.

The papers mentioned ten to twelve casualties and an equal number still missing. Nitya knew that at this stage most newspapers were getting their information from the police and other security agencies. Once things calmed down, the media would be able to independently verify the numbers. Old Delhi was still under curfew and would be for at least another thirty-six hours. This meant that no one would be allowed to either leave or enter the area unless there was an emergency. Nitya moved on to the other articles in the paper and that's when the phone rang. It was the guard informing her that Tilak had arrived with the car. She had already prepared the notes for her team members and written down the addresses for Tilak.

"Good morning, madam," Tilak said right away as she opened the door.

"Good morning, Tilak. Would you like some tea?"

"No, thank you."

"I hope your neighborhood was not affected by what happened yesterday."

"No, madam. I don't live in Old Delhi. I am quite far from where the riots happened."

"That's good. Well, I have a job for you. Here are the addresses of all my team members who don't have phones. I want you to take these notes to them," Nitya said, handing them over. Tilak went through the names and addresses carefully.

"I know these places and can reach all of them, except Shiv. He is in Old Delhi and there's a curfew on. I may not be able to get through to him."

"Yes, I figured that would be the case. Keep his note with you and if the curfew lifts tomorrow, then you can perhaps try to reach him, but only and only if it is totally safe. Otherwise, I don't want you to go anywhere near that area."

"Yes, madam, understood."

"Also, do you have a number I can reach you at in case of an emergency?"

"Yes, madam. I don't have a phone but my brother-in-law does. He is a private security guard in a factory and his company has given him one. He lives a floor above mine. He can get in touch with me if needed."

"Alright, give me a minute," Nitya said. She got her notebook from her desk and handed it over to Tilak. She was surprised to see that for his age, he had really good handwriting.

"Madam, do you want me to call you every morning to find out when I should come pick you up?" he asked as he handed back the pen and notebook.

"No, there is no need for that. I will tell you the time the night before when you drop me off. I'm keeping your number only for emergencies."

"Yes, madam," Tilak said.

Nitya sensed that he wanted to say something else but was stopping himself.

"Is there anything else, Tilak?"

"Yes, I was just thinking about Shiv. You can ask Moina. She probably knows how to get in touch with him."

"Oh, sure. I will ask her when I talk to her. Thank you, Tilak."

Once the chauffeur had left, she checked the clock to see if it had been more than an hour since she had tried to reach Moina. There was still some time left so she decided to make herself some tea.

Nitya had taken great pains to aesthetically decorate her apartment. Her bedroom was sparsely furnished, but she had splurged on an expensive bed and mattress. The desk and bookcase were a gift from her parents. They matched her bed and side tables. The walk-in closet was not enough for her clothes, so she had to use the one in the living room. The sofa set, dining room chairs, and carpet contrasted well with the floor. Since moving to Delhi, she had picked up a liking for indoor plants and there were several in her apartment. The kitchen was small and had an adjoining storage area. It was more than sufficient for her needs. To maximize space, she had bought a smaller fridge and refrained from buying too many utensils.

While making tea she thought of Moina and Shiv. She wondered if there was anything going on between the two. Although office relationships were not frowned upon, they were also not encouraged. It led to gossip and if things didn't work out well, could lead to complications that Nitya was well aware of following her short affair with Vijay. After finishing her tea, she called Moina again.

Moina picked up the phone and said, "good morning, ma'am. I am sorry I missed your call. I had gone out for a jog."

"That's alright, Moina. I am just checking in with everyone."

"This area doesn't seem affected at all. Most people are just going about their daily lives."

"I am sure you may have heard already that we are not expected back in the office until day after tomorrow, Thursday, that is."

"Yes."

"I will leave it up to you on how you want to spend the time. I am not expecting anyone to be working or following up on any stories that they are working on until we get back to the office."

"It's alright, ma'am. I brought home the files I was working on, and I will go through them."

"That's good."

"Do you think we will be assigned any story linked to what happened yesterday?"

"I don't know yet. I spoke to Manoj earlier today. He has something planned for our team and has asked to meet us first thing Thursday morning."

"Right."

"There is one thing I wanted to ask you. I have been able to reach almost everyone on the team, but I am not sure how to get in touch with Shiv. He is in Old Delhi, and I don't know the situation there. I just want to make sure he is fine."

"He is, ma'am. He called me this morning from a public booth in his building. He said that the police will lift the curfew tomorrow morning and then for the next few days there will only be a night curfew in place. He will be in the office on Thursday."

"Oh, I am so glad that he is fine."

"We couldn't talk for a long time, but I informed him of how our office building was attacked by the mob."

"Yes, scary, wasn't it?"

"Yes. He asked whether we were all okay."

"I think he should be the one we should all be worried about given where he lives. Well, I will let you go now. Unless something changes, let's aim to be at the office on Thursday by 9:30 a.m."

"Yes, ma'am. Thank you for calling and checking up on us. Bye."

"Bye."

Nitya was convinced by now that her instinct about Shiv and Moina was correct. She went back to her files and patiently waited to hear back from the rest of her team members. She knew it would take a while as Tilak would have to drive quite a distance to reach them all.

* * *

Meanwhile, in one of the many Old Delhi police stations, a tired group of officers was replacing another after their shift had ended. Manning the narrow streets in a jeep and on foot for twelve hours was mentally and physically draining. The last twenty-four hours had been stressful, and although the riots were largely over, they still had to make sure that the miscreants couldn't take advantage of the situation and loot stores, offices, and homes—a common occurrence in past riots. The police had to always deal with the aftermath of the riots. It was a sensitive time with loved ones looking for missing relatives and police trying to find the next of kin for the deceased. Most victims were usually innocent bystanders who had nothing to do with the violence. There were several police stations in Old

Delhi, but the one that bore the brunt of the riots and its aftermath was the Kotwali Police Station.

The walled city had been built in the sixteenth and seventeenth centuries and came into prominence during the reign of the same Mughal emperor who had built the Taj Mahal. Although much of the wall itself had either been taken down or disintegrated, most of the monuments were still intact and reflected the grandeur of the bygone era. After India's independence and the Partition, Old Delhi saw a wave of immigrants coming and settling there. In more recent decades, it had become a refuge for people from all over India who came to Delhi in search of employment and a better life. Compared to New Delhi, it offered cheaper rents, vibrant bazaars, a huge variety of street food, and a chance to live in a historic area. Most people living in the area were oblivious to the history and were busy earning a living and going about their daily lives.

The Kotwali Police Station was not far from the Old Delhi Railway Station. When the riots broke out, they had been caught unawares. Past riots had been preceded by inflammatory rhetoric from religious leaders. But this time around it had started suddenly, and the officers at the station were unprepared to deal with it right away. They focused on cordoning off the railway station and ensuring that there was as little damage as possible to human life and property. It was always a crowded area and even at the best of times, dealing with a large volume of people crammed into the narrow streets and alleyways was a huge challenge. Thankfully, the police from the other stations and the paramilitary forces had been able to quell much of the disturbance. They had rounded up the usual suspects and miscreants in the area for questioning and held them in custody until the situation improved. The last twenty-four hours had been challenging, but it seemed that the worst was over. Some violence that had spilled over to other parts of the city had also been contained. When the unruly crowd had started moving from Old Delhi toward Connaught Place in New Delhi, there was a danger of the riots spreading to other areas quickly, but after a few hours, the violence had subsided. This was also different from the previous riots, which had lasted for a few days. The Delhi police, the political leaders, and the public were relieved that this one hadn't gone on for days.

Shankar Sen was the officer in charge at the Kotwali Police Station. His boss at the station had been transferred and there had been no replacement. This wasn't surprising. Manning a station in Old Delhi was not a coveted post. No police officer looked forward to overseeing a station in an old, run-down, riot-prone area of the city that was a hotbed of criminal activity.

Officers who were able to pull some strings ensured that they avoided any posting at Kotwali or, for that matter, any station in Old Delhi. The ones who couldn't usually lasted a year or two before getting transferred to another, more peaceful area. Shankar Sen had lasted for almost three years. He had requested a transfer multiple times to no avail. He did not have any connections, and an incident prior to being posted at Kotwali had ruffled some feathers in the police hierarchy. That is why he had been penalized and transferred to Kotwali. He had seen successive officers come and go. In three years, he had had three different bosses, and after the last one had been transferred, he was now the most senior officer at the station. That's when the riots broke out.

It had been a night like any other. Shankar was in his police jeep patrolling the streets in and around the Old Delhi Railway Station. Everything seemed peaceful. A constant hum of trains arriving and leaving the station was drowned out by the noise of the crowds. Everyone seemed to be in a hurry although it was close to midnight. The street vendors around the station were busy catering to their customers' insatiable appetites for tea, savouries, and sweets. Shankar had asked his driver to stop the jeep at a crossing near the station. He had got off and bought some tea for himself and the driver. They decided to sit on one of the rickety wooden benches near the tea stall to enjoy their midnight snack and beverage. The other customers at the tea stall gave them quiet glances and made some space for them. A man in uniform was either feared or loathed in this part of town. During his tenure at the station, Shankar had managed to convince his peers and superiors to cultivate a network of informal contacts and informers. Most of them were street vendors or owners of shops in the bazaar. They had the most to lose in any commotion. Shankar had made them understand that if they were able to warn the station of any incident beforehand, then any physical harm or potential damage to their businesses could be minimized. Many had agreed and the initiative had produced mixed results.

Motiram, Shankar's driver, wiped down the wooden bench with his handkerchief before they sat down. The old man had been a fixture at the station for nearly two decades and had gotten fond of Shankar. Unlike other junior officers who were arrogant and cocky, Shankar seemed quiet, soft-spoken, and thoughtful. He also treated everyone with respect. Whenever they went on patrols, he would buy meals or tea for everyone who accompanied him, not just his fellow officers or superiors. Motiram also felt sorry that Shankar had to endure this post longer than others and at his unsuccessful attempts in getting a transfer to a better station.

"Lovely night, sir," Motiram said.

"Yes, it is," Shankar replied, drinking his tea.

"Do you want to head back to the station after this, sir?"

"No. I want to take one more round and then head back."

"Sure."

Shankar had noticed a group of people gathering at the entrance opposite the bazaar. Most of the stores were closed and the group that he had seen did not have any luggage with them. He couldn't be sure whether they were arriving or leaving the station, but something didn't seem right. It could be nothing of course, but he decided to take another look before heading back.

"Don't you have some vacation coming up?"

"Yes, sir. I was going to ask you if I could take a few days off in the last week of this month. I want to go to Varanasi to see my family."

"Sure. Put in the request and leave the forms at my desk tomorrow, and I will approve it."

"Thank you, sir."

Motiram's family was in Varanasi because he could not afford to bring his family to Delhi. Over the years he had made several plans to bring them over, but it had never worked out. His wife and son were well settled in Varanasi and as time went by, they got used to staying apart. They would come visit him every month and he would go visit them whenever he could. It was a relationship that Shankar couldn't imagine with his wife and son. But he knew that he belonged to a different India than Motiram.

By the time they finished their tea, the other customers had left and were heading for the station. There was a bit of a lull before a new group would come in. The owner of the stall asked Shankar and Motiram if they needed anything else. Shankar asked him softly if he had heard or seen anything that could be a sign of trouble in the area. He hadn't. Shankar didn't have any reason not to believe him. The tea stall owner was Motiram's cousin and had helped the police discreetly on many occasions. After they finished their snack and tea, they headed to the jeep. Before getting into the car, Shankar stopped and surveyed the area to see if he could spot anything suspicious. Everything seemed fine. He instructed Motiram to drive him around the station and stop briefly at the other entrances. There was nothing unusual at the main entrance. People were on the move and the vendors were busy. When they reached the back entrance, the group that Shankar had seen earlier was no longer there. *Probably a false alarm*, Shankar thought. He asked Motiram to park the jeep and wait for a few minutes. Everything looked normal. They decided to head back to the police station.

The Kotwali Police Station was calmer and quieter than usual. A few constables who were patrolling the streets had broken up some scuffles between teenagers and had brought them back to the station. Their parents had been called to come pick them up. They were going to be sent home with a warning. The teenagers feared their parents more than the cops. They had apologized profusely and begged the constables not to call their parents. But the constables were itching to see what would transpire when the parents arrived. As Shankar walked into the station and started making his way to the end of the hallway where his office was, he looked around and saw the four teenagers. A constable quickly came up and told him what had happened. Shankar nodded, glanced at the boys, and then continued toward his office.

Kotwali was a small police station with four officers and twenty constables. With his boss now gone, they were down to three officers and only half the staff was around at any given time for their shifts. At night, two officers and ten constables were plenty to deal with any unruly incidents. As Shankar settled into his office, one of the constables brought him tea. Shankar enquired whether anything from the area had been reported, but nothing had. Once he was alone in his office, he started reading through the stack of files on his desk. It was almost 2:00 a.m. The parents of the boys had already come and picked them up. The constables had enjoyed the sight of the fathers admonishing their sons. One of them resorted to slapping and scolding his kid before dragging him out by the neck. The constables had a good laugh.

There were four phones at the station, one on each officer's desk. They were mostly quiet during the night unless something serious happened. The constables manning the phones were having a hard time staying awake. Suddenly, three phones started ringing within a few seconds of each other. Shankar immediately sensed something was wrong. He grabbed one of the phones from the constable who had answered the call. It was the stationmaster from the Old Delhi Railway Station informing Shankar that a group who had gathered near a train that had just arrived had started burning one of the coaches. Another call was from the receptionist of a small hotel opposite the railway station, who had seen two men setting a few cars on fire in the parking lot. The third call was from the constable of a neighboring police station who needed help getting an unruly mob under control because they were breaking windows and shutters in a narrow lane near a bazaar. It seemed that the worst affected areas were all around the railway station.

The officers and constables at the Kotwali Police Station immediately sprang into action. They quickly placed urgent calls to the home ministry's control room and the police headquarters to apprise them of the situation. The headquarters had already received some calls from other stations in the area. Shankar was assured that police from other stations would be diverted to the affected area. One of his colleagues was informed that members of the Central Reserve Police Force would also be sent to deal with the law-and-order situation. A central command post had been established at the police headquarters as a one-stop shop for directing the forces, gathering information, sending emergency vehicles to the area, and dealing with casualties. After successive riots spanning several decades, this process had finally been streamlined. Shankar and his fellow officers also knew that the additional forces would take another hour or two to arrive. Till then they had to manage the situation on their own with the help of other police stations in the area.

They quickly began coordinating the local response. Shankar and a few constables decided to patrol the areas around the railway station, while the other officers were sent to man the other areas. The first order of business was to establish peace and after that they would deal with any casualties, making sure that the deceased and injured were transported to nearby hospitals. Depending on the number of casualties, they would have to engage hospitals and staff in outlying areas. Officers at the other stations in the area would round up the usual suspects who stoked religious tension and made inflammatory speeches. As they drove through the neighborhoods, they used loudspeakers on their police vans and jeeps to urge people to stay home, stay calm, and follow the curfew for the next few hours.

Shankar, Motiram, and two other constables quickly made their way to the Old Delhi Railway Station. A police van and fire truck followed them with additional reinforcements. Having a fire station next to the police station helped. The narrow lanes and alleyways leading up to the station were filled with burning tires, bricks, and debris. It was still dark, and as they slowly started making their way, they could see the smoke emanating from some shops that had been set alight. They could also smell the burning rubber from the tires and tar on the road. Shankar stopped near the shops that had been set on fire. There was considerable damage. Most shops in the overcrowded area were small and filled with goods from wall to wall. The ones that had been set alight were almost completely burned from inside. The firemen were trying to contain the blaze. In some buildings, the fire had spread to the upper floors to storage areas, offices, and apartments. Luckily, there were no casualties on the two main streets, although the damage to property was severe.

A few shop owners and their neighbors were on the streets, desperately trying to douse the flames with buckets of water and prevent the fire from spreading. Given the circumstances, the firemen did an admirable job containing the fire. Shankar used the loudspeakers to make announcements. He quickly rounded up the owners whose properties had been damaged. They were all nestled into the police van and taken to a nearby school that was going to be used as a makeshift camp. Shankar and the constables spent the next two hours surveying the damage and making sure the injured got the medical attention they needed. Most of the injured had got minor burns or had hurt themselves while trying to jump out of the apartments. An ambulance full of nurses had arrived and was parked at one of the barricaded crossings to provide first aid to the injured.

Shankar turned his attention to a narrow lane that was used mostly by pedestrians to reach a side entrance to the railway station. It was a long lane lined with buildings connected to one another. The street was too narrow for any vehicle to enter. Shankar could hear the commotion in the other streets, but this dark lane seemed eerily quiet. He could barely see the end of the lane that had a small gate for pedestrians. Suddenly, he saw shadows moving in the dark corner toward the end of the lane. He could hear footsteps in the distance, but then it turned silent. Something did not seem right. Accompanied by two constables with large flashlights, he slowly walked into the lane. They drew their revolvers for all to see. But when they reached the end of the lane, they found it was empty. They could see some inquisitive people peeking from the surrounding buildings, but it was very dark, and difficult for anyone to make out what was going on. At the end of the lane was a small pedestrian gate leading to the railway station. Shankar opened it. The platform was visible a few hundred yards away. The gate felt wet and greasy, though it hadn't rained in days. Shankar quickly wiped his hand on his handkerchief and used a flashlight to check what it was. His white handkerchief had turned red—blood!

One of the constables who had stopped a few yards away seemed to be smelling something. Shankar walked back to him, and they turned the flashlight in the direction of the stench. There was a large open pit for collecting garbage and inside it were the charred remains of two corpses. It was a horrific sight. The constable who had discovered the bodies threw up. Shankar stepped closer to get a better look. It seemed that the bodies had first been burned and then dumped in the pit. Shankar ordered two constables to guard the area and retraced his steps through the dark lane toward the street. A few people had come to their doorsteps, curious to know what was going on. Shankar instructed them to stay inside. On reaching his jeep, he used the police radio to inform the station what had happened.

There was not much they could do until the next morning. The priority was to maintain peace. The station informed him that there had been some casualties in other areas too. The injured were being taken to hospitals in Old Delhi, and the deceased were being transported in police vans to a central hospital in New Delhi for postmortems. Shankar wanted to investigate the scene of the crime for clues but he was instructed to leave the constables at the spot and continue patrolling the areas near the station. A photographer would be sent over and the bodies would be taken for postmortem.

Once back in the jeep, he continued his journey toward the station. Along the way, he saw small pockets of people gathered at crossings. He used the loudspeaker to convey instructions and they immediately headed indoors. As the jeep turned into the road leading up to the main gates of the railway station, he noticed a few more fire trucks. Constables, medical staff, and residents of the area were helping the injured who were seated on the sidewalks. Their faces expressed their sadness and anger at what had happened. Shankar asked Motiram to stop the jeep a few yards from the main entrance to the railway station. He wanted to talk to other officers from some of the other police stations. He walked up to the nearest officer he could find. The officer was talking on the police radio to someone at the headquarters. Shankar waited for him to finish. He turned and saw that the vans from the Central Reserve Police Force had just arrived and were putting barricades around the main gate and cordoning off a few streets. Suddenly, Shankar felt a tap on his shoulder and turned to see who it was.

"Kabir Singh from the Chandni Chowk Police Station," the officer said with his hand outstretched.

"Shankar Sen from the Kotwali Station," Shankar replied, as he shook Kabir Singh's hand.

"Yes, I know who you are. We were at India Gate four years ago when the incident happened."

Yes, the incident for which I am now stationed at Old Delhi, Shankar thought. The incident had made him famous for all the wrong reasons.

"Oh, I am sorry, I don't recall. There were so many of us."

"Don't worry, I was nowhere near where you were. I was at the other end on VIP duty, protecting one of the ministers from the crowd. I heard about what had happened afterwards. I am new to this area. I just moved to the Chandni Chowk station last week."

"Right. That's probably why we haven't met. I wanted to know how bad things are here."

"The worst seems to be over. I believe it started around 1:30 a.m. I came here a few minutes later. There was a crowd that has dispersed since then. We caught some people trying to rob the stores nearby. I don't think they started the riots, though. I think they were simply taking advantage of the situation," Kabir said, and then pointed toward the railway station.

"What am I looking at?" Shankar asked.

"That's what brought us here in the first place. You can't see it now because it's dark. We got a call from the station master that one of the coaches on the platform nearest to the gate was on fire."

"Oh. Any casualties?"

"No. That's the strange thing. It seems that whoever started the fire waited for all the passengers to leave first."

"So, no one was inside the train when the coach was set on fire?" Shankar asked thoughtfully.

"That's right. The fire spread quickly to two other empty coaches. Unfortunately, another train had arrived at the same time. People are saying that they heard a small explosion. That's when everyone started rushing out of the gates," Kabir said, pointing toward it.

"Any injuries?"

"Sadly, yes. Three people got injured in the stampede. They have been taken to the hospital. Some others have minor cuts and bruises and are being attended to on the sidewalk. We are trying to ascertain whether any of them need to be taken to the hospital."

"Well, I have been told to stay here for a few hours. It seems that the Central Reserve Police Force will then take over the security around the railway station. I see some of them have already arrived."

"Yes. That's what I heard too. Honestly, this is my first time dealing with a riot. It feels a bit strange and unnerving. Although I didn't witness the violence, I am still a bit fearful that anything can happen at any time."

Shankar nodded in agreement. He knew the feeling all too well. In the past, riots happened in phases. Once the first wave was over, there was a momentary lull and then there was an inevitable retaliation by the opposing group. But somehow this seemed different. In past riots, the police had to break up opposing groups fighting each other and deal with angry mobs hurling stones, bottles, and bricks at the police. Those were usually preceded by inflammatory speeches and threats by religious leaders. On many occasions, the police informers and the public were able to predict that things could get worse and shared their apprehensions with the press, the police, or both. Sometimes that gave the authorities time to prepare or even bring the opposing groups together to persuade them to reach an agreement or a compromise for the sake of peace.

However, once the riots started, they could last for days, and the initial number of casualties, especially the death toll, was always high. This time there was no warning or threat to suggest that trouble was brewing. In fact, things were going well, and even the leaders of the opposing groups were happy at this prolonged period of peace that had led to an increased sense of security and economic activity in the area, benefiting everyone. Shankar snapped out of his thoughts and turned to Kabir.

"Apart from the three people injured in the stampede, do you know of any other casualties?"

"Yes. The control room told me that there were two charred bodies near another side entrance. They were two shopkeepers from the Chandni Chowk area, although that is yet to be confirmed. It seems they were not able to get out in time. Three more died near the Red Fort."

"I know about the two near the side entrance to the station. My constable found them."

"Well, what do you think, Shankar?"

"I don't know. This is a strange one. I'd have expected a lot more confrontations with mobs, but that hasn't happened. If there are indeed only ten or so casualties, though tragic for the families of the deceased, I'll say that it isn't as bad as previous riots. It's still early though. I suspect we will have to be on alert for the next week or so at the very least."

"Yes, that's what I have heard too. Well, I must be off. I have been summoned back to the station. It seems all the known troublemakers have been rounded up and taken there. They need officers to start questioning them and take their statements. Let's catch up later."

"Nice meeting you, Kabir. Yes, certainly, we will catch up again once this is all over."

"Be safe, Shankar," Kabir said, and turned toward his jeep. Although it was still cold at this time of the night, Shankar noticed that Kabir's uniform was drenched in sweat.

Shankar spent the next couple of hours ensuring that the area around the railway station was peaceful. All trains had been cancelled. There was a curfew in place and the police barricades and men in uniform were now visible near all the major crossings and intersections. Shankar called the control room to find out more about the bodies he had found. He was informed that they had since been removed and taken for postmortem. The area had been photographed and visible clues had been collected by the constables from his station. Shankar knew that for the next few days they would mostly be involved in preventing any further violence. Investigating the death of the victims would take a back seat. He didn't approve of this, but it was out of his hands. At the best of times, the station was short-staffed. Even with reinforcements, things wouldn't change until at least a week of calm. As he walked back toward the railway station to take another look, a colleague of his arrived to replace him. They spoke briefly and then Shankar walked to the jeep to head back to the station.

The drive back to Kotwali was largely uneventful. The morning sun piercing through the thick Delhi fog made the aftermath of the riots all too visible. A flock of pigeons, a fixture in this part of the city, lined the rooftops and the trees. The fluttering of the birds was drowned out by the loudspeakers instructing the residents to stay indoors. There were very few people on the streets and lots of police and paramilitary forces everywhere. Shankar could see the tired look on the faces of the officers and constables. He waved at them as they drove past. There was still smoke emanating from some buildings. One thing that struck Shankar was how clean the streets were. There was some rubble, tires, stones, and bottles but nothing compared to what he had seen in past riots where the streets were filled with all sorts of debris. The riots had started quickly and unless there was going to be another wave, seemed to subside fast as well. As their jeep turned into the road leading to the police station, Motiram pointed to someone on his side of the road.

"Look at that idiot, sir. We have a curfew on, and this fool is outside taking pictures."

"Well, let's just give him a warning and tell him to get inside."

Motiram stopped the jeep and Shankar stepped out and called the young man over.

"You need to get inside. I am not sure if you know there's a curfew on and you need to stay indoors."

"Oh, I am sorry, officer. I just heard an announcement on the loudspeakers that we are free to move around until 8:00 a.m."

Shankar asked Motiram to check on the police radio. The young man was right. A police van had indeed gone by announcing that people could get supplies from the few stores that were open, or they could leave the area if they wanted. Some were taking advantage of this to get their provisions and a few families were packing up to leave, most likely to go stay with relatives in other parts of town. However, the families leaving the area had to get permission from the authorities and had to have a good reason. Most of them had ailing parents or infants and young children who needed constant attention. They also had to provide details about their destination and how they could be reached if required.

Shankar turned to the young man who was patiently waiting with his camera around his neck. He was not in a hurry but had a worried look on his face.

"Aright, just be back home by eight, and stay safe."

"Was it bad out there, sir?"

"Yes, it was, and we have to take every precaution. Please follow the police directives."

"Strange one this. Usually, things boil for a bit and there are angry mobs."

"Have you seen many riots?"

"Two before this, sir. But not like this."

"What's your name? What do you do?"

"My name is Shiv Kumar. I am a journalist."

"Which newspaper?"

"*The New India Courier.*"

Shankar knew the paper all too well. It's where Nitya worked. But he was exhausted and did not want to prolong the conversation.

"Well Shiv, I think you should head home and leave the handling of the riots to the police."

"I will, sir."

Shankar and Motiram went back to the station. Once he was back at his desk, a constable informed Shankar that his wife had called a few times. He called her back right away and reassured her that everything was calm and peaceful now. Shankar lived in a gated compound meant for police officers and their families. It was in a relatively safe area of New Delhi and quite far from the trouble spots.

After his phone call, Shankar turned his attention to the events of the past few hours. Being the most senior officer in charge at the station, it was up to him to coordinate the activities. He quickly called a meeting of all the officers and constables who had returned from the riot area. He ensured everyone was fine and took stock of all that they had learned and witnessed in the past few hours. He instructed them to make detailed notes and share any pertinent information with the other stations in the area, the police headquarters, and the home ministry. Then he looked at reports coming in from other areas and stations. Kabir Singh was right: ten people had died. They had all been taken to the Willingdon Hospital in New Delhi, where postmortems would be conducted before releasing them to the families. They had already started identifying the victims. The control room was fielding plenty of calls from families whose relatives were missing. The injured had been taken to various hospitals in Old Delhi and thankfully, most were not critical.

Shankar called the constable who had been at the site of the charred bodies and found that they had also been taken for postmortem. Since the victims were found in his area, it was well within his jurisdiction to investigate what had happened. Shankar wanted to get on it right away, but the directive from the home ministry was to first make sure that peace was maintained. This meant any investigation would have to wait, and that bothered Shankar. The prevailing wisdom among his superiors was that during riots some deaths were inevitable, but the priority was to prevent further deaths from happening. Once normalcy had returned, the deaths could then be investigated. Most deaths were almost always related to the revenge attacks among the groups involved. More often than not, the police knew who the culprits were, and eventually were able to apprehend them. There were times, however, when the perpetrators would not be convicted in court due to lack of evidence or witnesses.

Shankar decided to call Kabir Singh at the Chandni Chowk Police Station to find out if there were any leads from questioning the various religious leaders who had been rounded up.

"Shankar here, Kabir. How are things at your station?"

"Well, we are still questioning the folks whom we rounded up. But we are not getting anywhere. It's a bit odd."

"How so?"

"It almost seems like they were caught unawares as well. They seem surprised too."

"Do you believe them?"

"Under usual circumstances, I wouldn't. But it seems that all the groups that we have questioned so far are perplexed. There would have to be an amazing amount of coordination among them to be in this kind of agreement, and the thing is they don't even like one another."

"Yes, that is strange."

"Tell me, did anyone find out more about the deceased?"

"Unfortunately, not. We have got some calls from families whose relatives are missing, and we are still trying to connect the dots. I am sure you may have heard the directive is to establish peace now and investigate the deaths later."

"Yes, that's what I have been told as well."

"Are things calm near your station?"

"Yes, things appear to be under control. The worst seems to be over. How about Chandni Chowk?"

"Well, most of it was near the main bazaar. A few shops were burned down. The owners are angry, which is understandable. We will know more in the coming days. I have to be back on the road soon to enforce the curfew at eight."

"Thank you, Kabir. Let's talk again, and once this is all over, we can go for a drink."

"Certainly."

After hanging up, Shankar headed to the control room where there was a radio connecting all the stations in the area, the police headquarters, and the home ministry. He reviewed all the calls, directives, telexes, and messages coming through the wires. The latest was that a mob was headed toward Connaught Place in New Delhi, but the New Delhi police and paramilitary forces would be tackling the situation. Shankar wondered whether they would be able to reach on time. Usually, paramilitary forces were extremely effective in quelling any sort of protest, riot, or disturbance, but it took time for them to mobilize. If the mob was already close to Connaught Place, then the only forces who would be able to tackle them immediately were the police in the area, some of whom had been diverted to Old Delhi. His thought immediately shifted to Nitya. They hadn't spoken in a while. He decided to give her a call to check whether everything was fine. He couldn't get through. He looked at his watch. It was time for him to be back on the road to enforce the curfew near the railway station.

Aftermath

After two days, the people of Delhi were assured that the riots that had started in the walled city were behind them. There was still anger, sadness, and confusion among the residents who were impacted. The police had done their best to ensure that there was no subsequent looting by gangs who usually took advantage of such situations. Apart from a few sporadic incidents, they had managed to maintain peace. There was still a lot of police presence in the area where it started and where most of the damage was concentrated. The focus was now slowly changing to ensure that the victims' families were notified. The families of the injured were finally able to connect with their loved ones and there was a coordinated effort among all the stations in the area to investigate any other missing persons reported by their families. Shankar was finally able to go home to his wife and son after spending almost two days at the station. He was relieved that the worst was over. His superiors in the headquarters and ministry had insisted that all personnel involved in dealing with the riots be sent home for two days. Enough reinforcements had arrived and had been stationed in the area to deal with any aftermath.

* * *

Meanwhile, Nitya and her team were back in the office on Thursday morning, after being informed that the situation was under control. The large police presence in the area was reassuring. When the team met in the conference room, all the talk was about the events of the last two days. But they were happy to be back at work. The management was happy and relieved because no one in their organization had been affected too greatly by what had happened in the city.

Manoj planned to approach the riots differently than how the paper had in the past. He wanted to divide up the stories among the teams in the current affairs department. At the meeting in the conference room, after inquiring about everyone's well-being, he got down to business.

"Is everyone here?" Manoj asked.

"Everyone except Shiv and Suresh, sir," replied Swati. "They will be here in a few minutes."

"Well, let's get started. Nitya, maybe you can fill them in once they arrive."

Nitya nodded. She knew that they were going to be late. They had called in the morning and left a message with one of the secretaries manning the phones at the reception.

"Sir, can you please tell us a bit about how we will be covering the riots, and then maybe we can get into what our group should focus on?" Nitya asked.

When she had spoken to Manoj briefly over the phone, he had given her somewhat of an idea of what he wanted her team to do, but he hadn't offered any details on what the others were doing. It was important for Nitya and her team to know the larger picture.

"Sure Nitya. We have decided to divide up the work among the various teams in the current affairs department to address the riot from different angles. One team will be working on the actual events, and the sequence of incidents leading up to the riots. Another team will be working on the response of the authorities—the police, fire department, medical staff, etcetera, to see if the response was adequate under the circumstances, or if they could have done some things better," Manoj said slowly, pausing for it all to sink in. He could see some heads nodding around the table.

A gentle knock on the door interrupted him—Suresh and Shiv walked in.

"I apologize for being late, sir," Suresh said.

"Same here, sir," Shiv followed suit.

"No harm done. We just started. Please take a seat," Manoj said, pointing to some empty chairs at the far end of the oval table.

This was the first time Nitya was seeing Shiv up close since taking over the team. She had seen him in the office before but had never interacted with him. As he quickly made his way to one of the empty chairs, Nitya pondered on his general appearance. He did not seem like someone from Old Delhi. He was dressed in what seemed like expensive attire. His shoes were polished, and his clothes were clean and ironed. His upright stance made him look taller than he probably was and unlike the other men in the room, he was cleanshaven and didn't wear glasses. Suresh crouched right next to him in glasses and with a saddlebag still around his shoulder. They looked like quite an odd pair. Nitya remembered what Swati and Suresh had told her about Shiv, but she knew she had to approach each person with an open mind. Once they had settled in, Manoj continued with his monologue.

"Apart from the two teams that I just mentioned, there is another team that will be working on contacting the various political and religious leaders to get their take on what happened. I am sure there's enough blame going around, but their task will be to remove the noise and concentrate on what these leaders think of such incidents and most importantly, on how they can be prevented," Manoj said, pausing again and taking a sip of water from the glass in front of him.

"What are we expected to be working on, sir?" Swati asked before Manoj could continue.

"Yes, Swati. I am coming to it," Manoj replied patiently, with a smile.

"Sorry for interrupting."

"Don't worry about it. I want your team to work on a story on the victims and what happened during those fateful hours. Find out who they are and what their stories are. Most often the violence and mayhem dominate the reporting during the riots and the blame game in its aftermath. What is often overlooked is the actual lives that are lost, the victims just becoming faceless numbers. I don't want that to happen. From the reports that we have seen so far, there have been around ten deaths and a dozen injuries. I want all of you to tell their stories and the story of the impact on the families."

Manoj stopped and looked around the table. Nitya knew that her team probably had some questions and she wanted them to have the opportunity to ask them.

"Anyone have any questions for Manoj?" Nitya asked, looking around the room. She anticipated that many of her team members would feel shy or intimidated in Manoj's presence. Some were probably afraid that their question would come across as unintelligent. Finally, Swati broke the silence.

"How long do we have? This can take a while. We will have to question the families, and since they are grieving and angry, they may not want to speak with us."

"That's right," Manoj replied, "it's not going to be easy. But I am sure you are all up to the task. As to how long you have, well I'd say around two weeks or so. I want to start getting a few stories out in two weeks' time while the events are still fresh in the minds of our readers. They don't have to all come out at once. I will let Nitya decide how to go on from here, how to assign the stories, etcetera."

"It's a good idea, sir," Suresh said softly.

Manoj nodded and looked around the room. "Any other questions?"

"Yes, sir," Shiv said.

"What is it, Shiv?" Manoj asked. Nitya could sense that his tone had changed slightly from an understanding one to a demanding one.

"Are we free to engage members of other teams? Our stories could be linked to what others outside the team might be following up on."

"Yes, that's possible. I will leave it up to Nitya and the other managers to figure how that will work. Of course, we are one organization. We do need to collaborate as needed. It's not a competition," Manoj replied in a hurried tone, making it clear that he did not want any follow-up questions from Shiv.

The rest of the team also sensed that Manoj was not in a mood to field any other questions. He looked around the room, gave some customary words of encouragement, and left. Nitya could sense that her team had become a bit more relaxed after Manoj's exit. She quickly made some notes in her notebook while the team members started discussing with one another.

"Alright then, the first order of business is to make a list of the victims—the ones who were killed and the ones injured. I think the local news desk section should be able to give us that information. It has been three days already. I am pretty sure they have an accurate list, and we can cross-check it with the official police reports that have been made public. The same goes for the injured," Nitya said.

"Talking to the families that are still in mourning will not be easy," Suresh said. He was more confident and vocal now that Manoj had left. He was also senior to the other reporters on Nitya's team and wanted to make his presence felt.

"Yes, and that's why we have to tread carefully. We do not want to pester the families if they don't want to talk to us, but at the same time we must make them understand that their stories need to be told so that the public knows that the victims are not just numbers on a page."

"Yes, ma'am," Swati responded, "you are right." Nitya wasn't sure if Swati was really agreeing with her or just trying to make herself feel important. Knowing Swati, it was probably a bit of both.

"How will we divide up the work, ma'am?" Moina asked.

"Good question, Moina. Let me give it some thought. I want to pair everyone up with a few victims each. I know we are an odd number so one of you will end up working on your own to start with, but each member should be able to reach out for help when needed. I will let you know the teams by the end of the day. Meanwhile, I want you all to gather as much information as possible. It's critical that we get an accurate list of victims to begin with. We don't want to miss anyone. The worst thing would be to publish the stories and leave someone out. The family would think that we have forgotten about them. That must not happen. If they don't want to talk to us or don't want us to publish anything, that's fine, but we should reach out to everyone."

Everyone nodded in agreement.

"When do we start?" Shiv asked from the far end of the table.

"I am going to give everyone their assignments by the end of the day. Also, this will involve a fair amount of travel, so I want everyone to make use of the company cars and at all times, keep me and the rest of the team informed of your whereabouts. Is that clear?"

"Yes, ma'am," several of them replied in unison.

Nitya looked around the table and said, "the first order of business is to get that list. Let's try to get the list from as many sources as possible, and once we have it, I will start handing out your assignments. We have a lot of ground to cover in a short period of time. Any questions?"

The group was silent. Nitya could sense that they were trying to figure out all that needed to be done.

"Ma'am, should I contact the local news desk and our contacts at All India Radio to get the media reports?" Suresh asked.

"Yes, I want you and Moina to take the lead on that, while the others can start looking at other sources. Look at the other newspapers and what they have reported as well."

"Is there anything else you want us to follow up on, ma'am?" Swati asked.

"No, I think that's it for now. Let's head back to our desks and take some time to finish what we are working on at present. I have spoken to everyone individually except for Shiv. Shiv, I want you to come by my office in an hour. I have to make some calls and then we can have a quick chat."

"Yes, ma'am," Shiv replied.

Nitya was aware that the assignment her team had been given was not the most coveted in comparison to the other teams. However, she was the newest addition to the senior management team in the current affairs department. She had to make the most of it and decided she would actively engage with everyone in each of the stories. As soon as she entered her office, she heard the phone ring. She hoped it was not her mom calling for yet another conversation about finding a suitor. It wasn't. As soon as she picked up the phone, a friendly voice on the other end of the line made her smile.

"Hello Nitya, this is Shankar. How are you?"

"I am fine, Shankar. It's so nice to hear from you. It's been a while."

"Yes, I should have called earlier. I just wanted to check if everything's alright. I tried to reach you on Monday. I heard there was an unruly mob in your area. I heard from my colleagues that they broke windows and robbed some stores."

"Yes, it was scary for a while. But we managed well. Everything's back to normal now. Honestly, apart from the first hour when the mob was throwing stones, it has been peaceful. There has been no violence where I live."

"That's good. Yes, most of Delhi has been largely untouched by what happened."

"Yes, how about you Shankar? Your station is in Old Delhi, right? It must have been bad. I am sorry, I should have checked in on you."

"I am fine. The first night was bad, but things have settled down after that."

"I heard that there were casualties in and around the station. I hope you didn't have to deal with any mob attacks."

"No, thankfully most people abided by the curfew. There were some minor incidents, as there always are, of people taking advantage of the situation to rob and loot stores in the area, but things are better now. I'd say it's almost back to normal."

"I am glad. How are Rohini and Vikram?"

"Oh, they are doing fine. Vikram is growing up fast and is quite a handful now."

"We must meet up sometime. It's been ages since I have seen you."

"Certainly, we will. I need to get back to work now. As you can imagine, the next few days are going to be extremely busy, but things should settle down in a couple of weeks, and then we can meet up."

"Sure, it was nice of you to call and check up on me."

"Well, someone has to. You have a knack for getting into trouble."

Nitya laughed and retorted, "well, I am not the only one."

Shankar laughed and said, "bye Nitya."

Nitya recalled how she had met Shankar. Shankar was a new recruit in the police service and Callipur was his first posting. At the time, Nitya was working for *The Callipur Post*, a regional newspaper. They had worked together on a case involving the murder of an apprentice in an auto repair shop. The investigation spanned a few months and during that time, Nitya had grown fond of the handsome young police officer. Shankar was athletic, smart, and outspoken. She was impressed with his confidence and investigative abilities. At the time, Nitya was almost engaged to be married to her childhood friend, Raj. Raj and Nitya's families had decided that it was a great union, and most of Callipur was eagerly awaiting their marriage. But a lot had happened since then.

Shankar had got transferred to New Delhi, something that he had eagerly wanted. Nitya had broken off her engagement and accepted an offer with her current employer and moved to Delhi much to the disappointment and contempt of her mother. Raj, meanwhile, had married one of her friends and settled in Callipur.

Since moving to Delhi, Shankar and Nitya's careers had taken on different trajectories. While Nitya's had really taken off, making her a star performer within the organization with one promotion after the other, Shankar's career had initially started off with a lot of promise but had stalled due to an ill-fated incident three years ago. At the time, Shankar and his fellow officers were on duty near the majestic India Gate in New Delhi. A large labor union had planned a protest march in the area. The officers were manning the barricades to prevent any unruly incidents. The crowd was much larger than they had anticipated. Reinforcements had been called in but were slow to arrive. The unruly mob pushed through the barricades, hurled projectiles at the police, and soon there was an imminent threat that they would start making their way toward the parliament. Another section of the crowd was making its way toward the India Gate monument and the police feared that they would desecrate it. To make matters worse, some unruly elements within the crowd were harassing tourists visiting from outside Delhi. The situation deteriorated quickly when an empty bus and a few taxis were set ablaze, and the drivers were beaten up. Shankar and his fellow officers had no choice but to open fire on the crowd. Initially, they fired empty rounds in the air to disperse the crowd, but when that didn't work, they resorted to using rubber bullets. After almost two hours of intense physical confrontation, the mob was finally contained. But by then a few police officers and several protestors were injured.

The next day the papers carried full-page articles on the high-handedness of the police and their brutality while dealing with the "peaceful" protest. There were pictures of protestors being carried away in ambulances, interviews with labor union leaders demanding an independent probe of the incident, and politicians of all stripes asking for accountability from the police. The media was all over the police and Nitya's paper was one of them. In fact, she was assigned the story and was front and center in reporting it. There was an upcoming national election and the thirst for votes meant that the ruling party in power tried to absolve themselves of any wrongdoing. They squarely put the blame on the police. The home ministry and police were subjected to a judicial probe and although the officers on the scene were acquitted of any deliberate and premeditated wrongdoings, they were guilty of "negligence" largely due to a lack of training and resources. Members of the public and press, including Nitya, who were present during the protests were interviewed.

The final report was about how the police "could" have done their job better and "should" have been better prepared. Once the elections were over, things died down and public interest shifted to more recent events. However, some in the police hierarchy were upset with the officers who were posted at India Gate on that ill-fated day. The three officers in charge were swiftly transferred to other, less glamorous areas in the capital and other states. Shankar was one of them. He was sent to the Old Delhi Police Station in Kotwali, in a riot-prone part of the city, and had been there ever since. His career had practically stalled and his repeated attempts at a transfer request had been rebuffed. Nitya was sad about how things had worked out for Shankar and felt somewhat responsible that the press had not given the police a fair shake. She was worried that Shankar would hold it against her, but he didn't. He was always warm and friendly toward her, and Nitya sensed that he didn't want to discuss the incident but move past it.

On their personal fronts, Nitya and Shankar's lives had taken different turns as well. Nitya had been busy meeting up with prospective suitors that her mother had "arranged" for her and had an ill-advised, short-lived affair with Vijay in the office. While both had been engrossed in their work with little time for a social life, on one of his work trips to Mussoorie, Shankar had managed to start a courtship with one of his childhood friends, Rohini. When he had first moved to Delhi, a case would take him to Mussoorie quite often. It also gave him an opportunity to visit his parents and siblings in Dehradun. After six months, Rohini and Shankar got married and moved into their current apartment in New Delhi, in a housing colony for police officers. They were soon parents of a boy, Vikram, and everything seemed promising.

Then the incident at India Gate happened, followed by the posting in Old Delhi. It was all downhill from there. The long hours at work in a stressful station meant that Shankar was away from his wife and son for long periods of time. With Shankar's hours and Vikram still young, Rohini couldn't look for a full-time job. Her parents and in-laws were not in Delhi, and they had no other family or close friends. Rohini tried to make some friends with the wives of the other officers who lived nearby, but no one became that close. She was stuck at home, bored and without work, and started taking out her frustration on Shankar. Her parents were constantly encouraging her to move back and that was extremely tempting for her. Although she wanted to make it work with Shankar, her circumstances worked against her. All this put a lot of strain on their marriage. Rohini was now looking forward to her trip to Mussoorie. Vikram's holidays were coming up and she had decided to make the most of it and head back to her hometown for a couple of weeks. After the riots, she knew that Shankar wouldn't be able to join them. Her parents had even told her to look for schools for Vikram in Mussoorie. Initially, she had refused, but during her last conversation with them, she had relented. She hadn't spoken to Shankar about it.

Rohini had heard about the riots on the radio while listening to music late at night. Shankar was on one of his weekend shifts at the station and that meant lots of unwanted free time for Rohini to get bored and contemplate all kinds of negative thoughts. She just couldn't sleep. She had tried reading a book and then hoped that listening to the radio would relax her and help her sleep. When the announcement was first made on All India Radio, she immediately got worried. The reports were not dramatic or sensational, but Rohini knew that the government channels always downplayed what happened in communal riots. They did not want to cause any panic. The idea was to make it seem like the authorities were in charge of the situation and had a handle on what was going on. She had immediately phoned the control room at Shankar's station, and they had informed her that Shankar was out on patrol. She tried to get in touch with him repeatedly, but to no avail. She knew that Shankar wouldn't be back at the station for many hours and probably not back home until the next day. Riots were always stressful for the families of police officers. There were long periods of little or no communication, and things could suddenly take a turn for the worse. In the past, some officers and constables who had been dealing with riots in Shankar's station had got injured. Shankar himself had had some bruises and scratches, though nothing too serious. They were mostly during attempts to break up opposing mobs involved in street fighting or from objects being thrown at the police.

Suddenly, Rohini forgot about the strain in their marriage. Dread and panic engulfed her. Her only thoughts were about Shankar's safety and well-being. She did not know the wives of the other officers at the station because they were all new. She looked through the phone directory and called them anyway to see if they had any information. They didn't. Most were just as worried as she was, while a few found it strange that an officer's wife who did not know them would be calling in the middle of the night. But Rohini didn't care. She called the control room every hour and found out that Shankar had called them twice. She paced up and down the small apartment. Vikram had woken up and wanted his mother to get him ready for school, but since she didn't know how bad things were, she didn't want to send him to school. When Shankar finally called from the station in the morning to let her know that he was all right, part of her wanted to hug him, and another part of her, in equal measure, wanted to scream at him. She was relieved when he came home after two days. She wanted to know what had happened, but the look on his face made her feel sorry for him. When Shankar walked into the apartment, Vikram jumped on him and gave him a big hug. Once Vikram let go of him after repeated pleas from his mother, Shankar slumped into one of the armchairs in their living room. Rohini could see that his uniform was completely drenched, his eyes had dark circles, his face was covered in dust and soot, and he could barely stay awake.

"I will take a quick shower," Shankar said, as he slowly headed toward the bedroom.

"I have kept a fresh set of clothes on the bed. Once you are done, we will have some breakfast together," Rohini said.

"Sure," Shankar replied.

Rohini headed to the kitchen to help the cook make a big breakfast. Vikram was happy that he did not have to go to school for yet another day, but more so because his father was home. He was looking forward to playing with his father. Rohini knew that Shankar's visit home would be short. She was sure that he would be summoned back at the first sign of any trouble in the riot-hit area. After she prepared breakfast, she laid it out neatly on the table. She was looking forward to talking to Shankar about what had happened. Shankar was not always open about things at work, but she knew that the times when he did share, he felt more relaxed. She went to the bedroom to let him know that breakfast was ready, but found him showered and sound asleep in his nightclothes. She thought of waking him up, but looking at his tired face resting peacefully on the pillow, she decided otherwise. She slowly closed all the windows and drapes in the room to make sure it was dark and quiet. Then she gently placed a blanket over him, left the room, and closed the door from outside. She asked Vikram to play and read in his room and sternly reminded him not to make any noise or go into the bedroom where his father was asleep.

After a couple of hours, the phone rang. It was the police station. Shankar had been summoned back. He woke up, made some phone calls, got ready quickly, wolfed down the reheated breakfast, and headed out. Rohini packed him some fruits and food in a bag. It made him smile and a little sad that he hadn't spent more time with her and Vikram.

* * *

In the offices of *The New India Courier*, Nitya's team was busy gathering all the details on the victims. They confirmed that all the dead and those with serious injuries were taken to the Willingdon hospital in New Delhi. The latest reports in all the papers had reported ten dead and around fifty injured. All the missing, it seemed, had now been accounted for. Manoj asked them to focus on the deceased. Moina and Suresh quickly gathered all the information that they could from sources in their own paper. Others in the team read through the reports in rival papers and gathered information from public communications sent out on the radio. They scoured through all the police and media reports. All the dead had been identified, but not all the names had been made public, because the police were still waiting to inform the families of two victims. They had to make a formal identification first before their names could be made public. All reports seemed to suggest that the postmortems had been completed, and except for the two that were going to be identified and released later in the day, all others had been handed over to the families for the last rites. The victims, as always, spanned all religious denominations. Some were going to be cremated while others would be buried.

After the phone conversation with Shankar, Nitya immediately started working on the list of victims. To verify the list, she placed some calls to the Press Council of India, All India Radio, and the police headquarters. Once she was satisfied with the list she had got, she asked the team to convene in the conference room.

From her room, through the large glass windows and open door that faced the cubicles, she could see her team members interact with one another. Most were getting along fine, but it was quite evident that Swati and Suresh were avoiding Shiv. Shiv was mostly working on his own and occasionally speaking with Moina and members of other teams. He didn't seem to engage in long conversations with anyone. A few senior journalists who were now Nitya's peers came by to congratulate her on her promotion. Among them was Vijay. Things were as normal as could be between them, but some awkwardness naturally lingered.

"Congratulations, Nitya," Vijay said, standing at the open door to her office.

"Thank you, Vijay."

"I hear your team has been assigned to work on the victims' stories."

"Yes."

"Should be interesting."

"We will see."

"Is this your new team?" Vijay asked, pointing to the cubicles in front of her room, where some of the reporters could be seen standing and talking to others.

"Yes, pretty much and some others."

"Shiv too?"

"Yes."

"Oh, well, I am not sure what you have heard, but he is one outburst away from getting tossed."

"Well, I just took over. We will see how it goes with him and everyone else."

"The rest are fine, I think. Shiv's a misfit. You will find out soon enough. He has been with a few of us on some stories, and he is just too smart for his own good."

"I am sorry to do this, Vijay, but I need to get back to work. Perhaps we can catch up later," Nitya said, immediately regretting it. She didn't want Vijay to have the impression that she wanted anything to do with him outside of work anymore.

"Oh, that's fine. I must get going as well. Congratulations again and good luck!"

"Thanks."

A few minutes later, Shiv arrived for their one-on-one meeting. Nitya was swamped and asked him if they could postpone it to another day, and he agreed. After a few minutes, Nitya headed to Manoj's office for her first meeting with the senior team. They talked about the stories that everyone was working on, some expense-related matters, and other administrative items that were not a priority for Nitya at the moment. She wondered why they were wasting their time on this when actual work needed to be done. She decided to remain courteous as always and offer her opinion only when asked. She knew that if she had to get her foot into the old boys' club, she couldn't start alienating them right off the bat. But her mind was on the meeting with her team.

When she entered the conference room with the list of assignments, the others were already seated around the oval table. Nitya quickly handed out copies of the assignments and contact details of everyone in the team.

"Before I hand out the assignments, I want to reiterate that I must know where everyone is at all times while we are working on this story. Now, here's the most important part—I don't want anyone to go anywhere where they think there might be trouble. I know that the riots are over, and things are calm, but this kind of violence has a way of resurfacing. Is that clear?"

Nitya could see everyone nodding.

"What about transportation, ma'am?" asked Moina.

"Yes, I am coming to that. I have arranged for three company cars. We will be using those along with my car. There will be four groups, so each group will get their own car."

Nitya could see the relief on their faces. She knew that with the young reporters, transportation was a sore point since they constantly had to take buses, taxis, and auto-rickshaws. They had to keep track of all their commuting expenses and then claim them at the end of the month. The entire process was tedious and annoying.

"Are these all the assignments, ma'am?" Suresh asked, pointing to the papers that Nitya had handed out.

"Yes. They are based on the list that I received from you and Moina. You will see that two are yet to be identified, so I couldn't assign them to anyone now. Did we verify the numbers with multiple sources?" Nitya asked Moina and Suresh.

"Yes, ma'am, we did. There are ten victims," Moina replied.

"We called All India Radio, the Press Council, and the police headquarters, and they all confirmed the number," Suresh said. Nitya had called them as well and her figures matched with what her team was telling her.

"I checked with the hospital, ma'am," Swati said, "they confirmed the same number."

"So, we have names of all the eight victims, and two are yet to be identified?" Nitya asked.

"Yes, and we have the addresses of most," Swati replied, "and we will have the rest tomorrow, except for the two whose names are yet to be released, of course."

"Did anyone speak to our colleagues who reported the numbers?"

"I did, ma'am," Rakesh replied.

"And?"

"They confirmed the same number. They also gave me some more details about the injured. I know we are not focusing on their stories yet, but they may come in handy later," Rakesh added.

"Yes, they will," Nitya said, adding, "so are we all set for tomorrow? You know your assignments and who you are paired up with. You have your cars. We will all meet back here at 5:00 p.m. each evening to catch up and compare notes. Anything else?"

"Yes," a voice called out from the far end of the room. Everyone turned toward it.

"Is there anything you want to add, Shiv?" Nitya asked.

"Yes. There are eleven victims, ma'am, not ten."

There were visible signs of exasperation in the room. Suresh, Swati, and Rakesh showed some skepticism. The rest looked curious.

"How so? What makes you think there are eleven victims and not ten?" Nitya asked.

"Initially, when the reports came out, there was some confusion about how many people had died. That's understandable.

News from riot-hit areas is hard to come by and even harder to verify," Shiv said softly, pausing for the others to react.

"Get to the point, Shiv. We have verified through multiple sources that there are ten victims. Perhaps they made a mistake in the beginning and declared eleven, but then corrected it to ten. What makes you suspect that there are more?" Suresh asked curtly.

"Right, and that's what got me thinking. We have had so many riots in the past. In all instances, the numbers of the dead and injured were always revised upwards."

"So, maybe this time around it's different," Swati said, matching Suresh's tone.

"It is, in probably more ways than one. Both the police communiqué and All India Radio had initially said eleven but then went back down to ten."

"But we have verified it with them again and other sources too, even the hospital, and they all agreed that there are ten deceased," said Moina politely. Her tone was different from Suresh's and Swati's.

"Did you call anyone or find out anything else that would suggest that there are eleven victims? Otherwise, we are just running around in circles," Nitya said.

"Yes, ma'am. I did. I called the hospital as well. I spoke to the guard on duty at the gate. They keep a record of victims coming in through the gates. Of course, there are many people who are brought in, not just victims of the riot. But he had made a note in his register of all the bodies that came in ambulances from the riot areas. He doesn't have any names, just the numbers, and there are eleven."

"Maybe the guard made a mistake," Suresh said, this time in a much less confrontational tone.

"I also spoke to the orderly at the morgue. He also said there were eleven bodies."

"Again, he may have got it wrong," Swati said, sounding less confident in her assertion.

"Yes, they may have. You are right. So, I decided to call the crematoriums and burial grounds in the city. There are five of them altogether. They have to keep accurate records or else they will be in trouble in more ways than one. There are hundreds of people who die each day in this city. I asked them if they could tell me how many had come in from the riot areas. They wouldn't give me details, but they did give me a count. They add up to nine. There are two still in the hospital. That makes eleven victims, not ten," Shiv said, and paused.

There was utter silence in the room. Nitya had been quiet for a while. She could see that everything Shiv said was slowly sinking in.

After a pregnant pause, she decided to break the silence.

"Alright, Shiv. From what you have said, it is possible that there are eleven victims. But where do we go from here?"

"If you don't mind, ma'am, and if it is fine with Rakesh, we can take on the additional victim."

Rakesh nodded in agreement. The rest of Nitya's team was still silent.

"Well Shiv, you have certainly earned it. The eleventh victim is all yours," Nitya said.

"Thank you, ma'am."

As they got up and slowly left the room, Nitya realized that she had to keep an open mind about Shiv. She had heard all sorts of things about him, most of which were not positive, but it was hard not to be impressed with him after what had just happened. Based on what they had just heard, she was convinced there were eleven victims, although she didn't say so in as many words. The investigative journalist in her knew that there could be more to this story than what met the eye, and she was glad that Shiv was on it.

Stranger

When Shankar arrived at his police station, he wanted to find out more about the two charred bodies that were found near the railway station. He knew that in order to make any headway, he had to start the investigation right away. However, his superiors were more interested in maintaining peace and ensuring that there was no subsequent rioting. There was good reason to believe that could happen. Shankar was happy that the unlawful incidents had abruptly come to an end. Security reinforcements that had been swiftly deployed to the area from the other parts of Delhi had helped curb any mass looting and violence. At the same time, he was convinced that they were missing something. All accounts seemed to suggest that the first reported incident was the burning of the empty railway coach on the tracks. That seemed odd. Usually, riots started due to scuffles between communities or mobs. Then there were the killings. All of them happened in and around the station. While the area was a hotbed of communal activities, in the past the casualties were spread not just across Old Delhi but adjoining suburbs as well.

Once he was in his office, he called his constable to get him some tea, and called Kabir Singh again. Kabir had told Shankar that the leaders of various religious communities were being rounded up and being held at the Chandni Chowk Police Station, which was larger and better equipped to hold miscreants.

"Hello Kabir, this is Shankar again from the Kotwali Station."

"Yes, of course," Kabir replied.

"Any progress in questioning the folks you have rounded up?"

"Nope, still the same."

"They know nothing?"

"Yes, they are still holding the line and saying that they were caught unawares as well."

"So, no one seems to know what triggered this?"

"They are confused. I mean they all automatically blame the opposing groups, but that's their first reaction anyway. They are not convinced themselves how this started."

Shankar was quiet as he tried to absorb it all.

Then he asked, "I am sorry to ask you this again, do you still believe them?"

"Usually I wouldn't, but, as I said yesterday, this time I am tempted to believe them."

"Are they still being questioned?"

"No, I think it's over now. We are holding them until we can ascertain their whereabouts last night and check if any of them were near the affected areas. Then we will have to let them go. They have already requested legal representation and once the lawyers arrive, it will be a matter of time before they are let go, unless, of course, we are able to link any specific incidents to them."

"What about the casualties?"

"What about them?"

"Are they known to the police? Do they have any connections to the folks who you are currently holding?"

"We are trying to determine that. But at first glance, I'd say no. None of the victims have any past records."

"A bit strange, isn't it?"

"Yes. I have to say that even the officers in our station are a bit stumped."

"Thank you, Kabir. Do you mind if I drop by your station on my way back home? I need to see if I can get more details on the two bodies that I found near the railway station. I know all the details are being sent to your station, but these two are under my jurisdiction since they are from my area. I am interested in finding out what's going on with them."

"Certainly. My understanding is that the investigation will start as soon as the top brass is convinced that things are under control."

"Understood."

"I will see you in the evening," Kabir said and hung up.

It was a rehash of the same conversation that Shankar had with Kabir earlier. Questioning the folks that had been rounded up had not yielded any results. Shankar spent the next few minutes looking through the files, which had information on all the informers from his area who had been rounded up and brought to the station. He called for his constable.

"Have we rounded up everyone?"

"Yes, sir."

"Are they being held separately?"

"Yes, sir."

"Alright, please send them in one by one."

Shankar spent the next three hours questioning all the police informers. The detailed line of questioning was to ascertain whether they knew anything prior to the rioting that could help the police understand what could have triggered it. The responses were remarkably consistent. None of them had heard or seen anything that could help. Usually, at least some would be eager to share information with the police even if the others were guarded, but this time around none of them could offer any insights on what triggered the events in Old Delhi. Shankar spent some more time looking over the reports of all the incidents. He went to the control room to pick up all the messages from the night of the riots and started putting together a chronology of events. He didn't have the full picture, of course, because his was only one of the many police stations in the area. After spending another hour or so going over the rest of the messages from the control room, he decided to eat the lunch that Rohini had prepared for him. Then he called out for Motiram since it was time for them to go out on patrol.

Their first stop was the side entrance to the railway station where they had found the two charred bodies. The surroundings looked very different now. There were hardly any visible remnants of the riots. The streets were clean. All the debris had been removed. Pigeons were on the rooftops, their large number only matched by the number of people walking the overcrowded lanes and bazaars. Motiram was having a hard time making his way through the lanes, and although people were giving way to the police jeep, it was taking him a long time to navigate the congested roads. On reaching the end of the lane, Shankar asked Motiram to park the jeep and started walking slowly to the other end of the lane along with the pedestrians who were heading toward the railway station.

The buildings on either side were full of people. A few shops were open. Most people knew that there was a night curfew that would start late in the evening and were in a hurry to get back home. Shankar knew that the public resented the curfew and wanted to go back to their daily lives. As he slowly walked up to the gate, Shankar shifted his gaze upward toward the higher floors of the buildings. He could see some people staring at him. But a policeman in uniform was not uncommon in the area. Since the area was recovering from a riot, a police presence meant that things would probably take longer to get back to normal.

On reaching the end of the lane, Shankar surveyed the street in each direction. The gate leading into the railway station was narrow, and a constant flow of people were getting in and out. Across the gate was a pathway leading up to the station. On either side were patches of overgrown grass. He looked over to the side where the bodies had been discovered. He could find remnants of police tape. On the opposite side, he found some street vendors, a small pharmacy, and a tea stall where people had gathered. He walked up to the tea shop and spoke to the owner. He wanted to find out whether he knew anything, though Shankar knew well enough that no one in the area would talk freely to someone in uniform. Despite their reluctance, the owners and tenants in the building approached Shankar to ask him whether the situation was still tense. They wanted the night curfew to be lifted. Shankar informed them that it would depend on whether there would be any more unlawful activities overnight. He asked around whether anyone had seen anything near where the bodies had been found, but no one was forthcoming with any information. Once he had finished talking to a few locals, he headed back to the jeep. He instructed Motiram to tell the pharmacist and tea stall owner to meet him at the police station in two hours. Since Motiram was not in uniform, he could talk to them discreetly without raising any eyebrows.

After setting off Motiram on his errand, Shankar surveyed the crossing and the road where his jeep was parked. It was clear to him that the two people were either killed and burned where their bodies were found, or they had been brought there through the pedestrian gate leading to the railway station. It would be impossible for anyone to bring the bodies in through the road where he was standing without being noticed by the residents in the buildings. However, the lane was dark at night. If indeed the victims had been killed there and their bodies left to burn, the people in the surrounding buildings would have at least smelled something. The tea stall and pharmacy owners would know if something happened. Tea shops and medical stores were open till late, and Shankar was confident that they would let him know if they had seen anything when he interviewed them one-on-one. Once Motiram was back, they carried on through the overcrowded streets toward the main entrance to the Old Delhi Railway Station. They passed two main roads and an avenue that led to the entrance. At each crossing, they found police barricades with the officers and constables in uniform checking vehicles, trucks, and rickshaws. Being in a police jeep meant that they were let right through without being stopped at any checkpoints.

Once they reached the railway station, Shankar decided to check the platform where the coach had been set on fire during the riots. He asked Motiram to stay near the jeep. The station was still not fully functional. Only a handful of trains were being allowed to use the station, but there was still a large volume of people on the platforms. The coach that had been set alight had been removed. On asking the stationmaster, he was informed that it had been taken to a shed at the far end of one of the other platforms. He decided to go take a closer look. He found some police officers combing the debris in the coach for clues. Some of them were from other police stations in Old Delhi. Since this was a riot, the central agencies had taken over the investigation. The officers were busy at work but acknowledged Shankar's presence with a few greetings and nods. Shankar decided to stay out of their way and asked the constable standing guard to prevent anyone from entering the area. The constable recognized Shankar right away.

"Good afternoon, sir."

"Good afternoon. When was the coach moved here?"

"Oh, just about an hour ago. We had to clear the platform for trains arriving and departing from the station."

"Anything inside?" Shankar said, pointing to the coach.

"Nothing so far, sir. It seems they burned an empty coach."

"I smell petrol."

"Yes, sir. They found a few cans inside. It seems they poured it and then set the coach on fire."

"No victims?"

"No, sir."

"What was burned inside?"

"Mainly empty seats and paper sir. Lots of paper. They are all burned. We can't make anything out. All reduced to ashes, sir."

"Hmm. Who first reported it?"

"The stationmaster, sir. He called your police station and the other ones in the area."

"What about the railway police? There is an outpost here. Why weren't they called?"

"It seems there was an incident on another platform that they were looking into. A fight had broken out between two groups, and they went across to break them up."

"So, they left this platform completely unguarded?"

"Yes, sir. It seems that way."

"Where can I find the constables who were on duty that night?"

"They are in the control room near the main gate, sir."

"Yes, I know where that is."

"They are not too happy about what happened. They were already reprimanded by the commissioner this morning, sir."

"Right. Thank you," Shankar replied, and turned to retrace his steps to the platform and then to the main gate toward the police control room. He really wanted to be a part of this investigation, but central agencies, mainly the Central Bureau of Investigation, had taken over. There was good reason for it too. The investigation of past riots had been bungled by local stations in the area. The lack of coordination between the stations hadn't helped either. Ultimately the home ministry had decided that the CBI would take over the investigation while the police would focus on maintaining peace, enforcing the curfew if there was one, and assisting in the investigation rather than leading it. Shankar did not like this.

The constables in the police control room at the main entrance of the Old Delhi Railway Station recognized Shankar right away. They immediately stood up to greet him. Shankar asked the head constable to take a walk with him and chatted a bit with the others. He could sense that they weren't in a good mood after having been admonished by the commissioner. They were defensive and understandably a bit nervous about what had happened. It was quite evident that they had realized their mistake. They shouldn't have all rushed to the scene of the fight when it first started. Some of them should have stayed back and manned the other platforms. The head constable who was in charge that night was also visibly upset at what had happened and wondered why Shankar was questioning him when the investigations were being led by the CBI. But he liked Shankar. In the past, Shankar had helped him maintain law and order in and around the railway station. Once, when there was a stampede, Shankar and officers from his station had helped in controlling the crowd and transporting the injured. Their help had reduced the number of people who had been injured. The chief constable also knew that Shankar wasn't the type of police officer who would point fingers or lay blame.

"Which platform did the fight break out on?" Shankar asked.

"The one on the other side of the station, sir."

"Who was involved?"

"Two groups of people. When we got there, there were at least twenty people going at one another with knives, hockey sticks, and broken bottles. There were a lot of people on the platform. It was a busy time, sir. Two trains had just arrived, and one was leaving. There was a lot of pushing and shoving. It took us a while to calm things down."

"Was anyone injured in the two groups?"

"A few bloody noses, torn shirts, and trousers. We saw a few people sitting on the platform but don't know if they were injured in the scuffle."

"Did you take down their names and addresses? Did you manage to bring some of them in for questioning?"

"That's the thing, sir. When the coach on this side of the station started burning, everyone panicked. There was suddenly a lot of screaming and shouting and the crowd started running. When the fight stopped, everyone was trying to get away at the same time. People started heading toward the exits, and our focus shifted to the burning coach. We all hurried back to help extinguish the flames. We didn't know at the time that the coach was empty. It took us and the fire brigade almost an hour to bring the fire under control and make sure that no one was inside."

"What happened to the two groups of people who were fighting?"

"They had all left."

"So, you didn't book anyone or question anyone, from the two groups? You don't have any details whatsoever on who they were, where they came from ... nothing?"

"No, sir," came the feeble response.

"Could you make out whether the two groups belonged to two different communities?"

"I can't say, sir."

"What was the fight about?"

"Sorry, sir, I don't understand."

"What were they fighting about?"

"We don't know, sir. When we reached, they were in the midst of it, and then the coach started burning on this platform. People started screaming and running for the exits, and we hurried to deal with the fire."

"Had everyone dispersed once the fire was put out? Couldn't you find anyone from the groups that were fighting?"

"No, sir. I am sorry, sir. I wish I could help you more."

Shankar paused for a bit and tried to understand what had happened. Then after a couple of minutes, he said, "I want you to think about this very carefully. When you arrived at the scene of the fight, did you see the people involved in it carrying any luggage?"

The constable thought for a while before replying, "I can't say for sure, but I did see some luggage on the platform."

"What kind of luggage?"

"Rice bags, sir ... big bags in which one usually carries rice or mattresses."

"How far is the pedestrian gate from the platform where the fight broke out?"

"You mean the side entrance to the lane on the other side?"

"Yes."

"Not far, maybe a few hundred yards away."

Shankar was trying to piece together all the information. Meanwhile, the constable was being called by one of his colleagues and had to head back to the control room. Shankar thanked him and slowly started making his way to the parked jeep. Motiram had dozed off in the driver's seat.

"Motiram."

"Yes, sir. Sorry, sir," Motiram replied, a bit startled.

"It's alright. Next stop, Chandni Chowk Police Station."

"Yes, sir."

As they made their way through the overcrowded streets of Old Delhi toward Chandni Chowk, Shankar could see the tired look on people's faces. They all seemed in a hurry to get somewhere. He could see the street vendors attending to customers and food stalls full of people talking to each other, enjoying their snacks and tea. Although the distance was short, because of the narrow streets and the large volume of people that the jeep had to navigate, it took them almost half an hour to reach their destination. They could have probably walked the distance in the same amount of time. Many police cars, jeeps, vans, and trucks were parked outside the Chandni Chowk Police Station, and there were barricades to keep protesters away.

Shankar made his way through the two sets of barricades to the police station, where the constables at the entrance immediately stood up to greet him. After exchanging a few pleasantries, he asked them to direct him to Kabir Singh's office. The office was at the far end of a long corridor, past a big hallway with the offices of the more senior officers on one side and interview rooms and a large holding area for troublemakers on the other side. The police station was housed in a large, old, renovated building with a courtyard in the middle. The courtyard had a few wooden benches for visitors. They were empty today. Shankar could sense from the hustle and bustle among the constables and workers constantly carrying tea and snacks in and out of the various rooms for a number of senior officers from other locations that were at the station for meetings. This was a much larger and important station than Shankar's, and it was quite evident that it was busier than usual in the aftermath of the riots. The door to Kabir's office was open. Shankar walked right in and was met by a secretary furiously typing away. When he saw Shankar, he stopped typing and informed him that Kabir was in a meeting in another room. He led Shankar through a set of doors to an inner office and offered him some tea, which Shankar politely refused.

Shankar made himself comfortable on a chair across Kabir's. He looked around the empty office and was surprised at how clean it was. Usually, offices in police stations were an utter mess. One other thing that caught his eye was the pictures hanging on the walls. Police stations were filled with pictures of political leaders, ministers, and freedom fighters. This one was filled with black-and-white pictures of Old Delhi. He got up and walked over to see what they were and was surprised that many were newspapers clippings from the 40s, prior to India's independence. The pictures showed the grandeur of the old mansions and *havelis* in all their pomp and glory. There were also pictures of the iconic Red Fort and Khari Baoli, the famous spice market. As he marveled at the pictures, Shankar could hear Kabir talking to the constable outside. Kabir walked into the office, smiled, shook Shankar's hand, and pointed to the chair across his desk for Shankar to take a seat.

"Nice to see you again, Shankar."

"Thank you for seeing me. I know you are busy, and I promise this won't take long."

"Oh, don't worry about it. Would you like to have some tea?"

"Sure," Shankar replied. He knew that he could spend some more time this way. Kabir stepped outside and asked his secretary to get some tea.

When he returned, he asked, "tell me, what brings you here?"

"Oh, two things really. First, I want to find out more from you about the questioning of the informers who you had rounded up. Did they tell you what might have triggered the riots?"

"Not really. We finished questioning everyone and let them go. They seemed to have been stumped by the riots as well."

"What about the victims? Did they know any of them?"

"No. That's the other surprising bit. We shared the names of those we identified, but none of them had any knowledge about these people."

"Strange, isn't it?"

"Very."

Before they could continue, Kabir's secretary brought their teas in two small glasses and placed them on the desk. They thanked him and waited for him to leave. After taking a sip, Shankar continued.

"The other reason I am here is to find out about the two charred bodies that I found near the station. I think all the victims were taken to Willingdon Hospital and your station is informing all the relatives, right?"

"Yes. All of them have now been identified. Their bodies have already been taken from the hospital directly for cremation or burial, as the case may be, and I think their last rites have been performed in the presence of their families."

This was standard practice during riots. It was impossible to gauge how long curfews would last and what the aftermath would be. Once the victims had been identified and their postmortems completed, their families were informed. If they were from the riot-hit areas, they were taken to the hospital, where the police and the hospital staff made arrangements with crematoriums and burial grounds nearby to perform their last rites in the presence of the family members.

"What about the postmortem reports?"

"As you know, the investigation has now been taken over by the CBI. They are the ones leading it."

"I understand. There are two deaths that happened in my jurisdiction. I want to know more about those."

"You would have to talk to the CBI. By the way, I am not sure they will care too much about local jurisdictions."

"Understood. I was reviewing all the telexes and messages from the control room. It seems there were eleven victims. It is sad, of course, but at least the number is not as high as one would expect in a riot. I am happy that this time around, it wasn't worse."

"Yes, that's right. I am new here, but from what I have heard from other officers, both the carnage and loss of life were much less compared to other riots. Some shops were looted and robbed, but the violence started and stopped fairly quickly."

"Yes, that's a bit surprising," Shankar said, taking another sip.

"And there were ten victims, not eleven."

"Sorry?"

"I said there were ten victims, not eleven."

"That's not what I read in the written reports and the messages from the control room. You must have all of them since we are all on the same secure police channel. You can check."

Kabir was curious as he hadn't thought of this. It could be possible that he had got the number wrong at such a busy time with multiple messages coming in quickly. It was a chaotic night, after all. He asked his secretary to bring the file containing all the transcripts of the messages from that night. In the meantime, Shankar and Kabir spoke about their respective stations and about the upcoming visits from various political leaders that would keep them busy. They were not looking forward to it. In the aftermath of the riots and once things had calmed down, leaders of all parties made it a point to visit the affected areas to show their support and give long speeches on unity. For the police, that meant being on duty during their visit, making sure that they were safe and secure, and avoiding untoward incidents.

Kabir's secretary brought in a thick file with the transcripts and handed it over to Kabir, who immediately started going through them. After a few minutes, Kabir looked up from the file and said, "I see what's happened here. Initially, they thought there were eleven victims based on the number of bodies that had been taken to the hospital. But there are messages here that the number is actually ten. There is a confirmation from the control room here and someone at the hospital as well."

"Just out of curiosity, can we check how many victims were taken from each station and tally them up?" Shankar asked.

"Sure."

Kabir tallied up the count from the various stations and softly added them as he leafed through all the pages.

"I am sorry I am making you do all this, Kabir."

"No, no. I am curious myself after what you said," Kabir said as he finished counting. "It adds up to ten, Shankar. It's all there. Go ahead, take a look." He handed the file over to Shankar.

Shankar read through the file and scrutinized the numbers that were reported from each station. Then he looked up, went back a few pages, reviewed them again, and leafed all the way to the end.

"This doesn't make sense," Shankar said with a strained look on his face.

"What doesn't?"

"I reported two charred victims from my station. They were taken to the hospital. The transcript clearly shows what I said over the police radio. But look at the final number that the hospital confirmed from my station—one. I know there were two. So, what happened to the second victim?"

"That is strange," Kabir said with a worried look on his face.

Just then the assistant commissioner of police who was in charge of the station entered the room without knocking. Shankar and Kabir immediately got up to greet him.

"Orders from above. Everyone needs to be at their stations. Shankar, please report to Kotwali immediately. What's all this?" he asked, pointing to the file with all the transcripts.

Kabir started explaining what they were trying to do but was abruptly interrupted. They were both sternly reminded that investigating the deaths was not their concern, as the CBI was on it. Their priority was to maintain law and order in their areas. Shankar nodded and made his way back to his jeep. During his drive back to the station, he was convinced that there was something wrong with the tally of the victims. He wanted to find out more from the hospital, but he had no choice but to head back to the station. He decided to call the hospital later.

When he reached his police station, he found the tea stall vendor and pharmacy owner waiting for him. He called them in one by one. He took his time questioning them to find out whether they had seen anything that night. Both said that they had seen a group smoking at the corner of the lane. The group had been there for a while. What stood out was that they seemed to be just loitering near the gate. A constant stream of people would always be either leaving or entering the station but hardly anyone would be standing in a corner where there were no shops or stalls. The area was dark, and the shop owners couldn't make out how many people were in the group much less see their faces. Once Shankar finished questioning them, he told them to keep an eye out to see if they saw the group again and inform the police. Once they left, Shankar went back to reviewing all the files and messages on his desk. A number of senior officers had called from the headquarters while he was away. They probably wanted to know the latest status. He knew he had to spend the next couple of hours returning all the calls. He sighed, picked up the phone, and started calling them one by one.

* * *

In the offices of *The New India Courier* that morning, Nitya was busy trying to ensure that her team had everything they needed to start working on their stories. She was happy to see that they were energized and ready for what lay ahead of them. All of them had come to work before her, and that was a good sign. She reiterated her directive that the team would meet in the evening daily to take stock of the progress that had been made. She hoped that most of the families would agree to have stories written on them. Once her team had left for their assignments, she made her way back to her office and found Manoj's secretary, Charu, waiting for her.

"Good morning, Charu. How are you?"

"I am fine. I need to talk to you about your new office."

With the events that had happened following the riots, Nitya had forgotten about her move. She was happy to have a bigger office. At the same time, she did not like the fact that she was going to be on another floor and further away from her team.

"Is the office ready?"

"Yes, it will be by the end of the day. We need to move your stuff upstairs. When can we do that?"

"Can I let you know tomorrow?"

"Sure, also there is something else," said Charu, as she handed over a file to Nitya.

"What's this?"

"A copy of your promotion letter signed by Manoj and an HR letter for Shiv."

Nitya opened the file. She quickly put her promotion letter aside. She had already read it. She started reading the letter for Shiv. It was a warning letter signed by the head of HR. It clearly stated that he was being reprimanded for unprofessional conduct and was being put on probation. If there was to be a subsequent incident, it could mean an immediate dismissal without any notice period. She sighed as she read it, and then turned to Charu.

"What is the issue with Shiv?"

"It seems that he is too outspoken and gets into arguments with senior journalists. It has happened one too many times. They have reported it to HR and hence the letter."

"Has Shiv ever lodged any complaints?"

"No. He hasn't complained about anyone. The complaints are against him."

"Is he aware of this letter?"

"No. You are his manager now. You have to discuss it with him and give it to him. Make sure he understands the content. It's pretty clear anyway."

"Yes, it is.

"Will you give it to him?"

"Yes, in my own time. Tell me, Charu, just between us, what do you think of Shiv and all these complaints. What's his side of the story?"

"What do you mean by his side of the story?"

"Did HR never bother to find out his side of things?"

"Not that I know of. I don't think the process works that way."

"Hmm. Something wrong with the process then."

"Perhaps, but from what I have heard from many senior journalists, Shiv is not a good fit for the organization. He is not a team player and is always asking questions and stirring up trouble."

"What do you think? I mean, you have seen him in Manoj's office quite a few times," Nitya asked, pointing to the letter in front of her.

"Yes, I have. To be honest, he has always been polite with me and treated me with respect. Now that I think about it, it seems strange that he has so many issues."

"Alright, anything else?"

"Yes, one more thing. You have a meeting later today with the senior team about budgets for the rest of the year, and then another in the afternoon with Manoj and the HR director about your team. You know raises, promotions, and all the other interesting stuff."

"I will be there."

"It's good to have you on the senior team now," Charu said with a smile.

"We will see," Nitya replied with a smile as Charu left the room. She read the HR letter for Shiv once more and placed it in the bottom drawer of her desk. She wasn't sure what to do with it just yet. She knew what the letter meant. It would always be on Shiv's record. Any future promotion or raise could be denied based on it. Nitya hoped that she didn't have to deal with it right off the bat, as she had just started managing a new team.

Nitya spent the rest of the morning following up on all the stories that she was working on before her promotion and the current assignment that Manoj had tasked her team with. She had already prioritized them based on what she would be tackling herself and those she would be assigning to her team members. She knew that she couldn't distract them from their current assignments. It was her first project after her promotion. All eyes were on her. Some wanted her to succeed, some were jealous, and a select few wanted her to fail. But all that was not in her hands. She was determined to make a good start in her new role.

The rest of the day was busy in meetings and that was frustrating for Nitya. It took time away from what she wanted to focus on. But attending the meetings was crucial. Perception and visibility were important in her new role. By late afternoon, some of her team members had returned. Many of them wanted to come to her room right away and let her know what had happened. She politely asked them to wait until everyone was back and use the time to put their notes on paper.

After her later afternoon meeting with Manoj and HR, Nitya went to check her new office on the second floor. She surveyed the newly painted office. The old cabinets and tables had been replaced with a new, sleek desk. The windows had been cleaned, and the room still smelled of fresh paint. The carpet had also been cleaned and she could see that the wires for a phone were hanging from the wall. She was happy with her new office.

Once she was back in her current office on the first floor, Moina came by to inform her that Rakesh had called from the Willingdon Hospital and wanted to talk to her. He had been trying to reach Nitya for a while and then had called Moina in desperation. Rakesh and Shiv were working on finding out more about the eleventh victim, if indeed there was one. She had given them her car, and Tilak Singh was driving them for the day. Moina transferred the call to her.

"Hello, Rakesh. Is everything alright?"

"Yes ma'am. Everything is fine. I am at the Willingdon Hospital, and I wanted to know if I could go straight home instead of coming back to work. I was just informed by my cousin who is a nurse here that my mother is not well. I need to bring her to the hospital. It was sheer luck that I met my cousin here."

"Absolutely. Ask Shiv to drop you home on his way back."

"Oh, Shiv has left already."

"What do you mean by he has left?"

"Ma'am, he told me to keep the car so that I could go home after talking to you. He has to go to a few other places before heading back to the office. He will be late. I don't think he will be able to make it on time to the meeting this evening."

"He should have kept the car with him and dropped you off."

"Yes. We tried calling you, but you were not at your desk."

"Yes," sighed Nitya. She was upset with Shiv for going off on his own without informing her of when he would show up in the evening.

"Thank you. Tilak will drop me home and then head back to work."

"Yes, thank you. Please take care of your mother."

"Thank you. I may have to take a couple of days off."

"I understand completely. Don't worry about it. Just keep me posted on how things are. We will take care of things at work."

"Thank you, ma'am," Rakesh said. Nitya could sense the relief in his voice.

Everyone was back in the office and in the conference room by 6:00 p.m. Everyone except Shiv. Since Rakesh had already warned Nitya that Shiv would be late, they didn't wait for him. Nitya didn't want the rest of the team to stay on till late at night. The team assignment was progressing reasonably well. Suresh, Swati, and Moina had been able to contact the families of the victims they were assigned to. Some had agreed to tell their stories, others were still in mourning and did not want to talk to the press. No one had denied their request outright. There were a couple who needed more time to think. But every family wanted to know what triggered the riots and who was responsible. They were both sad and angry. They were also adamant about finding out whether it could have been avoided. All of this was understandable. The victims were mostly from the same area. At first glance, it didn't seem like they had much in common other than being at the wrong place at the wrong time.

The families had been given the postmortem reports, and although they didn't share all the details with Nitya's team, they had shared enough to let them know how the victims had died. Nitya's focus was to tell their stories and not on how they died. The idea was to share with the readers about the innocent lives that had been lost in the tragedy, the impact on the ones that were left behind, and the meaninglessness of it all. The team spent almost two hours talking about the events of the day. Nitya could sense their youthful excitement coupled with the sadness they felt about what they were reporting on. Finally, around 8:00 p.m. she asked everyone to go home and start working on their contacts, scheduling interviews, and getting more details on the victims. She also reminded them to be sensitive in their reporting and vet any information with the families before it was published.

After an hour of work, Nitya was ready to leave too. Just as she was about to leave, she saw Shiv walking toward her room from the far end of the hallway. She waved at him to come over and then pointed to the chair across hers so he could take a seat. She could see the exhaustion on his face. Nitya wanted to scold him for letting go of the car, but after looking at his face, decided against it.

"How did it go, Shiv? I need to talk to you about something. It's not related to what you are working on, but first, I want to hear how things went today."

"I don't know, ma'am."

"What do you mean?"

"I am certain of one thing. There were eleven victims, though the official tally is ten."

"I am not sure I understand."

"The hospital received eleven bodies that night. Of that, I am sure. The official number that they confirmed was ten. I am not sure why. They are hiding something."

"Are you sure? What about the cross-checking that you had planned to do?"

"I did. That's why it took so long, and I am sorry I couldn't make it back in time for the meeting."

"That's fine. Tell me what you found out."

"The names of all the victims have now been made public and we know who they are."

"Yes. Ten names."

"Right, ten names have been made public. I went to the crematorium and burial grounds where they were taken for their last rites."

"And?"

"They add up to eleven from the Willingdon Hospital. I tallied the names against the ones from the records of the crematorium and burial grounds."

"And?"

"Ten names matched with the official list. The eleventh name is Avneesh Trivedi."

"Did you find out anything about him?"

"Only his address in Old Delhi from the record in the crematorium and where his last rites were performed. I will go there tomorrow."

"Hmm. There is no record of him in the hospital."

"So, that's the thing. I am sure Rakesh told you that his cousin is a nurse at the hospital. She was on duty that night. She recalls two charred bodies arriving. The other victims were not arson victims. She knows that postmortems were done on all of them, but in the morning, she and her colleagues were informed by the hospital management that there was only one charred body. She didn't want to ask too many questions."

"That's definitely weird."

"Yes, ma'am. I also spoke to the guard at the ER gate. He mentioned that one of the bodies was taken away in the middle of the night well before the others were released. It was whisked away in an unmarked van, and he couldn't be sure whether it was a police van. This is off the record, of course. The guard does not want to get into trouble and will surely deny things if questioned."

"That's understandable," Nitya said, lost in thought.

"If you don't mind, I will go to the address that I found for Avneesh Trivedi and try to find more details."

"Yes, but Rakesh will not be with you."

"That's fine, I can go on my own."

"No, you won't. I will come with you. You are right about something weird going on here. It seems almost like an attempt to hide this victim, but I am not sure why."

"Yes, ma'am. I'll take your leave then. I will see you tomorrow," Shiv said and got up.

"Wait, how will you get home? It is almost 9:30 p.m."

"I have a bike, ma'am."

"What?"

"A motorbike I will be fine."

"No. I will ask one of the office cars to drive you home."

"But …"

"I don't want to hear anything, Shiv. Old Delhi is recovering from a riot. I don't want you riding back on a bike at this time of night."

"Yes, ma'am. Thank you."

"Tomorrow, let's see if we can find out more about Avneesh and why no one wants us to find out that he was killed in the riots."

"Right."

"Good work today."

"Thank you."

"Well, I will leave as well," Nitya said, and started arranging all the papers on her desk.

"Ma'am, you said you wanted to talk to me about something."

"What?"

"When I came into your room …"

Nitya glanced at the bottom drawer of her desk cabinet where she had kept the letter from HR and then looked at him.

"Oh, that can wait," she replied and got up to leave the room.

Old Delhi

The next morning, Nitya's team was busy scheduling interviews with the victims' families, friends, and colleagues. She could see them working away on the phones. Shiv was waiting for her at his desk when she reached. She let him know that they would be leaving in an hour. She spent the next hour rescheduling her other meetings. Nitya was happy to be getting away from the office to work on a story. She missed being in the field and was looking forward to the rest of the day outside the office. When she sat at her desk, she saw a handwritten note from one of the secretaries at the reception. Rakesh had called to let her know that he would be away for the rest of the week. She had guessed as much from her conversation with him the day before. Another note was from Charu, asking to let her know when she would be moving to her new office. She quickly signed a few other forms approving cars for her team. While she was going over the notes that her team had left her, the phone rang. She picked it up and immediately had a big smile on her face. It was her younger sister Kavita calling from Bombay.

"How are you, Kavita? It's so nice to hear your voice."

"I am fine. Did you get my letter?"

"Yes, I did. It was so serious. What's going on?"

"I don't know," Kavita said, her tone suddenly changing. Nitya could immediately sense something was wrong and began to worry.

"What is it? You are not sick or anything, are you?"

"No, no ... I am completely fine. It's just that married life is not what I thought it would be."

"Are things okay between you and Sanjay?"

"I am not sure."

"What happened? Did you have a fight? Did you have an argument?"

"We seem to be arguing and fighting all the time."

"Did something happen? I mean, what triggered it?"

"Honestly, I can't say. I just think that we are not compatible with each other. We seem to argue over everything and all the time."

"You are getting me worried now."

"I don't know what else to say. Anyway, I am calling you to let you know that I will be in Delhi for a seminar."

"Yes, I know. Oh, it will be so good to see you. When are you coming?"

"I still have to book my ticket. I will be reaching either on Wednesday or Thursday of next week and I will leave the following Sunday so that I can be back here by Monday."

"I am looking forward to it. I am guessing you will be coming alone?"

"Yes, thank God for that. I don't want Sanjay to be on my case there as well."

Nitya did not probe any further. She could understand that Kavita was unhappy and maybe the change of venue, albeit for a few days, would help.

"Okay, let me know the details of when you will be arriving. I will pick you up at the station. If I can't make it, I will have my driver pick you up."

"Oh ... so exciting, now you have your own car and driver," Kavita screamed, and for a moment she was her old, lively self, the one that Nitya adored and knew so well. When they hung up, Nitya thought about their conversation and felt worried. She glanced at her watch—it was time to head out. She quickly called Charu to let her know that she would be out for most of the day and that the movers could come and pick up her things except for the papers that were locked in her desk cabinet. She requested a box so she could carry them herself. When she went over to Shiv's desk, he was making notes on his writing pad. He quickly got up when he saw her, and they headed toward the parking lot.

Tilak was waiting for them and immediately opened the back door of the Ambassador for Nitya. Shiv went over to the front to sit beside Tilak. But just as he was about to open the door, Nitya asked, "What are you doing?"

"I was going to sit in the front."

"Why?"

"Habit."

"I am sorry?"

"Well, that's where I usually sit because the senior journalists that I have worked with have always asked me to sit in the front."

"Well, you are going to sit next to me."

"Yes, ma'am," Shiv said, and then came over to the back and sat beside Nitya.

The car quickly sped through the wide avenues in Connaught Place and headed toward Old Delhi. The distance wasn't much but the two places in the same city were very different, almost as though they were two separate countries. As the car turned toward a road that led to the walled city, Nitya turned to Shiv.

"Have you given Tilak the address?"

"Yes, I gave it to him this morning."

"When?"

"When you were on the phone in your room, ma'am. We also spoke to some other drivers and confirmed the location. It's a crowded area, and it's not always easy to find an address there."

They could see the change in the neighborhoods as they moved further away from their office. The roads were getting narrower and more congested and the spacious offices and high-end stores were now behind them. These streets were lined with bazaars and buildings competing with each other for every inch of space. Tilak had to slow down, and the car had to move at a much gentler pace, trying to make its way through the sea of cycles, autorickshaws, cows, people, and of course, other cars. They hadn't reached Old Delhi yet.

"I wanted to ask you something."

"Yes, ma'am."

"You told me that Rakesh and you visited the hospital and then the crematorium and burial grounds."

"Right."

"I can understand that Rakesh's cousin who works at the hospital helped you with your inquiries there but what about the other places? I mean the offices at the crematorium and burial grounds are not always forthcoming in giving out details."

"No, they aren't."

"So how did you manage to get the details from them? I mean you are not a family member. I can't imagine that they were ready to share the details with you knowing you were from the press."

"No, you are right. If I had told them I was from the press, it would have been difficult."

"So how did you get the details?"

Nitya could sense from Shiv's body language that he had become slightly uncomfortable. She could also see in the rear-view mirror that Tilak was smiling while driving.

"Ma'am, in each location I found someone who could give me the details."

"How?"

"Um, well, I sort of had to give them something and then they agreed, provided I didn't point fingers at them. And they were clear that they would deny everything if it ever came to it. In any case, they didn't give me any papers. I was just comparing the names that we had compiled with their records, that's all."

"Still doesn't answer my question. What did you do to get the details, Shiv?" Nitya asked, more firmly this time.

"I found some people in each location who would give me the information if I gave them something."

"You mean you bribed them!"

"Well, yes, but I wouldn't word it so crudely, ma'am."

"Really! How else would you characterize it? I want to know."

"I helped them, and they helped me…"

"Oh my God, Shiv, you are just digging a deeper hole for yourself now," Nitya said exasperatedly.

"I know, but we got the details that we needed. In the end, we managed to find out something that may be of some relevance."

"I am not disputing that. But it's a slippery slope if you go down this path. The ends don't always justify the means."

"I totally understand. But I couldn't think of any other way of getting the information. I didn't tell them where I work. They don't even know my real name. Rakesh and Tilak were waiting in the car which was parked at a distance, and there's no way to trace it back to us. In any case, I don't think they would want to advertise the fact that they gave us the details. Most people I managed to get information from were peons or guards. You will be surprised that most of them are actually quite honest. It was actually hard to find someone whom I could convince to share the information with me."

"Unbelievable. You should be happy that most folks are honest and don't take bribes."

"I am, ma'am. So that's why it took more time, you see. I had to find that one person in each location who would agree."

"I don't even know what to say to you, Shiv. I think you already know that what you did was wrong. You probably knew it even before you did it. And yet …"

"I understand, ma'am. I am sorry. I really didn't want to tell you, but since you asked …"

Nitya sighed. She was upset with Shiv for what he had done, but she was also impressed with his ingenuity and perseverance.

"Shiv, I want you to understand that I cannot have people in my team bribing members of the public to get information. It puts us in an awkward situation. Our reputation as journalists, and that of the newspaper itself, would be harmed if this were to come out."

"I understand. It won't happen again."

"Also, even if I want to, I cannot reimburse you for what you paid. It's not an expense anyone can justify."

"I was not looking to get reimbursed."

"You absolutely shouldn't for what you did. The point I am trying to make is that next time try to find better ways of getting the same information. We could have contacted them officially as part of the newspaper to get the details. It may have taken longer. They may have had to contact the families to release the information. But, eventually, it would come our way."

"Right, ma'am."

"Just out of curiosity, who did you say you were when you asked them for this information?"

"Insurance."

"What?"

"Insurance salesman, ma'am. I told them I was from the Life Insurance Corporation of India, making sure of all the details of the deceased before payouts were made."

"Oh, my God, Shiv."

"It worked."

"Yes ... but that doesn't make it right. I am surprised they didn't ask you for your ID. Don't tell me you have a fake ID?"

"Well, no. It's a real ID for something else, but I show it from afar and no one really bothers to check up close."

"Unbelievable."

They were now right in the middle of Old Delhi. The loudspeakers outside were competing with one another, blasting Bollywood songs, hymns, ghazals, and speeches, all at the same time. Adding to the cacophony of noise were the vendors in the bazaar shouting out prices for their wares. The air was filled with the smell of spices and food being prepared by the street food vendors in the open-air restaurants. This area was known for its street food and an amazing assortment of delicacies.

The car was hardly moving. Nitya asked Tilak to park near a street corner and decided to walk the rest of the way. Shiv had his notepad with him, and he was trying to understand the addresses in the congested lane with Nitya following a few steps behind. He constantly looked back to make sure that she was keeping up with him. Shiv stopped at a couple of stores to ask the shopkeepers for directions, and finally, after a few minutes, they found themselves standing outside an old, run-down *haveli* that looked dark amid all the lights and colors flooding the rest of the lane. Shiv knocked on the door but there was no answer. They decided to wait and after a few minutes, he knocked again. This time the door was opened by an old gentleman wearing thick glasses. His age and frail stature seemed to resonate with the building. They could see an old lady behind him.

"My name is Shiv Kumar. This is Nitya Chaturvedi. We are from *The New India Courier*. Is this the residence of Avneesh Trivedi?"

"Yes, it is."

"We are running some pieces in the paper on the riots."

"Avneesh is dead. He was killed," the old man said.

"I understand, sir. My sincerest condolences to you and the family. We are trying to contact the families to see if they want us to write something about their loved ones. We don't mean to pry, sir, and we won't publish anything without your consent."

"What good will that do? It won't bring Avneesh back to us, will it?" said the old man with tears in his eyes and anger in his voice. Shiv stayed silent. The old man turned and walked back inside. The old lady came to the door and asked them to come inside. She introduced herself as Avneesh's mother. Inside, the *haveli* was dark and the dim lights on the high ceilings made it look even darker. The bright sun outside could hardly make its way inside the thick walls of the old building. The walls looked as if they had never been painted. The cracks on the ceiling and the wall were all too visible. The fans on the high ceiling belonged to another era. There was no living room as such. There was a big, open courtyard in the middle and the two-story house was built all around it. The old lady pointed to a few wooden chairs in the courtyard and gestured Nitya and Shiv to sit. Nitya and Shiv could survey the house from this central vantage point. The doors to the rooms were all open. They were all dark. The curtains on the large windows were all drawn. They could hear a toddler on the upper floor. The old man regained some of his composure and introduced himself as Avneesh's father. He offered them some tea, but Nitya and Shiv politely declined. The couple sat on the chairs across from them. Nitya broke the silence.

"Ma'am, sir, please accept our condolences. I know it is the worst possible time in your lives and we certainly have no intention of intruding on your privacy. But we would like to know if you are open to sharing some stories about your son. We have been contacting the families of those who have lost their loved ones and some of them want us to publish stories about them. It's their way of remembering them and letting people know that these senseless events lead to tragedies for the families. If you don't want to share any details, we will gladly leave."

The old couple sat silently with a distant look on their faces. There was a noise from one of the rooms on one side of the courtyard. All four of them turned toward it. A beautiful young woman in a sari was standing at the edge of the courtyard looking at them. She seemed out of place in her surroundings. She was in her early twenties and dressed impeccably. She was looking at Nitya and Shiv. Her gaze fixated on Shiv for a while and Nitya thought that she may have recognized him from the streets of Old Delhi, although it was unlikely. Before the woman could start speaking, the old man introduced her.

"This is Madhavi, our daughter-in-law, Avneesh's wife."

"Hello Madhavi, I am Nitya, and this is Shiv. We are here from *The New India Courier*."

"Hello," Madhavi said in a soft but clear voice. They could see the sadness in her eyes.

"If you don't mind, Nitya-ji, I will let Madhavi speak with you. We will go inside. Honestly, I am not sure if printing anything about our late son will be useful to anyone. I am sad and angry and can't think clearly. It doesn't matter to me one way or the other. I will let Madhavi decide," said the old man as he slowly got up and made his way into one of the rooms.

"I understand, sir," Nitya said, but he had already turned and walked away.

The old lady then turned to Nitya, "can you please find out what happened to Avneesh?"

The question took both Nitya and Shiv by surprise. Nitya looked at her affectionately before replying, "yes ma'am. Didn't the police or the hospital give you any more details?"

"No. Two people came to our house at night and told us to accompany them to the crematorium. I don't remember much really. We were in shock. We would have preferred to have a proper ceremony, but it was too late. The last rites had to be performed that night. The people who had taken him there informed us that due to the riots and curfews, this was the only way we could perform his rites," she said amid tears. She was about to collapse and hit the floor, but luckily Shiv caught her. He gently held her in his arms and handed her over to Madhavi who took her inside.

While Madhavi was helping her mother-in-law to her room, Nitya and Shiv tried to piece together what might have happened that night. Some of it made sense. But the bit about being taken to the crematorium and insisting that the last rites be completed right then didn't. Usually, families were given an option and it was well within their rights to insist that the ceremony be performed on a date and time of their choosing. As they were mulling this over, Madhavi returned to the courtyard. They could see that the recent exchange had affected her, and she had tears in her eyes as she spoke.

"I am sorry about that."

"Oh, don't be. This is all so sad, and honestly, we can't imagine what all of you are going through," Nitya said in an understanding tone.

"This was all so sudden. What makes it worse is not knowing what happened."

"Does Avneesh have any siblings?"

"Yes, a sister who lives in Bangalore. She got married recently and moved there a few months ago. She is here now but has gone out to get some supplies. She is helping us a lot."

"Do you work, Madhavi?"

"Yes, Nitya-ji. I am a teacher at a school. I have taken a few days off. My in-laws and parents help with our son, Rahul, while I am at work."

"If you don't mind my asking, where did your in-laws work?"

"My father-in-law is a retired professor. He taught at Delhi University. My mother-in-law is a homemaker."

Nitya could see the tired look on Madhavi's face. It was clear that the family was going to be under some financial strain. A retired professor's pension and a teacher's salary would barely be enough to maintain a *haveli*. Shiv, who had been surprisingly quiet for a long time, decided to join the conversation.

"Didn't the police or the hospital tell you what happened to Avneesh? Did they share the details of the postmortem report?"

"No. We were told that he was killed during the riots. My in-laws were told that the postmortem report would be shared with them, but we are still waiting for the death certificate. Someone from his work came over the next day to give some money as compensation. I only came to know of it the day after when I returned," Madhavi said, looking at Shiv.

"I am sorry, were you not here that night? Didn't you go to the crematorium?"

"No. I was staying at my parents' with our son. I had gone over for a couple of days. Avneesh said that he was going to be traveling, so I took Rahul to visit my parents."

"Where do your parents live?" asked Nitya.

"In Old Delhi itself, not far from here, near the Red Fort. I wish I was here that night," Madhavi replied, her voice quivering.

"Where did Avneesh work?" Shiv asked.

"In Hauz Khas. He is ... was a manager in a clothing store."

"How long had he been working there?"

"About six months. He was happy with his new job. He said he was working on something important and was expecting some news. He told me that it would make everyone proud of him. I was certain that he was going to get a promotion."

"You said he was going to be out of town, right?"

"Yes, he told me he was going out of town for work and would be back in a couple of days. He said it was important."

"Where?" Shiv asked.

"I am sorry," Madhavi replied, confused with the question.

"Where did he travel to?"

"Ah, yes, Dehradun."

"Were the people who came and handed over the money to your in-laws from his workplace?"

"That's what my mother-in-law said. I have tried to get more details, but it has been so difficult for us to have a conversation. All I know is that someone came and handed over an envelope, took Avneesh's work-related files and papers, and left."

"Envelope?" Shiv asked.

"Yes. Envelope with the money."

"Would you happen to know anyone from his workplace whom we can get in touch with?"

"Well, that's the thing, he only started a few months ago and he didn't talk much about his work. He was almost secretive, now that I think about it. Avneesh was not very forthcoming about his workplace details and activities. He left work at work and I kind of liked it that way. Now I wish I knew more," said Madhavi, suddenly becoming quiet.

Nitya was a bit surprised at how quickly Madhavi had opened up to Shiv. She would have thought that Madhavi would have engaged with her more. But Shiv was closer to her age and that probably made her feel more comfortable.

Shiv and Nitya could see through the open door into the room where the old couple had retreated to. They were trying to console each other. It was hard not to be moved by the poignant sight. Madhavi turned to Shiv again and as she started speaking, a child's cries could be heard from upstairs.

"I am sorry, I have to go upstairs. I think Rahul is awake now. He is probably hungry."

"Of course. Before you go, do you have the address of Avneesh's workplace?" Shiv asked.

"Unfortunately, my in-laws handed over all the details to the person who had visited from his workplace. I know he has a notebook, and it must have some details. If I can find it, I'll let you know. I know the name of the showroom. It's called the Royal Textiles and it is in Hauz Khaz. He never took me there, but I am sure you will find it if you ask around."

"Where did he work before that?"

"In another showroom called Apparel House. It is also in the same area but on the other side of Deer Park."

"Yes, I know where Deer Park is."

Shiv noted down the names and then on a fresh page quickly wrote something, tore off the paper, and handed it to Madhavi.

"Here are the numbers where you can reach us. If you do find the notebook or remember any more details that might help us, please do let us know. You don't mind if we start making some inquiries, do you? We won't publish anything without your approval," Shiv asked.

Madhavi thought for a moment before replying, "I know my in-laws didn't say it, but we want to know what happened. My mom-in-law said that they were shocked at the sight of Avneesh's body. It was burned and they could barely recognize him. His face and some birthmarks were visible, but seeing him that way completely broke them. They can't get it out of their mind, and then after the visit from Avneesh's colleague the other day, they sort of don't want to talk about what might have caused his death, but I want to know. I know it's not going to bring him back, but I want to know the truth."

"We will try our best," Nitya replied.

"I promise you we will find out what happened to your husband," Shiv said.

Madhavi thanked them and then turned and headed upstairs to be with her son. Nitya and Shiv slowly walked toward the room where Avneesh's parents were sitting. They thanked them and quietly made their way outside to the street.

The hustle and bustle outside was a welcome change to the solemn atmosphere in the old *haveli*. They walked back to where Tilak had parked the car. Once inside, Nitya turned to Shiv.

"Shiv, we cannot go about making promises that we might not be able to keep."

"I understand, ma'am. I think this family needs some answers."

"Yes, I agree, but it may not be up to us to find all the answers for them. We can make them get in touch with the right authorities and they can provide the details to them."

"Ma'am, don't you think there is something strange going on here?"

"On that, we agree. There is something weird and I can't put my finger on it. We should definitely find out more."

"Whatever happened inside, the way the family spoke to us, or rather, what they didn't say was also very strange, don't you think?"

"How so?"

"I mean, I know that they are grieving, but it almost seemed like Avneesh's parents were not just sad but also scared. Then there's the bit about one of his colleagues handing over money to his parents. I mean, why in cash?"

"Yes, I agree, it's unusual. Then again, it is a family in mourning, and we can't expect them to behave normally."

"There are other things too. Avneesh not telling his wife about his work, being secretive, not letting her know what he was working on even though it could make his family proud, and then his colleague collecting all the work-related papers the very next day … I mean, why the urgency?"

Nitya was quiet. She knew Shiv was right. Finally, Tilak broke the silence.

"Where to, ma'am? Back to the office?"

"No. Take us to Kotwali Police Station. Do you know where it is?"

"Yes, ma'am."

"That's our next stop."

As Tilak slowly started backing up the car in the narrow lane, Shiv asked Nitya, "ma'am, why are we going to the police station?"

"I have a friend there who might be able to help us with this. This area probably falls under his jurisdiction."

"You have a friend who is a policeman?"

"An officer, yes. Why is that surprising?"

"It isn't. I am just asking."

"I know him from Callipur. He was stationed there, and we worked together briefly on a case."

Nitya and Shiv looked out the window and marveled at the sea of humanity crisscrossing the narrow lanes and alleyways, the bazaars full of merchants, and the vehicles waging battle with everything on the street to make their way. They weren't far from the police station, but the congestion made the commute horrendously slow.

"Do you want to walk the rest of the distance, ma'am?"

"Yes, why not. This is why I don't like coming here. So many people ... It is so different from the other parts of Delhi. Such a different city, a different India."

"Yes, it's actually many Indias rolled into one."

Nitya asked Tilak to park the car near a main road so that they could leave quickly. Then they slowly waded through the crowded bazaar and onto the lane leading to the police station. Once they reached the entrance, Nitya asked for Shankar. The constables at the station were surprised to see a well-dressed, good-looking journalist with a young aide in this area. Nitya and Shiv's presence set off some uncouth comments and remarks which they chose to ignore. After a few minutes, the constable came out in a hurry and asked them to accompany him inside. They made their way through a long corridor to a large sitting area. They could see some officers at their desks, secretaries typing away, and constables coming in and out of the various rooms that were around the hall. After a few minutes, Shankar came in, and on seeing Nitya, greeted her with a big smile and a slight embrace. He led them to his office, which was small but looked spacious. It was surprisingly clean for a police station with very few papers and files on the desk and sparse furniture. Shankar asked them to have a seat and said, "It is so nice to see you after such a long time, Nitya."

"Yes."

"It is a busy time for us as you can imagine, and I have to start making my rounds and go out on patrol again. What brings you here?"

"We won't take long, Shankar. This is Shiv Kumar. He is on my team, and we are following up on something that we are hoping you can help us with," Nitya said, while Shiv nodded along and smiled slightly.

"Yes, we have met," said Shankar with a smile.

"Really?"

"Yes. We met on the day after the riots. Shiv was out taking pictures. Am I right?"

"Yes, sir," Shiv replied.

"Taking pictures? During the riots?" Nitya looked at Shiv sternly.

"Well, ma'am…"

Before Shiv could continue, Shankar came to his rescue.

"It was during a break in the curfew. He wasn't really creating any trouble," Shankar said slightly amused with Nitya's tone and stern demeanor.

"Well, I wouldn't put it past him," Nitya said, looking right at Shiv who knew he was up for a scolding at some point.

"So, what can I help you with?"

Nitya took the next few minutes to explain the stories they were working on. She then mentioned what Shiv had managed to find, the anomaly in the reports regarding the number of deceased, and finally how they had been able to track down Avneesh Trivedi. Shankar listened to all of it without interrupting them. Nitya then turned to Shiv and asked him to summarize what happened at the Trivedi residence. Shiv carefully laid out all the details. He shared how he felt the family seemed scared and how it was strange that no one from the hospital or the police had shared any information with them. Shankar was impressed with how well both Nitya and Shiv had dug up all the details. He knew from his experience that Nitya was thorough and articulate, but he was particularly impressed that Shiv had figured out who the missing victim was even before the police could. He was also pleased that someone from the press was following up on stories about the victims.

Once both Nitya and Shiv had finished explaining the details, Shankar asked Shiv, "you said that Avneesh Trivedi was taken to the Willingdon Hospital and then was whisked away to the crematorium before any of the other victims, right?"

"It seems that way, sir."

"Do you know how he died?"

"Not really, sir. The postmortem report was never shared. All we know from his mother is that Avneesh's body was burned, and it was hard for them to see him that way."

"Hmm. That must have been tough."

"Also, after the rites were performed, they were not given a death certificate. Usually, the crematorium gives one to the family. His parents were told that they would be given one the following day. But they are still waiting."

Shankar took his time to speak. "I have to admit all this is rather strange."

"What do you think, Shankar? It does seem like someone wants to hide the fact that he was killed in the riots."

"Or maybe they want to hide any link or involvement he may have had to the riots," Shankar said.

"I know you may not be able to tell us much about an ongoing investigation, but is there anything you could share with us that will help the family know what actually happened that night?" Nitya asked.

"Well, the investigations on the deaths of all the victims are being conducted by the CBI. We can only assist when requested."

"That's bollocks, sir," Shiv blurted out, showing his visible disappointment.

"Language, Shiv! What's wrong with you?" Nitya asked in a raised voice, looking straight at him.

"Pardon my language, sir. I am really sorry, but this happened in your jurisdiction and under your watch. After what we told you now, you should be investigating this," Shiv continued.

Shankar seemed to be lost in thought, oblivious to Nitya's anger toward Shiv. Nitya was still upset with Shiv's outburst.

"Shiv, you are in no position to tell the police how to do their job. Shankar is a good friend and he certainly doesn't need any advice from you on how to do his job," Nitya said. She then turned to Shankar and said, "I am sorry about all this."

"No, that's fine," Shankar replied in an understanding tone. Before he could continue further, Nitya looked at Shiv angrily, wanting to admonish him further.

"Shiv, wait for me in the car. I will finish talking to Shankar and meet you outside."

"Yes ma'am," Shiv replied as he got up. "Once again, I am sorry, sir. I didn't mean to offend you in any way. If I did, I do apologize."

"Don't worry about it, Shiv," Shankar said. "You did well to find the identity of the victim."

Shankar stretched out his hand and after they shook hands, Shiv left the room. Nitya looked at Shankar apologetically.

"Once again, I am sorry, Shankar. Shiv has a habit of causing trouble. He doesn't really fit in, you know."

"He shouldn't have to."

"Sorry?"

"Fit in. What is that? Why should he have to fit in?"

"I mean, look at the way he behaved."

"Granted, he shouldn't have said 'bollocks.' But other than that, I can't really blame him for anything else."

"Really? What about his totally unsolicited opinion on what you should be doing?"

Shankar smiled before replying, "I don't know Shiv, and I have absolutely no idea what kind of journalist he is, but I can tell you one thing—he is right about the fact that something is strange about this victim. Something's not right. Shiv also found out the identity of the victim, and I am sure that required some ingenuity. Now, I will tell you something off the record."

"Yes?"

"I know there were eleven victims that night, but all the official figures are hell-bent on saying there were ten."

"Could they be right? Is it possible that you and Shiv are wrong?"

"No. I found two charred bodies on the night of the riots. They were both sent to Willingdon Hospital. Then it became one. They could not have confused these two with the other victims. None of the bodies of the other victims were burned."

"Oh my God! Does that mean that they are deliberately trying to hide something?"

"Yes, and I can't officially investigate this because it's in the hands of the CBI. I can go to them with what you have told me, but I know how they work, and I am not exactly in the good books of my superiors, the home ministry, or the CBI. So, no one will listen to me."

"Right."

"I will tell you what, Nitya, let me make some inquiries and I will see what I can find. Meanwhile, I don't want you or Shiv or anyone at your paper impeding a police investigation. Is that understood?"

"Yes. But if we do find something and it's in the public domain, we will publish it with the consent of the victim's family, of course."

"Agreed," said Shankar, with a smile. His phone started ringing and they could hear some officers and constables waiting outside his room. Nitya knew that she had to leave.

"Thank you for your time, Shankar. Please say hi to Rohini and little Vikram. I am sure he is not that little anymore."

"I will, and I will let you know if I find anything that I can share."

"Thank you."

"And please go easy on Shiv. He really didn't offend me in any way. If you really must know, I agree with him and I want to investigate this myself. Instead, I have to now prepare for a minister's visit and babysit him during his tour of the riot-affected areas."

"Take care Shankar, and good luck!"

"Thanks! You too!"

Shankar opened the door for Nitya and instructed one of his constables to accompany her to her car. Shiv was waiting for her outside. He hadn't walked to the car as she had instructed him to. They walked back to the car together. Tilak quickly opened the back door for Nitya to get in. Shiv stood on the other side and gently opened the door to get in beside her. Before he did, he asked Nitya, "do you still want me to sit next to you, or should I sit in the front?"

"You can sit with me. I was mad at you and still am, but it's okay. You are safe around me for now."

"I am glad, ma'am," Shiv said, and that brought a smile to Nitya's face.

As the car slowly waded through the crowds back to New Delhi, Nitya and Shiv discussed what they had learned. Nitya told Shiv that Shankar had confirmed that there were indeed eleven victims, but that, for some unknown reason, the authorities were fixated on stating the official number as ten. She also informed him that Shankar would be making inquiries and letting them know if he found anything. When the car slowly gained speed after leaving the confines of Old Delhi, Nitya rolled down her window and looked outside. She felt the cool, refreshing breeze on her face. She turned to look at Shiv sitting beside her. He was also looking out the window, lost in thought. She recalled their conversation with the Trivedi family and thought of how, despite all his faults, Shiv was resourceful and someone who just could not be ignored.

* * *

At the police station, in the middle of his meeting with the other officers, Shankar was lost in thought after what he had heard from Nitya and Shiv. He was convinced about investigating the death of Avneesh Trivedi, even if it meant doing so without the consent of his superiors or the CBI. There were too many unanswered questions. He wished that he had a better reputation among his senior officers and wondered if anyone would help him in his endeavor. He also had to prepare for the minister's visit. While the other officers were discussing the details and putting forth suggestions to make the visit go off smoothly, Shankar wondered if he could use this to his advantage. He reviewed the plans of the upcoming events with his colleagues and then decided to call for Motiram for his routine patrol of the areas near the station.

As usual, the crowded streets made the drive to the railway station excruciatingly slow, but this time Shankar was in no hurry. In his head, he was playing out the conversation he had with Nitya and Shiv. Once the jeep reached the station, he walked toward the main entrance and the police control room near the gate. He spoke to the constable there briefly. They were no new incidents to report. There was also no information about the miscreants who had been fighting on the platform the night of the riots just before the coach was set on fire. He hadn't expected any in any case. He slowly walked back to his car. Things had returned to normal in a hurry. He had read all the messages from the other police stations in the area. There were some minor incidents being investigated, but they would be categorized as routine. All the officers had been asked to be present in their areas, either manning their stations or patrolling for the next few days. Before stepping into his jeep, Shankar stood beside it and surveyed the area. Then he got inside and turned to Motiram.

"Next stop, Willingdon Hospital."

"But that's outside our area, sir."

"I know," Shankar said. Motiram had been Shankar's driver long enough to sense the tone of urgency in his voice. He knew something was on his boss's mind, and he also knew that this was not the time to ask questions.

As they left the confines of the walled city and drove into the big leafy avenues of New Delhi, Shankar realized how desperately he wanted a transfer out of his current posting. Once they arrived at the hospital entrance, Shankar asked Motiram to park the car outside the main gates and headed straight for the emergency. Seeing an officer in uniform, the guards at the entrance and reception let him right through. They didn't bother to check his credentials and saluted him on his way in. At the ER reception, he asked for the nurse and doctor on duty. He was asked to wait in a waiting area reserved for VIPs. As he walked through the long corridor to the waiting area, he could see that the hospital was not that busy. There was a constant stream of people coming in and out of the main entrance being stopped by the guards. He figured most of them were relatives of patients. There were a few others in the waiting area. He sat in one corner and waited. After about half an hour, a doctor in a white coat entered the room and walked right up to him. Shankar got up and stretched out his hand.

"I am Dr. Chahal. How can I help you?"

"Hello, doctor. My name is Shankar Sen. Can we speak in private?"

"Yes, we can go to my office."

"Sure."

Shankar followed the doctor into his office, which was small and in an utter mess with files and papers on top of each other. They sat across a small desk.

"Mr. Sen, how can I help you?"

"Oh, just Shankar would be fine, doctor. I want to have a word with the doctor or the chief resident who was on duty the night of the riots."

"That would be me. I was the one on duty."

"That's great. Then this won't take long."

"I have already spoken to the officers who came from the headquarters and the CBI."

"Oh, I am not interested in that. I am actually here on behalf of one of the family members of a victim who was brought here that night."

"Who?"

"Avneesh Trivedi."

"I am sorry, that name doesn't ring a bell. I don't remember that name being in the list of victims."

"He was one of the burn victims. I think there were two victims whose bodies were charred. I am the one who found them near the Old Delhi Railway Station. They were sent here for their postmortem."

"Yes, I remember that."

"What happened to him?"

The doctor suddenly turned quiet and seemed lost in thought. He looked toward the door to make sure that it was closed and then after a brief pause, he looked at Shankar and said, "look Shankar, I have already told your colleagues and the CBI what I know. There is really nothing more I can add. You should find out more details from them."

"I understand, doctor, and I will, but I want to know what happened to him."

"I really shouldn't say more."

"There is a family out there who have lost a loved one and don't know what happened to him. They haven't been given any details from the hospital and they are still waiting for the death certificate."

"And I am sorry for their loss, Shankar, but it was your colleagues who sealed my lips. You must speak to them."

Shankar realized he was not getting anywhere, and he was skeptical whether his superiors or the CBI would share anything with him. He decided to shift gears and try a different approach.

"Well, doctor, if I were you, I'd be expecting a visit from the victim's family, and also from the press. They will be contacting you to find out more."

"What do you mean?"

"Well, you were the doctor in charge that night. You better have a good answer ready when they ask you how the victim died and why the hospital hasn't shared any details with the family."

The doctor immediately seemed worried. He didn't want to get entangled in any controversy. He was already unhappy about the way things had unfolded with this victim. He had not been in favor of releasing the body but had been forced by the police and his superiors. There was no paper trail to suggest anything, and he knew that something wasn't right. The policeman in front of him knew more than what the authorities had told him, and although they had assured him that his name wasn't going to be dragged into any controversy, he wasn't convinced.

After a pregnant pause, the doctor looked at Shankar and chose his words carefully. "Shankar, if I am asked anything in an official capacity, I will have to deny everything. There is no paper trail for this victim. I don't even know his name. We did the postmortem and were forced to release his body to the authorities."

"I understand, doctor. I am not here to get you in trouble. I just want to know what happened that night."

"You are right, Shankar. He was brought in along with the other victims. He was one of the two burn victims, and they were among the first ones to arrive. Much of his body was charred and it was a ghastly sight. They seemed to have been covered in jute bags, you know, like the ones used for carrying rice. His face was partly visible. We cleaned him up as much as we could. When we were in the middle of his postmortem, we saw policemen arrive to pick him up. Initially, we refused, but they called our superiors on the phone and forced us to release him. They took all his belongings and the partial report. Unfortunately, we did not have time to finish it."

"Did you see the people who came to pick him up again afterward?"

"No."

"How do you know they were policemen?"

"Well, one of them was in uniform and the others, I suspect, were plainclothes policemen. It was a busy night. We didn't have time to cross-check. They filled out their names and identifications on the register at the nurses' station, the one that you saw on your way in. Their details should all be there."

"I will look at it on my way out."

"I will make it easier for you. Give me a minute," said the doctor, and picked up his phone. He instructed the nurse to bring the visitor register and after hanging up, he took out a file from a drawer and handed it over to Shankar.

"What am I looking at, doctor?"

"These are all the victims. No harm in sharing this with you. Their families have been informed and even the papers know about them. We were able to identify them fairly quickly, except the one that we are talking about."

"Did they all die during the riots?"

"These ones in the file. Yes, some were stabbed; others were shot."

"There was another burn victim."

"Yes, he is the second one on the list," the doctor said, as Shankar wrote down his name on a notepad.

"What was the cause of death?"

"He was stabbed, most likely in a fight. He had bruises all over his body and face that showed that he may have been in a fight."

"And the time of death?"

"A few hours earlier the same night."

"I am curious, doctor, wasn't there a police presence outside the hospital as the victims were brought in?"

"Yes, I am surprised you are asking me that question."

"So, they didn't see who came and took Avneesh away? Didn't they speak to the gentlemen who came to pick up his body?"

"They weren't here at that time."

"What do you mean? You just said there was a police presence when the victims were brought in."

"Initially, yes, but then they left. It was strange. I asked our guard who was on duty at the gate what had happened. He told me that the police stationed here got a call from the control room to go to Old Delhi. It seems things were getting worse over there and they had to leave. I am surprised you are asking me this. You should know this already."

Before Shankar could ask his next question, there was a knock on the door and a flustered nurse entered the room. Shankar thought a new case might have been brought into the ER.

"Doctor, we can't find the register."

"What do you mean?"

"The register that has the visitor's log from that night is missing."

"How is that possible?" the doctor asked, irritated.

"Well, the logbook is usually kept at the nurses' station. Someone may have picked it up. We have looked at all the cabinets and it is missing. We can't find it anywhere."

Shankar asked the nurse, "tell me, has this happened before?"

"No, never."

"Do you have a register or logbook for each day?"

"Yes, sir, one for each day."

"Did you found out that this was missing only today, when the doctor asked you for it?"

"I don't know, sir. Maybe someone saw that it was missing and put a new one in for the same day. I don't know. All I know is that the book for that night is missing."

The doctor's exasperation was all too visible. He told the nurse, "Please call security immediately. Tell them what has happened, and when the nurses in the current shift have completed their rounds, tell them to stay back and conduct a thorough search for the logbook."

"Yes doctor," the nurse said, still a little shaken up.

"You can go now," the doctor said, and the nurse left the room.

Shankar was looking through the file and when the nurse left, he said, "If you do find the logbook, please do let me know.

I don't think you will find it, doctor. It has probably been stolen."

"We have never had this problem before. I mean it's a hospital, not a bank, and there isn't much security. The nurses' station is always manned. We keep our equipment, supplies, and medicines locked away, but not logbooks. This is strange," said the doctor, lost in thought.

"You are right about the security. When I walked in no one checked my credentials."

"What are you suggesting?"

"I can't say anything for sure at the moment. Something strange did happen that night."

The doctor got up from his seat to leave the room. He looked at Shankar and said, "well, I need to get back to what the taxpayers are paying me for. I need to do my rounds. Before the nurse entered, you were about to ask me something. What was it?"

"Ah, yes," Shankar said as he got up. "I know you don't have the postmortem report, but when I asked you who the victims were who died that night you looked at the file and used the word said 'these.' Why is that?"

"Right, well that's the strange bit. This unknown victim, well not unknown anymore I guess, now that we know his name ... what was it again?"

"Avneesh Trivedi."

"Yes, Avneesh Trivedi," the doctor said, as he wrote it down on his pad. He continued, "it seems Avneesh Trivedi was not killed that night."

Shankar had just opened the door to leave the room, but he suddenly stopped in his tracks.

"What do you mean he wasn't killed that night?"

"He was shot in the back of his head at least a day before the riots. Unlike the other victims, he was not killed the same night."

Faith

Nitya and Shiv had returned to the office by late afternoon. Shiv started looking through the directories to find more details on Avneesh's workplaces. Nitya spent the rest of the day calling each of her team members one by one to check on their progress. The rest of the team had been fairly successful in contacting the families of the victims that they had been assigned. Many had already gathered some material, and most had scheduled interviews with friends, co-workers, and families of the deceased to get more details. Nitya reminded them that their articles had to be reviewed by her and the senior team and most importantly, vetted by the families. Although Nitya wanted to directly follow up on the investigation around Avneesh's story, she had a lot of meetings lined up the next day. In any case, she knew that Shiv was quite capable of handling interviews at Avneesh's workplace. What worried her was the secrecy around his death, and she hoped that Shankar would find something that could help.

Around 7:00 p.m., some of her team had left for the day, she quickly looked over the schedule and called Swati into her room.

"Is Shiv still here?"

"No, he left half an hour ago."

"Alright. I need to talk to you about something. I know it's late, but I won't keep you for long."

"That's alright, ma'am. I am not in a hurry."

"You know that I had paired Rakesh up with Shiv, right?"

"Yes."

"Well, Rakesh will be gone until next week because his mother is still in the hospital.

"Yes, he called while you were away, and he spoke to Suresh and me."

"Right. I need the rest of the team to pick some of his work."

"Does that mean I have to work with Shiv?" Swati asked, with a worried look on her face.

"Yes, at least tomorrow. I cannot go with him. I have looked over your schedule and you have no interviews planned for tomorrow. I want you to accompany him to the offices of the riot victim, Avneesh, whom we followed up on earlier today."

"Ma'am, why do you want me to go with him?"

"What do you mean? I just told you."

"Why can't it be Moina? She gets along with him. Why don't you want to send her?"

"Because Moina is busy tomorrow. Swati, we will not have the luxury of choosing who we can work with on every project. Shiv is a member of the team. I need you to fill in for Rakesh and both of you will be following up on Avneesh Trivedi," Nitya said sternly. It was clear to Swati from Nitya's tone that the topic was not up for discussion. Still, she persisted and decided to give it one more try.

"I have never really worked with Shiv. Everyone seems to have problems with him, but not Moina. I am a bit surprised that you would pair him up with me."

"Yes, well, I just gave you my reasons and that should be enough. Is that understood?"

"Yes, ma'am."

"Good, you will have Tilak with you tomorrow, and he will drive you and Shiv wherever you need to go. Now, do you have a ride back home?"

"Yes," Swati replied.

"Good. Then I will see you tomorrow. Good night!"

"Good night, ma'am!"

Once Swati left, Nitya worked through some of the papers on her desk. The movers had come and taken all her stuff upstairs to the new office and left an empty box for her. She quickly unlocked her desk drawers, took out all the remaining papers, put them in the box, and headed upstairs to her new room. When she reached the top floor, she could see that most people had left. Some were on their way out and nodded at her as they walked by. Her new desk looked large and clean in the spacious office. The movers had placed all the items in the right places, more or less. Charu had left a note informing her that the phone on the desk was working now and had the same number as the previous phone. She picked up the receiver and indeed there was a dial tone. She found a new table lamp and turned it on. She could see the bright streetlights outside the large windows behind her desk. She went over and looked out the window. It was a clear, starry night, and she could see people enjoying themselves outside, strolling under the arches of the various blocks in Connaught Place. After a few minutes, she sat on her chair and slowly started arranging all the papers from the box she had carried upstairs. While she was busy settling in, she heard a gentle knock on her door. It was Manoj.

"Hi, Nitya."

"Good evening, sir."

"Settling in, are we?"

"Yes."

"Good. I am glad they got your office in order."

"Thank you."

"Well, I am just leaving. I wanted to ask you a couple of things."

"Yes," Nitya replied. "Would you like to sit down, sir?"

"No, this won't take long," Manoj replied, still standing near the open door. "How is it going with the stories on the victims?"

"We have made good progress."

"That's good. I am glad. So do you think we will have something ready in a couple of weeks?"

"For most of them, yes. There is one that is a bit strange. We are still working on it."

"What do you mean strange?"

"I know you are in a hurry. I can fill you in tomorrow."

"Yes, please do. We have a number of meetings tomorrow. Let's talk during a break."

"Sure, sir. What's the other thing?"

"I am sorry?"

"You said you wanted to talk to me about a couple of things. What's the other thing?"

"Oh, yes. We are meeting the board members on Saturday evening at the Gymkhana Club. You are now a member of the senior team, so we expect you to be there. There's going to be a cocktail and then dinner. It starts around seven, but everyone shows up fashionably late around eight. Please be there."

"Thank you, sir. I will."

"That's all then. We will talk tomorrow about your 'strange' thing," Manoj said with a smile as he picked up his briefcase.

"Good night, sir."

"Good night!"

After Manoj left, Nitya realized that she was exhausted too. She put the remaining papers back in the box and then stashed the entire box in one of the filing cabinets and locked it up. She decided everything else could wait until the next day, which was also going to be a long one with endless meetings. She picked up her purse and headed down the two flights of stairs past the reception and then out into the parking lot. The cold Delhi air was chilly but refreshing at this time of the evening. The parking lot was nearly empty and Tilak spotted her coming out of the building immediately. He quickly started the car and opened the back door for her. She asked him to stop by a sandwich place for her to pick up something to eat and then they were on their way to her apartment. In the car, they spoke briefly about Old Delhi and their plans for the following day. It was a leisurely and enjoyable drive back home.

"Did it go well today, ma'am, what you and Shiv were working on?"

"I am not sure Tilak. We still have to keep at it."

"Shiv's a smart boy."

"Yes, he is," Nitya said, slightly amused.

"I know he got into trouble with you, but he is a good boy. I have heard what other people say about him, but he is not like that. I know."

"How do you know?"

"I am from Agra, ma'am."

"Yes, you told me, and Shiv is from Bangalore. Not sure I see the connection."

"My family is still in Agra. A few months ago, my wife fell ill. She was very sick and had to be taken to the hospital. At the time I was not able to drive. I had fractured my hand and was doing odd things around the office."

"Yes, I remember you had a cast on your hand."

"Yes. When I came to know what had happened to my wife, it was already late and there was no way to catch the train. All the drivers had left for the night, and I was trying to see if anyone could give me a ride to the bus station. A few people were still working on the second and third floors. Most of them offered me money for a taxi to take me to the bus station from where I could take a bus to Agra. Then Shiv approached me and told me to wait downstairs. I thought he was going to give me a ride on his bike to the central bus station. He came down after half an hour. He had called a friend to bring a car. He borrowed his friend's car and drove me from Delhi to Agra that night. It's a long drive. It took us almost four and a half hours to get there. After he dropped me off, he drove all the way back to be here for work the next day. I will never forget the gesture."

"That was indeed kind of him."

"Yes, ma'am. I have worked here for a long time and interacted with a lot of people. I don't know what he has done to irk so many people. All I can say is that he isn't as bad as people make him out to be."

"Hmm," Nitya said, as she looked out the window when the car turned onto the avenue where her building was located. Once they got past the gates, Tilak stopped the car and they both got out.

"What time should I come to pick you up tomorrow, ma'am?"

"Nine."

"Right, ma'am."

"Tomorrow you will be driving Swati and Shiv to a few places. They will give you the addresses."

"Sure."

"Good night."

"Good night, ma'am."

Once home, Nitya ate quickly and decided to go to bed early. She cursorily reviewed the files that her team had given her on the progress they had made. She was happy with them. The only missing link was Avneesh Trivedi. The journalist in her was convinced that there was more to his story than what met the eye. Unfortunately, there wasn't much to go on unless new leads opened up from his workplace or through Shankar. As she turned in for the night, her thoughts shifted to her conversation with her sister, Kavita. Nitya was worried about her and knew that their mother would throw a fit if things didn't work out between Kavita and her husband.

* * *

Meanwhile, on the other side of town, in Old Delhi, Shankar was finishing his shift. Things hadn't gone particularly well for him since he had returned from the hospital. While he was away at the Willingdon Hospital, the police commissioner had paid a random visit while inspecting all the stations in Old Delhi. The constables and officers informed the commissioner that Shankar was out on patrol. He had called the police control room at the station and waited for almost an hour. He spoke to the constables and officers at the station, but Shankar was not at the railway station or any of the other police stations in Old Delhi. Shankar's constables had tried desperately to look for him at the usual places but had failed to locate him. When the commissioner left, he was visibly upset and that didn't bode well for Shankar. Upon his return from the hospital, he called the commissioner right away, but he didn't take Shankar's call.

What preoccupied Shankar's mind was what the resident doctor had told him about Avneesh. He had been killed before the night of the riots. It made Shankar wonder whether Avneesh's killers had taken advantage of the riots to dump his body in Old Delhi to make it look like he was one of the victims. But then who were the people who whisked his body away in the middle of the night? Where was the postmortem report? Where was the register with the details of who took away his body? Who took the family to perform the last rites? There were too many unanswered questions. The biggest one was why were the police and the home ministry so adamant that there were ten victims and not eleven.

As he was about to head home, the phone on his desk started ringing. He picked up hoping it would be the commissioner and he would get the opportunity to explain why he was not manning his station during his visit. But it wasn't the commissioner. It was his counterpart from the Chandni Chowk police station, Kabir Singh.

"Good evening, Shankar. I hope I didn't catch you on your way out."

"Hello, Kabir. That's alright. We can chat for a few minutes."

"Good. It's really about that elusive eleventh victim that we were discussing earlier when you were here."

"Yes?"

"Well, it bothered me as well and I started digging. I have a colleague who works at the home ministry, the same batch you see, and he has been looking at what happened as well. As you can imagine, there are multiple agencies involved in the investigation."

"Yes, that's normal, I guess."

"Yes, well, I asked him about the number of victims and specifically about Avneesh Trivedi."

"And?"

"Firstly, he did confirm that there were eleven victims, not ten. They know that the eleventh victim is Avneesh Trivedi, but they cannot make it public just yet."

"Why not?"

"That's where things are a bit murky. He is not sure himself. He thinks that Avneesh was an informer."

"Informer for whom? I don't recall him being on our list or for that matter any of the stations in the area."

"No, you are right. He wasn't. They are saying it could be the CBI or some other security agency."

"Really?" Shankar asked rather surprised. He knew that the CBI and other agencies had been active in recruiting agents and informers in the area. These central agencies didn't always keep the police informed, lest there be leaks through the local officers and constables in the area.

"There is one more thing."

"Yes?"

"They still don't know who took Avneesh's body to the crematorium and who took the family to perform the last rites."

"This is all good information. I must thank you for looking into this, Kabir."

"Your turn now," said Kabir. Shankar could sense that he was smiling on the other end of the phone.

"My turn?"

"Oh, come now. The police commissioner shows up at your station, you are not there, and no one knows where you are. He calls every station in the area and you are nowhere to be found. Well, when I called the hospital to ask about Avneesh, they told me that another police officer had visited to question the resident on duty. It's not hard to figure out who that officer might have been."

"You are right. I was there," Shankar admitted. He was happy to see that Kabir was interested in finding out the truth about what happened.

"What did you learn?"

"The doctor on duty confirmed that Avneesh was taken away by an officer in uniform and some other people who had CBI badges. They wrote their names and details on a register that has since been misplaced. And yes, they also took all his belongings and the postmortem report."

"Wow. If indeed it was not us, I mean, none of the government agencies or the police, it was quite a daring act ... but wait a minute, there must have been a police patrol car and constables at the hospital as the victims were being brought in."

"Yes, initially there was and then they were called away to Old Delhi. It seems there was a request on the police radio to have them redirected to the troubled areas."

"That is strange. That means someone from within the system knew what was going on."

"Yes, it would seem that way," Shankar said.

Both of them paused for a bit to ponder on what they had discussed.

Then Kabir broke the silence. "What do you think happened, Shankar?"

Shankar weighed his words carefully before answering. "I think there is a rogue element in one of the agencies or in the police. There must be. Otherwise, all this doesn't make sense."

Kabir was silent. They knew what the ramifications of this were. They had to tread carefully and there was no way to know whom to trust. After a moment's pause, Kabir broke the silence.

"What's the connection with the riots?"

"I have been thinking about that. The doctor told me that Avneesh was killed at least a day before the riots."

"If that's the case, then he must have been killed in Old Delhi and his killers took advantage of the riots by leaving his body visible to the public so that everyone would think of him as a riot victim."

"Yes, I thought about that. His body was burned and maybe they expected that it would not be easily identifiable and in a worse state. Since we discovered it quickly, the postmortem was able to reveal that he wasn't killed during the riots. Who knows? There are still many open questions. There must have been something that led to this man's killing and then the need to take him away to be cremated so quickly, take away his belongings, and the postmortem report … we are missing a piece of the puzzle, or several pieces, I think."

Kabir was trying to absorb what Shankar said. A lot of it made sense. It was now time to tell him what the orders from his senior officers were, something that Shankar would also be told the next day.

"Is there anything else?" Kabir asked.

"Yes, the riots."

"What about it?"

"It wasn't started by the usual suspects. We know that. All the people we questioned were surprised by it. None of the informers knew about it. That's strange, don't you think?"

"Yes, it is. What do you think happened?"

"The constables at the railway station told me that on the night when the train was set alight, there was a fight that had broken out on the platform farthest from the police control room."

"Yes, I remember that."

"When they went to stop the fight, they saw the coach burning at the other end of the station and they ran back to douse the fire."

"So?"

"Well, when they went back, the people who were fighting had left. They couldn't take down their names or any details."

"So, you think the fight was staged to divert attention."

"Well, in an actual riot, criminals don't set fire to empty coaches."

"You are right. I am guessing there's no news on the groups that were fighting?"

"No, but I am sure of one thing."

"What?"

"Avneesh's body was brought on the train that was on the platform where the fight broke out."

"How can you be so sure?"

"The doctor told me the postmortem showed that the burned body might have been wrapped in jute bags that are used to carry rice. The constables said they saw similar bags on the platform where the groups were fighting. The train had arrived on the platform a few minutes earlier. I checked the schedule. It had just arrived from Dehradun. And that's the platform where the commotion started. The train on the other platform, the one whose coach was burned, had arrived half an hour before, and all the passengers had alighted from it already. It was just about to be taken to the yards for cleaning and maintenance. It was the group that was on the platform from the Dehradun train that started the melee."

"Why would they draw attention for the police to come to the same platform?"

"Good question. Think about it. The train arrives and everyone gets off. People head for the exits in all directions. There are guards at each exit. Anyone carrying big rice bags would immediately be noticed. So how could they get them past the gate without getting noticed?"

"By creating a diversion."

"Exactly. I think the fight and the fire were deliberately started to simulate a riot-like situation so that the body could be burned and dumped. When everyone panicked and headed for the exits, Avneesh's killers headed for the pedestrian gate with the big bags. The people were in a hurry to get out. The guards had converged to deal with the fire. In the meantime, the gang set the bags on fire outside the gates. Remember we found his body near a garbage dump which is set on fire on a regular basis to burn the trash. So, no one would suspect anything. Everyone would think that he was a riot victim and not bother to check anything else. What they didn't realize was that the body wouldn't burn completely. There really is a dangerous gang of people coordinating this. Their main objective was to hide the murder and Avneesh's body, and they almost succeeded."

"Well, that is possible."

"Yes, it's a theory at this point with lots of loopholes. There is another possibility, of course."

"What's that?" asked Kabir.

"Whoever started this knew that police and reinforcements from all over Delhi would end up here. I mean there would be skeleton forces in other areas, but most of the focus and manpower would be here."

"So?"

"That would leave vast swaths of the city unguarded. If anyone wanted to commit crimes in other areas, this would be the perfect time and opportunity."

"You are right. I hadn't thought of that."

"I need to take a look at reports from other areas to see if any criminal activities stand out from that night."

"I need to tell you something about that," Kabir said. Shankar knew from his tone that he wouldn't want to hear what came next.

"What is it?" Shankar asked.

"We have been told, and you will be told too, that no one should be investigating the deaths except the CBI. No one. Our only task is to man our stations and patrol our areas. Nothing else. Our primary objective is to keep the peace and make sure that the junior home minister's visit goes off peacefully without any incident," said Kabir. He could hear Shankar sighing at the other end.

"Just when we thought we had made some headway into the investigation," Shankar said exasperatedly.

"I know, but we have been told clearly, no more investigations into the victims. That's all being done by the CBI."

"Yes, so it would seem."

"Well, I need to go home now, and I am sure you do too. Good night Shankar."

"Thank you for all this, Kabir. We will talk again. Good night!"

Shankar leaned back into his chair, folded his hands close to his lips, and thought about what Kabir had told him. He was convinced that there was a rogue element in either the police or other investigative agencies like the CBI or even the home ministry who was involved in this cover-up. He didn't know whom to go to for help. Kabir was the same rank as Shankar. Going to their superiors would result in them being sternly reminded that this was not their case. Any attempt to approach the other agencies directly would mean involving the commissioner, and Shankar was not in his good books either. Then there was the junior home minister's visit and the order from his superiors on focusing on their priorities. After a few minutes, he called out for Motiram to head home. He decided to visit Avneesh's family the next day to find out more about him and continue with his investigation.

* * *

When Nitya walked into the building in the morning, she saw Swati and Shiv waiting for her at the reception. She told them that Tilak would be driving them to Haus Khaz and reminded them to be back in the office to let her know of any progress, even if it was late. Given that Haus Khaz was in New Delhi, she knew it wouldn't take them long. She watched them walk out of the building toward the parking lot. She could see from Swati's body language that she was still not happy to be paired up with Shiv.

Moina and Suresh were waiting for her in her new office. They had made good progress with their assignments and were helping others with their interviews. They were working well together and seemed to complement each other. They were also keen to please Nitya. She spoke to them for half an hour and then headed to her meeting with Manoj and the senior team.

The meetings were long and seemed to drag on forever. Everyone had an opinion even if they knew nothing of the subject. The longer the meetings lasted, the more they became about making themselves feel good and important. Manoj tolerated it to some extent, but she could see that as things dragged on beyond lunch, he was getting tired too. Finally, the meetings ended around 3:00 p.m. There were a few short breaks, but Nitya didn't get a chance to speak to Manoj alone. During her allotted time, she told the group about the progress she was making. They had a few questions, but they were mostly happy with her team and the work they had done.

By the time she returned to her room, Nitya was exhausted. She asked for some coffee and turned her attention to the ever-increasing files and paperwork on her desk. There was also a note from the reception about the calls she had missed. She decided to take a breather for an hour before returning the calls. She needed to stretch her legs. She took her coffee mug and decided to check in on her team. They were happy to see her and only too eager to tell her about their progress. Swati and Shiv were still not back. Moina informed her that someone had called for Shiv. In his absence, she had picked up the phone but the woman on the other end of the line hadn't left her name or number. After her break, she headed back upstairs and heard the phone ring as she made her way to her room through the long corridor. She rushed inside and picked it up at the last minute.

"Hello."

"Hello, is this Nitya Chaturvedi?"

"Yes, it is. Who is this?"

"It's Madhavi, ma'am, Avneesh's wife. You had come to our place."

"Yes, of course, Madhavi, is everything alright?"

"Yes, everything is fine. I was trying to get in touch with Shiv. I have found Avneesh's notebook with some numbers and names. I don't recognize any of them. I don't know if it will help."

"It might."

"I tried calling Shiv, but he is not at his desk. So, I decided to call you."

"You did the right thing. I am glad you found the notebook."

"I am afraid I can't bring it over to you. I can't leave my son with my in-laws for too long and I am tutoring some kids."

"Yes, I understand. I will ask Shiv to pick it up from your place. He lives in Old Delhi, and he can go and pick it up tonight or tomorrow. Will that be fine?"

"Yes ma'am."

"Is there a number where we can reach you? I just want to make sure he calls before he goes."

"No, ma'am. We don't have a phone at home. He can come any time. Someone is always at home, and I will be here too."

"Alright, don't worry, I will ask him to go pick it up."

"Okay," Madhavi replied softly. Nitya could make out the background noise in the public phone booth. She wasn't sure if Madhavi wanted to say anything else.

"Is there anything else you want to say, Madhavi?"

"Ma'am ...," her voice trailed off. Nitya wasn't sure if she was still there, but the line was active since she could hear others in the background.

"What is it, Madhavi?"

"Did you find out what might have happened to Avneesh?"

"Not yet, but we are looking into it. Is everything alright?"

"Yes, ma'am. I just wanted to know," Madhavi replied. Nitya could sense the sadness in her voice. She tried to reassure her as much as she could, but she knew it was difficult. After hanging up, Nitya felt sorry for her. She knew that the family was stretched financially. The fact that Madhavi was tutoring in addition to her teaching job meant that the family needed the additional income, and with Avneesh gone, it wasn't going to get any easier. Nitya knew that small private schools in Old Delhi didn't pay well and wondered if it was better for her to apply as a teacher in a government school where jobs were more secure, and she would be assured a pension.

Around 4:30 p.m. Swati and Shiv were back from their visit to Haus Khaz. Swati entered Nitya's office first with Shiv following her slowly with a pensive look on his face. Nitya was on the phone, but she pointed to the chairs across her desk for them to sit while she finished her call.

"So how did it go today?" Nitya asked once she had hung up. Swati responded hurriedly while Shiv sat back with folded hands and a thoughtful look on his face.

"Seems like we went to the wrong place, ma'am. At least the first address was wrong. The other one where he worked before was correct."

"I am sorry, Swati, but you are not making any sense."

"Ma'am, there was no one who worked at the first address by the name of Avneesh Trivedi. When we went to the second address, the one on the other side of Deer Park in Haus Khaz, they confirmed that he had worked there, but he had left the job six months ago to work somewhere else. That's all that they told us," Swati replied. Nitya then turned to Shiv, expecting a clearer answer. Shiv looked at Swati who gestured that she had finished and then he began talking.

"Madhavi told us that Avneesh had worked in two shops. His most recent workplace was Royal Textiles and he had started there six months ago. Before that, he worked at Apparel House. We went to both places. When we went to Royal Textiles, they told us that they don't know anyone called Avneesh Trivedi. No one by that name ever worked there.

Then we went to Apparel House, and they confirmed that he had worked there, as Swati said, and had left his job six months back to work somewhere else."

"Hmm," Nitya said thoughtfully. "Does that make sense?"

"Yes," Swati replied. "We went to the wrong place."

"Shiv?" Nitya asked.

"No, it doesn't make sense."

"Oh, yes ma'am, Shiv has a theory. He spoke to some lorry drivers at a tea stall near the Royal Textiles office and he found out something, although I don't know if it's even relevant," Swati replied. Nitya was getting a bit impatient with Swati's long and winding answers, but she didn't show it.

"Shiv?"

"Yes, ma'am."

"What did you find?"

"I wish we had a photograph of Avneesh with us. When I went to have tea at the stall just across the showroom of Royal Textiles showroom, I struck up a conversation with the vendor and some lorry drivers who transport goods in and out of the showroom. I told them I was looking for my uncle who worked there, gave them Avneesh's name, and then described him as best as I could from the photograph that we saw at his house in Old Delhi. Of course, there are many people who match his description. It's hard to say for sure, but it seems that there could have been someone matching that description who worked there but hadn't come to the tea stall for a few days."

"What do you think?"

"I don't know, ma'am. We need to show them a picture and find out for sure. As I said, I wish we had his photograph."

"Yes, well on that, I got a call from Avneesh's wife, Madhavi. She found his notebook and is willing to give it to us if it helps. I suggest you pick it up from her this evening or tomorrow morning. I told her that you live in Old Delhi and can drop by. Is that okay?"

"Yes, ma'am."

"You can also ask her for a photograph. Hopefully, they will have no objection to sharing one with you."

"Yes, I will ask for one."

"Is there anything else?"

"Yes," Shiv said.

"What is it?"

"We spent some time talking to some of his ex-colleagues at the other place he worked before Royal Textiles."

"You mean, Apparel House?"

"Yes, ma'am."

"What of it?"

"Well, it seems he was quite happy there. They all liked him, and he enjoyed working there. The only problem was that it didn't offer a good salary, and when he got a new opportunity, he left."

"Nothing wrong with that," Nitya said.

"They all knew Madhavi. He had taken her over during festivals and other family events. Some of his colleagues considered Avneesh a close friend, but when he left, he didn't keep in touch with any of them. He didn't tell anyone where he was going. Don't you find that surprising, ma'am? I mean it's not like he left with any hard feelings or any animosity. There was also no indication that he had done anything wrong. From the conversations we had with them, it seemed like he was a model employee, honest and friendly. When we told them that he had been killed in the riots, they were genuinely sad and some of them said they would visit his parents and Madhavi to offer their condolences. They were shocked and saddened."

"Hmm, yes it's strange that he hadn't shared any information about his new employer with them."

"Right. If you recall, Madhavi had told us that she didn't know anyone from his new workplace, nor had Avneesh ever taken her to visit the new office. I'd have thought that if indeed he was moving to a new employer who offered a better salary and prospects, he would share some details with his wife and parents."

"True," Nitya said thoughtfully, while Shiv turned to Swati who wanted to add something.

"Well, ma'am, Shiv is right about that. They were all sad to hear the news and were surprised that he hadn't kept in touch with them after he left."

"Yes, seems strange."

"Let's say for the sake of argument that he didn't work at Royal Textiles but somewhere else, ma'am. Why the secrecy?" Shiv asked.

"What are your thoughts, Shiv?" Nitya asked.

"I am not sure, ma'am, but something doesn't make sense here. I need to go back with a photograph and ask around in Haus Khaz to find out where he worked. We also need that notebook. Maybe it will reveal something."

"Yes, it might. I will let you get on with it then. Make sure you get them both and then we will see how to proceed. There is something we are missing for sure. I can't put my finger on it. There are still too many open questions. Then there's the whole thing about how hurriedly he was taken away from the hospital to be cremated."

"Yes, any news from Mr. Shankar Sen?"

"Nothing yet," said Nitya, "I will let you know if I find out anything."

"Will that be all, ma'am? I will see if I can pick up the notebook and photograph now."

"Sure," Nitya replied. Shiv got up nodded at both Swati and Nitya and left the room.

"Strange day for both of you, wasn't it?" Nitya asked, and Swati nodded in agreement.

"Well, this one victim is taking a lot of time," Swati said with exasperation in her voice.

"It's not always a race, you know. Sometimes these things take time."

"Yes, ma'am."

"Well, let's go over the victims you were following up on and your notes on them."

"Yes, ma'am," Swati said with a smile. She had made a lot of progress on the ones that were assigned to her, and Swati spent the next hour or so discussing how she was approaching the interviews and what she was planning to write. Nitya offered her suggestions but for the most part, agreed with Swati's proposals. She was also happy to see that Swati was getting better at her writing. Once they had finished and Swati was ready to leave, Nitya looked at the schedule for the next day.

"Alright, Rakesh will be calling me tomorrow morning. If he is back, he can accompany Shiv to Haus Khaz or wherever else they need to go to follow up on all that you worked on today. You can go back to your own work."

"I don't mind, ma'am," Swati said in a much softer tone.

"What do you mean?"

"I mean if you want me to go with Shiv, it's okay, I will go with him."

"Really? What happened? Yesterday you didn't want me to pair you up with him and today it seems you are fine. What a difference a day has made," Nitya said with a smile.

"He is fine to work with; quite nice actually. Maybe I was wrong about him," Swati said apologetically.

"Well, I am glad to hear that. It does say a lot about you that you can change your opinion. I am happy."

"Yes, ma'am. I am sorry I said those things about Shiv. I really don't know him, and I shouldn't have."

"That's alright. Well, you are back with him tomorrow then. We will talk again tomorrow evening once both of you are back, hopefully, with a clearer picture."

"Yes, ma'am," Swati said as she got up to leave.

* * *

Death in the Walled City

In Old Delhi, Shankar was having little luck getting through to the commissioner to provide an explanation as to why he wasn't at the station during his last visit. The commissioner was giving him the silent treatment by not entertaining his phone calls or granting him an appointment. The CBI was well into their investigations but was providing very little by way of details of what happened that night. Shankar had visited the Old Delhi Railway Station earlier that day and spent a good two hours surveying the scene where the coach had been burned and where the scuffle between the two groups had broken out. He had also had a lengthy conversation with the station master and the constables at the police outpost to carefully go over the chain of events that night. Finally, before heading back to the police station, he had walked to the pedestrian gate where the charred bodies had been found. He spoke to the residents in the nearby buildings and the shopkeepers in the area.

Once he was back in his office, he spoke to Kabir. It seemed that most investigations were progressing well. They still had very little information on Avneesh's murder, though. Shankar contacted the CBI directly and was told that the investigations were ongoing and that they would be sharing the details with the police stations when they were ready. When he had asked specifically about the secrecy around Avneesh's death, they were particularly coy and reiterated that no information was to be made public until the investigations had concluded. That raised even more alarm bells for Shankar.

He recalled his conversation with Avneesh's family from earlier that day. His parents, sister, and wife were understandably devastated. He had noted down details of Avneesh's employers. While it was not a long conversation, Shankar got the impression from Madhavi that they were also in the dark about what happened. He asked Madhavi to make a formal request to investigate what had happened and he would then start looking into it using that request as a pretext in case he was questioned on it. It wouldn't be enough to convince his superiors, but it would be better than nothing. The other thing that he couldn't shake off from his visit to Avneesh's family was that they all seemed really scared. Although they didn't explicitly say it, it was quite evident from their mannerisms and guarded responses. It almost seemed like they had been threatened by someone. Madhavi had quickly come by the station and filled out the forms. The FIR or First Information Report contained all the relevant information that the family knew about what happened that night, how they had been informed of Avneesh's death, how his parents had been taken to the crematorium to perform the last rites, and the names and descriptions of the individuals who had taken them there. The form also mentioned that they were still waiting for a formal death certificate and a postmortem report from the hospital.

Madhavi mentioned that someone from the CBI had come to take down all the details and had informed them that they were investigating his death, but she hadn't heard back from them. Shankar realized that Avneesh's death had had an immediate and serious impact on the family's finances, and even in their grief and sadness, the focus of the remaining members had shifted to figuring out what to do next to secure their future. Although they were desperate for answers, the pressing economic realities meant that they had very little time to follow up on the investigation.

The files in front of Shankar were copies of reports of the activities from other police stations in Delhi. Shankar wanted to review them to understand what had been reported from the other stations, and to see if there was anything there to suggest that the miscreants may have used the riots as an opportunity to carry out criminal activities elsewhere. He went through them one by one. There had been some break-ins and petty thefts in some industrial areas, but nothing major. A few shop owners had reported that their stores had been broken into and some goods had been stolen but, again, nothing that raised any eyebrows.

Once he had finished with the reports, he started looking at the reports from the various checkpoints in the city. Usually, these were manned by police and transport authorities who inspected goods leaving the city and ensured that the paperwork was in order. There was a large stack of papers in multiple files from various checkpoints. On that night, the constables at the checkpoints had all been asked to head to Old Delhi. That meant that there was no inspection of cargo or goods that night. The officials manning the border checkpoints were simply doing a routine check—checking the paperwork, reading the shipment information, doing a quick count of trucks leaving the city, taking down the details of the drivers, making them fill out the details of the source and destination of the goods, and then letting them go.

What caught Shankar's eye was the unusually high number of trucks that left from Haus Khaz that night. He knew that Haus Khaz was not an industrial area and didn't have any factories as such. A large number of lorries leaving from there to destinations in other states seemed strange. He spent the next two hours calling different police stations and transport officials at various checkpoints to get a better understanding of how many trucks usually crossed the border each night, where they started from, and where they were headed. Slowly it became clear to Shankar that the number of trucks that had left from Haus Khaz the night of the riots was indeed an anomaly.

He focused on the trucks leaving from the Haus Khaz address and turned his attention to some of the addresses that had been provided in the forms that the drivers had filled out. The destinations were in different states. Some were in Shimla in Himachal Pradesh, some in Chandigarh and Ludhiana in Punjab, some in Srinagar in Jammu and Kashmir, and a few others in Dehradun in the foothills of the Himalayas. All of them seemed to contain either clothes or furniture. He then looked at where the trucks had picked up their goods from in Haus Khaz. They were all from the same place. He called the number. It was a clothing store called Royal Textiles. The gentleman informed Shankar that nothing had been shipped from their store. He was surprised at Shankar's questions since they were a showroom and not a manufacturer. Shankar then called a few numbers that were listed under the destination details in the forms with no luck. He called the central and state telephone exchanges and quickly realized that the numbers did not exist, and that all the destination addresses were fake. Finally, his gaze fell upon the signature of the shipper in all the forms. He noticed that they were all the same. The person who had signed off on all of them was the victim whose family he had visited earlier in the day—Avneesh Trivedi.

True Colors

When Nitya arrived at work the next day, she summoned Shiv and Swati to her office right away. She was happy with the progress the rest of the team had made but there still weren't any clear answers on Avneesh's death. She could see that something was on Shiv's mind too and he seemed distracted.

"Did you get the notebook and Avneesh's photograph?" Nitya asked.

"Yes, ma'am," Shiv replied.

"Did you learn anything new? Was the family more forthcoming this time?"

"Not really."

"Who did you speak with?"

"Mostly Madhavi and a little with Avneesh's father."

"So, we learned nothing new?"

"I wouldn't say that ..." Shiv replied thoughtfully, his voice trailing off.

"What is it, Shiv?" Nitya asked while Swati remained uncharacteristically quiet during the entire conversation. Shiv reached into the big brown envelope containing the notebook, took out a paper, and handed it over to Nitya.

"What's this?"

"It's some kind of a notice or advertisement that I found in the notebook and another one exactly the same was taped in one of the inside pages, ma'am."

Nitya took her time reading the paper and then said, "this is a strange flier."

"Yes," Shiv said, as Nitya handed it to Swati. Swati tried to figure out what was wrong with the flier. It looked like any of the other countless fliers distributed across the city and glued on walls, notice boards, stores, and doors and windows.

"Did you ask the Trivedis about this?"

"Yes, but it seems that Avneesh was secretive about his notebook."

"Hmm. Anything else?"

"Yes, I went to the address mentioned on the flier. It is two streets over from the Trivedi residence. It is a shop, but the shutters were down. I asked around and the neighboring store owners and employees told me that it has been shut for a while. I spoke to the landlord of the building who lives in an apartment on one of the upper floors and he told me that a government agency had rented out the place for a few weeks, paid their rent in advance, and then left suddenly."

"That is strange. Didn't the landlord try to find out more?"

"No, he didn't. The entire rent was paid in advance and then they just left. Ma'am, these places rent out these small stores and get paid in cash. I don't think they really want authorities to know about this. Plus, there weren't any complaints. Apparently, the store was used as an office for this agency. A few people would visit every day for what seemed like interviews and then they left."

"Hmm. I am guessing we don't know which government agency."

"No. I don't think it was a government agency. It makes no sense."

"You are right."

When both Nitya and Shiv paused, Swati decided to join the conversation.

"What's wrong with this flier, ma'am? We get these at home all the time from different companies, from the government, and even as announcements for new establishments opening in the area."

"Yes, but look at this one. It doesn't mention anything. It has an emblem of the government but doesn't specify which agency or even a phone number or a contact name," Nitya said.

"Yes," Swati replied slowly, realizing the lack of details and specifics in the paper that she was still holding. It was a colorful flier that seemed like a poster from the Government of India. It didn't specify any agency. It was an advertisement stating that an agency was hiring individuals for entry-level jobs. The ad mentioned exciting growth and travel opportunities. It wasn't out of the ordinary for the government to make such announcements. But usually, the advertisements were clear about the positions, the department, and had a name and number to contact. This flier looked official, was extremely well made, but offered very little detail. The only detail that was provided was the address of the shop that had been the recruitment office for a few weeks.

Nitya turned to Shiv and asked, "anything in the notebook?"

"I went through all the numbers and called them one by one. There aren't that many. I think there are around ten numbers. Five of them are in Delhi. They are mostly public phone booths."

"You mean those open public telephone booths in shops and stores?"

"Yes, ma'am."

"That's weird. Nothing from his workplace in Haus Khaz?"

"Nothing."

"This just keeps getting stranger."

"Yes, ma'am. One other thing."

"What is it?"

"Mr. Shankar Sen also visited the Trivedi residence and got details about Avneesh's workplace."

"Hmm. I am surprised they didn't give the notebook to the police and instead gave it to you. Who gave the notebook to you?"

"Madhavi," Shiv replied, "but she told me that she had copied the contents of the notebook and has given Mr. Sen a copy too."

"Alright. Well, the police have to do their job and we have to do ours. Are both of you heading back to Haus Khaz today with Avneesh's photograph to see if you can get more details?"

"Yes, ma'am," Swati and Shiv replied almost in unison.

"Well, off you go then. Tilak is waiting for you in the parking lot."

"Thank you."

Nitya saw Shiv and Swati walk out through the corridor. Swati was leaning over and seemed to be asking Shiv a lot of questions. Nitya could see that any misgivings that Swati might have had about working with Shiv were now all gone and in fact, their body language seemed to suggest that they were getting along well.

* * *

Shankar called his station from home to let them know that he would be late. He had been summoned by the minister who was going to visit Old Delhi. The minister's secretary had called the station heads at the various police stations in Old Delhi and had made appointments for them to speak with him. The minister had requested Shankar to meet him in his office that morning. Shankar arrived early and was still undecided on what to tell the minister. He knew that he would need help from other investigative agencies to find out what was going on. His attempts at engaging them directly had been thwarted.

As Motiram drove the jeep up to the Central Secretariat in New Delhi and parked near the North Block, Shankar sat back and marveled at the grandeur of the buildings. The Secretariat, as it was called, comprised of the North and South Blocks and the home ministry was in the North Block. It was built by the British during the early part of the twentieth century. It housed the most important ministries of India. The buildings comprised over a thousand rooms and offices belonging to the most important departments in the government. Shankar could see the vast array of shiny cars with their flags and red lights on top. As he got down and started walking toward the entrance, he could see ministers, members of parliament, and bureaucrats going about their work with their papers and briefcases in hand.

After a few customary security checks, he entered a long corridor leading to the minister's office. He got some glances from a few people. He was in uniform and some of the senior officers walking past him greeted him with a nod. The high ceilings and the imposing structure of the building made everything and everyone around look small. This was the seat of power and everyone entering the building knew it. Anyone who ever worked in the government wanted to work here at some point. Working at the Secretariat, no matter in what rank, was something that could not be quantified. It was no different for Shankar. Ever since he had moved to Delhi from Callipur, he wanted to be posted in New Delhi and eventually work in one of these offices. This was a different India. Although it was only a few miles from his Old Delhi Police Station, in reality, it was another world, one he desperately wanted to be part of.

His visit today was to ascertain whether he could engage the minister in gaining access into the investigation of the mysterious death of Avneesh Trivedi. It was a risky proposition. It was never a good idea to solicit help from a minister directly without the consent of his superior officers. If things didn't work out, it could backfire enormously. Ministers were elected officials that came and went, but his superiors were here to stay. Alienating them for the purpose of an investigation had its own risks. Shankar was well aware of the pitfalls, but he had a plan. Much of it was dependent on the minister himself and to what extent he could be convinced to get involved. What was working in Shankar's favor was that Ghanshyam Das, the junior minister in the home ministry, was a different kind of elected official.

In a country where most politicians and ministers of all stripes were in their 60s and 70s, Ghanshyam Das was in his late forties. He was young, articulate, and someone who was respected across the political spectrum. He also did not have a family pedigree in politics. He came from a modest background and was well educated. First, he was a student leader in college, and then, he was a lawyer in a private firm for many years before he entered politics. When he had initially run for office, he had done so as an independent candidate and had won against more established parties. This had surprised many people, but not his constituents. He represented a different type of politician, one who was not afraid to challenge the status quo.

After winning the elections, the ruling party had courted him, and he promptly decided to join them in exchange for a ministerial berth in the home ministry, albeit in the role of a junior minister. His constituents had initially seen this as a betrayal. However, he worked hard to get things done in his area and his constituents were happy to see that. The ruling party viewed him with suspicion. If he had jumped from one party to another, he could easily switch to another if things changed. Many in the party were also unhappy that an outsider had been given an important berth instead of members who had been with the party for a long time. The senior ministers and politicians knew that it was important to have someone like Ghanshyam Das within the cabinet than in opposition or in the backbenches. This way they could keep an eye on him and keep him in check.

As a minister, he hadn't disappointed. There were occasions when he had disagreed with his senior minister and others in the cabinet, but he had done so discreetly without stirring up any controversies. His pragmatism had ensured that in situations where things could have gone out of hand, a compromise was always reached. It was an uneasy dance, but so far it had worked out well for Ghanshyam Das and other senior members of the ruling party.

Shankar was aware of Ghanshyam's background and standing within the party. He liked the fact that he was young and didn't mind stirring things up. In a country where politicians were mostly loathed, Ghanshyam was liked by the public and the press alike. Shankar also knew that the minister was a wily politician and wouldn't hesitate to throw him under the bus if things went wrong. However, if there was anyone who would lend him an ear and find a way to solve this mysterious death, it would be Ghanshyam. There had to be something in it for him of course. This is where Shankar felt he had some leverage. Old Delhi was Ghanshyam's constituency. The minister had a vested interest in making sure that he was seen as someone who was going the extra mile for his constituents and getting them justice when any crime had been committed. This is precisely what Shankar was counting on. After half an hour, he saw a few people filing out of the minister's room. He recognized some of them. They were senior officials from the home ministry, police, and other investigative agencies. Once they had all left, the secretary ushered Shankar into the minister's room.

Ghanshyam liked Shankar. He knew about Shankar's past and had always felt that he had not been treated fairly by the senior officers. But since it was a matter within the Indian Police Service, he knew better than to intervene in the workings of the bureaucracy unless there was something for him to gain from it. He knew Shankar was a good officer, at times too outspoken for his own good, but at least he spoke his mind. They met regularly during his visits to Old Delhi, and he made it a point to invite all officers from his constituency over to his residence during get-togethers and festivals. Today's meeting was a routine one to get a view from Shankar on the law-and-order situation in his constituency. Ghanshyam knew that Shankar was the one who would give him the most candid view of the situation.

Unlike other minister's offices, Ghanshyam's was sparsely furnished. This made the large office look even bigger. As he entered the room, Shankar could see Ghanshyam on the phone behind a large mahogany desk at the opposite end of the room. There were a few files arranged in neat piles on one side of the desk. Behind Ghanshyam's chair were portraits of Gandhi and Tagore. One side of the room had a large bookshelf with more files, papers, a few books, and some journals. On the opposite side was a coffee table surrounded by some chairs and a sofa. The moment Ghanshyam saw Shankar entering the room he waved at him and gestured toward the sofa. The minister's secretary was still in the room trying to arrange a stack of files on the desk. After he hung up, Ghanshyam quickly walked over to Shankar with a big smile on his face. Shankar sat on one of the cushioned chairs while Ghanshyam sat on the sofa. They exchanged a few greetings and then the minister got down to business.

"How is the situation now, Shankar?"

"Much better, sir."

"Terrible thing, these riots. I wish there was some lasting solution to this."

"Yes, sir."

"As you are aware that I will be visiting my constituency. I'd like to visit your station as well and the Old Delhi Railway Station."

"Right, sir."

"I really don't want to make too much of a fuss, but you know how things are. We politicians must walk a fine line and if our constituents don't see us often, they feel that we are not doing anything," Ghanshyam said with a smile.

"Understood, sir. All arrangements are in place."

"I know they are. I have full confidence in you and all the officers in Old Delhi. All of you have done a splendid job in bringing the situation under control so quickly after the riots. I must commend all of you."

"Thank you, sir."

"I have already reviewed the situation a few times with my ministry, your superiors in the police department, and the investigative agencies. It seems things are back to normal."

"Yes, sir. They are."

"Strange one this time around, don't you think, Shankar? I mean past riots have always lasted a few days. This one lasted only a few hours and things were back to normal within a couple of days. I mean I am not complaining. I am thankful and happy that things didn't get worse. I feel awful for the victims and their families. Still, it was rather strange how quickly things deteriorated and then went back to normal. Don't you think?"

"Yes, sir. I am glad you brought that up. There is something I want to talk to you about," Shankar said looking at Ghanshyam and then at his secretary who was still arranging files. Ghanshyam immediately got the cue and turned to his secretary.

"Could you please get us some tea? Thank you," Ghanshyam said as his secretary nodded and left the room. Ghanshyam then turned to Shankar and continued, "what is it, Shankar? There is obviously something on your mind."

"Yes, sir. It's about the death of one of your constituents, Avneesh Trivedi. I visited his residence earlier this week and spoke to his parents and widow."

"Sad business. How did he die?"

"Well, sir, that's what I wanted to talk to you about. I found his and another victim's body by a pedestrian gate near the railway station. They were badly burned. Their bodies were found near a garbage dump."

"Yes, I saw that in the reports in the review meetings. I was told that the victims' bodies have now been released to the families for cremation or burial as the case may be. In this case, cremation, of course."

"Yes, sir, but before I get to the details, I wanted to ask you what you have been told about the total number of victims."

"Ah, so that's what you are getting at. Well, I have been told that there were eleven victims, but the official line is ten. Apparently, there's still some investigation going on regarding this eleventh victim. My understanding is that it will be made public once the investigation has been concluded. I am guessing this eleventh victim was Avneesh Trivedi?"

"Yes, sir."

"Well, there may not be much to it. I have been informed that he may have been mixed up in something illegal and then was killed that night in the riots."

"Not quite, sir."

"What do you mean?"

"He was not killed on the night of the riots. I spoke to the doctor at Willingdon Hospital who did his postmortem. He told me that Avneesh had been shot to death at least a day before the riots."

"Are you sure?"

"Yes, sir. His body was whisked away from the hospital in the middle of the night, and he was cremated within a few hours. His parents were brought over from Old Delhi for the cremation, but they weren't given any opportunity to perform any sort of ceremony. What's more, they haven't been given a death certificate or any report from the hospital telling them how he died. They are completely in the dark as to what happened to their son. The postmortem report is also nowhere to be found," Shankar said. He could immediately see Ghanshyam's expression change as he tried to absorb all of this. After a few seconds, Ghanshyam got up, walked across toward the window. Then he turned back and looked right at Shankar as he spoke.

"Who took him away from the hospital? Wasn't there a police patrol car present at the hospital?"

"Yes, there was, but they were called away to deal with the situation in Old Delhi."

"Called away? By whom?"

"The police control room informed them that they had to head to Old Delhi as the situation was getting worse."

"But it wasn't. Things were getting better after the first few hours, right?"

"Yes, sir."

"And we know nothing about the people who took Avneesh away from the hospital?"

"No, sir. Except that one of them was in uniform. The register where they wrote all their names and details is also missing. The resident doctor had initially refused to release the body and quite rightly so, but then he got a call from someone higher up in the department to let him go."

"Which department?"

"His own sir, a senior doctor, sir. I checked, and apparently, the senior ER doctor had received a call from the police to release Avneesh's body."

"Do you know who had called this doctor?"

"Not quite. It could be an officer or someone impersonating an officer from the commissioner's office."

"Unbelievable."

"Yes, sir."

"I can't believe that they released the body just like that."

"I do believe the doctors, sir. A lot of victims were being brought into the hospital. It was a chaotic night, and they were overworked and understaffed. If things looked official, they took it at face value. They may have been duped, but I don't think there was any malicious intent on the part of the hospital staff."

"Obviously, you have done a fair bit of investigation on this. Let's hear it. What do you think happened?"

Before Shankar could continue, the minister's secretary walked in with some tea and biscuits. He carefully poured some for Ghanshyam and Shankar while the minister seemed lost in thought. Shankar was pleased to see that the minister was taking this seriously, and he knew from the look on his face that he wasn't going to let it go. Once the secretary left, Shankar continued.

"Sir, you were right in saying that these riots were a bit strange compared to the other ones that we have had to deal with in the past. We have questioned all our informers and contacts in the area. None of them have any inkling as to what triggered this. The usual suspects were just as surprised as we were."

"Do you know what happened or at least do you have a theory?"

"Yes, sir, a theory. I think the riots were started by a criminal gang for two reasons. One was to divert police from other areas to Old Delhi. The second was to hide the murder of Avneesh Trivedi, which was completely unrelated to the other deaths."

"Do you have some evidence of this?"

"I am still investigating, sir, but this is where I need your help. The investigations are being done by the CBI and the home ministry, but each time I try to engage them, I hit a wall."

"What do you know so far?"

"I know that there were several trucks that left Haus Khaz that night and were heading toward Punjab, Himachal,

Jammu, and Uttar Pradesh. Due to lack of manpower, their paperwork wasn't checked thoroughly and none of them were inspected."

"And on the second?"

"The doctor confirmed that Avneesh was not killed that night. I think he was killed in Dehradun and his body was brought back on the train to Delhi. I believe that night at the railway station a fight was staged between two groups to deliberately start a fire in an empty coach of a train on another platform, and while the police were busy dealing with it, some miscreants took advantage of the chaos and dumped Avneesh's body near the gates and set it alight. They must have forgotten something and that made them come back to the hospital, and that's when they stole his body, took away the reports, and cremated him."

"Yes, but once they got the body from the hospital, why didn't they just take what they needed and then dump him somewhere else?"

"Right, sir. I thought of that, but as I said, I am still investigating."

"Do you have some paperwork to justify your points about the trucks?"

"Yes, sir."

"What's the link to Avneesh Trivedi on that one?"

"All the trucks left a warehouse in Haus Khaz and the signature of the shipper was Avneesh's."

"Hmm. Do you think he was involved in all this? Maybe part of the same gang?"

"Maybe, sir. I don't know. If he was involved in this, why was he killed? If he was a member of the gang, why would they kill one of their own?"

"Hmm. Good point. Lots of unanswered questions."

"Yes, sir. If you don't mind telling me—what have you been told during your review meetings?"

"Well, most of them were focused on bringing the situation back to normal and maintaining peace. We haven't spoken much about the victims and how they died. The summaries that I have seen so far seem to suggest that they were all killed during the riots, and I had no reason to question them. The families are distraught, of course, but they have been provided with the details of what happened."

"Except for Avneesh."

"Yes, except for Avneesh. I regret not asking more questions about him. How are things with his family?"

"They are devastated, of course. His widow has lodged an FIR with my police station to get more details, and she has formally made a request to the police and the hospital for the postmortem report. By all accounts, they are not a well-connected family, nor do they have the resources or time to follow up. There's also the matter of the press."

"What do you mean the press? Have the papers got a whiff of this?"

"Yes, sir. At least one paper. The family has contacted them, and I wouldn't be surprised if the story comes out. If we don't have the answers, then as you know, sir, the press will be left to speculate as to why the authorities are treating this with abject negligence."

"Oh, my God. That's the last thing we need. Alright, I will pay a visit to the family tomorrow. I want to speak to them privately. No press. I want you to accompany me, no other officers or agencies. Is that understood?"

"Yes, sir."

Lost in thought, Ghanshyam Das paced up and down the room for a couple of minutes. The phone on his desk started ringing but he let it ring. His secretary came in and wanted to tell him something, but he waved him away. Shankar could see that the minister was quickly trying to ascertain how to deal with the situation. The fact that one of his constituents had lodged an FIR, and that the press was involved was clearly weighing on him. Shankar knew Ghanshyam well enough to know that he also wanted to find out the truth for his own sake. He stopped walking and then turned to Shankar and took a few steps toward him and then broke the silence.

"From what you have told me so far, do you think there is someone involved on the inside in all of this?"

"It would seem that way."

"Right. We have to find out the truth. If there's a traitor in our midst, we must nail him right away."

"Yes, sir, I couldn't agree more. That's why I need your help with the investigation."

"Yes, yes, I understand. You don't have to worry about that. I will make sure you get all the help that you need. You do realize that if we are wrong about this, then both our heads are on the line and our bosses won't hesitate to leave us out to dry."

"Yes, sir. I understand, but I think I am right."

"I hope so, Shankar, for both our sakes. Let's keep things between us for the moment. If indeed there's someone involved on the inside, then I only want a small circle of people looking into it. Indian bureaucracies have more holes than the Titanic."

"Yes, sir, understood."

"I want you to come by my house in the evening after my visit to Old Delhi. I will have some other people there as well and I will make sure you get the help you need for this investigation."

"Thank you, sir."

"Will that be all?"

"Yes, sir," Shankar took the cue and got up to leave.

"I am glad you brought this to my attention, Shankar. We must do the right thing, of course, and for Avneesh's family as well. I will make sure they get what they need from the hospital."

"Thank you, sir," Shankar said as he turned to leave. Just as he was about to open the door, Ghanshyam called from behind.

"Oh, before you leave, Shankar."

"Yes, sir?"

"Which paper?"

"I am sorry, sir?"

"You said that the family had spoken to reporters from a newspaper?"

"Yes, sir."

"Which one?"

"*The New India Courier*. I wouldn't be surprised if other papers know of this as well."

"Hmm. Well, I am supposed to be at their office tomorrow. They are having me inaugurate a new wing at their office in Connaught Place."

"Right, sir."

"Well, thank you, Shankar."

"Yes, sir."

"Please don't forget, I do want to meet the Trivedi family to offer my condolences and let them know that we are going to get to the bottom of it. If indeed he was an innocent victim in all this, it's horrific the way things have unfolded for them."

"Right, sir. Thank you," Shankar said.

Shankar walked back through the hallowed halls and corridors of the North Block toward the exit. He was happy at how things had turned out. He knew from Ghanshyam's reputation that once he was onto something, he would see it through. This one had a direct bearing on his political future. It involved the mysterious death of a constituent, a possible cover-up by the police, a suspect within the ranks of his own department, and a potential scandal in the papers that could be damaging to his reputation. Ghanshyam had to get to the truth and get ahead of the story. His ambitions, reputation, and fallouts aside, part of him also wanted to do right by the family that had suffered an irreparable loss.

* * *

The New India Courier was abuzz for most of Friday preparing for the inauguration of their new wing. Decorations were being put up with large pictures of key publications over the years. There were posters and cardboard cutouts showing key achievements and the growth of the paper since it first started. The staff had been informed that the junior home minister would be the special guest. He would be cutting the ribbon of the new wing that would house many departments that were now on the ground floor, along with copy machines, a new cafeteria, a leisure room for the employees to relax, and a library. The staff was extremely happy with all the new additions. It reflected the paper's success and its financial sustainability.

Nitya spent most of the day in meetings going over what had been planned for the following day. Ghanshyam Das would cut the ribbon in the morning and then give a short speech. All employees were expected to be present. Manoj would then give him a brief tour of the office and the new wing. The minister would then have tea with the senior journalists and leave. In all, the visit was expected to last a little more than two hours. There was a cocktail and dinner at Delhi's Gymkhana Club that only the senior staff had been invited to. That had nothing to do with the minister's visit. It was more of a celebration and a way for Prakash and Manoj to show their gratitude to the senior staff.

Nitya found some time to talk to Manoj and apprise him of the progress on her assignments. Manoj seemed impressed and was happy to hear that the first drafts would be available for him to review the following week. He was curious about

Avneesh's death, but his mind was preoccupied with the preparations for the inauguration, and he left Nitya to deal with it as she deemed appropriate.

Nitya was glad to be back in her office and called her team one by one to find out where things were on their respective assignments. It was nearly 7:00 p.m. but Swati and Shiv were not back, and she was starting to get worried. They had left in the morning with Tilak, and she hadn't heard back from them since. She had asked the rest of her team to inform her as soon as they returned. Seven turned into eight and everyone started leaving. By eight-thirty, Nitya's entire team had left for the day but Shiv and Swati were still not back. She paced up and down her room and started checking the parking lot. Finally, around 9:00 p.m., when she was about to have a panic attack, Swati and Shiv walked into her office. They could see the concern and anger on her face. Before they could talk about their day, she scolded them for not letting her know that they would be late.

"Next time you are going to be this late, I expect you to find a public booth and let me know. Do you understand?"

"Yes, ma'am," they said in unison, and they knew better than to argue with her when they heard her stern tone.

"Alright, what happened today? What took you so long? Tell me."

"I will let Shiv explain, ma'am. It's a long, complicated story and he is better at explaining things," Swati said, turning to Shiv. Nitya knew Swati was right and was relieved that she had left it up to Shiv to explain the events of the day.

"Ma'am, our first stop was Avneesh's most recent employer, Royal Textiles. We showed them his photograph, but they told us that he had never worked there."

"You mean he was never an employee there?"

"That's right, ma'am."

"So, they have never seen him?"

"Not quite, ma'am. He had visited the store a few times and they had seen him in the area. Some of the store employees had also run into him at the roadside tea stall in the area. It seems he worked in the area and frequented the tea stall but was not an employee of Royal Textiles."

"Why would his wife think otherwise?"

"Yes, that is indeed a bit strange. So, we started visiting a few stores, offices, and establishments in the area. Although many had seen him, no one knew where he really worked. Finally, a street vendor who sells sweets and juices told us that he worked in a warehouse located in one of the lanes near Deer Park."

"A warehouse? For what?"

"We went to the establishment. It's a makeshift warehouse, completely run-down, more like a large shed, almost hidden behind some stores and not visible from the main street. It was completely empty. We asked an auto shop owner about the warehouse, and he told us that he had serviced a number of trucks a few weeks ago and that most had been in and out of the warehouse. Although he wasn't entirely sure what the trucks contained, he was told by some of the lorry drivers that it was some kind of tools and machinery."

"Hmm, this warehouse was just that? A storage facility of some sort?"

"It seems they were assembling things and putting them in crates and boxes, and then sealing them, and shipping them out."

"The lorry drivers knew what the crates contained?"

"No, they weren't told either. They were given the paperwork to take the trucks to different cities in the north and were assured that everything was in order."

"The trucking company never bothered to find out the contents?"

"This is the thing, ma'am. I tried to find out which trucking company they were using so that we could visit them. It seems there wasn't any one specific transport company being used by the warehouse. They were using different companies, mostly freelance, owner-driven trucks."

"That is strange indeed. I'd have thought that if there were so many shipments, then they would have gone with one or two companies."

"Yes, but we haven't even come to the interesting part yet."

"What is it?"

"When we showed people Avneesh's picture, many said that they had seen him around, especially at the tea shop. We couldn't find anyone who worked in the warehouse. Apparently, it had been really busy for a few weeks and then was abruptly closed. Everyone left suddenly. What's strange was that this warehouse was well-guarded and on the night of the riots several trucks left the establishment. By early morning everything was empty and there was no trace of anything having been there at all."

"So, they decided to move everything overnight, the same night as the riot in Old Delhi?"

"Yes, ma'am."

"Hmm, how is this related to Avneesh?"

"We finally found two people in a shop nearby that Avneesh frequented for cigarettes and snacks. They recognized his picture right away, but told us that his name was Rajeev Lekhi, not Avneesh Trivedi."

"That's weird. Did you check with others in the area?"

"Yes, we went back and forth a few times and it seemed more people recognized him as Rajeev Lekhi than Avneesh Trivedi."

"So, he was using another name?"

"That's right, ma'am. We also came to know that he frequently visited the tea shops and other establishments with men who looked like they were from the government or the police, but they are not sure."

"What about the warehouse? Did you go and check it out?"

"Yes, ma'am, we did. It's an abandoned shed with lots of rusted tools, industrial parts, and remnants of oil from the trucks that had been there a few days ago. There were also some broken crates with pieces of wood everywhere but there were no labels to suggest what may have been in them."

"And anything that would tell you who owns it?"

"There is an old notice board that states that it is a disputed property and there was a phone number. We called the number. It belongs to a company in Baroda. It's a family-run company and the land is currently in dispute between the brothers who own the company and is being litigated. The case is in the courts and has been going on for years. They informed us that they haven't used this property in years and neither has it been rented out to anyone."

"Wow, this gets even murkier," Nitya said thoughtfully, trying to absorb everything that Shiv was telling her.

"After finding out all of this we were ready to leave, till Swati said something that struck me."

Nitya looked at Swati who was listening to everything carefully. She seemed happy to hear Shiv give her credit.

"What was that?"

"She reminded me that Avneesh had worked in another firm on the other side of Deer Park. We thought it would be worth checking out if they knew anything about all this. We had already heard that he hadn't kept in touch with them, but it was worth a shot."

"So, you went back to his previous employer?"

"Yes."

"And?"

"Firstly, they all identified him as Avneesh and not Rajeev. So, we got that out of the way. Secondly, and more importantly, they told us that they had forgotten to mention that Avneesh had a school friend working in a company not far from Deer Park and that we should go check with him. While he was working for his previous employer, he had mentioned this friend quite a few times and even brought him over during lunch outings and picnics."

"I am guessing this is what took you so long."

"Yes, we went over to this friend's place. His name is Baljit Sandhu. Baljit went to school with Avneesh and knows the family well. He is an architect who works in an office not far from Deer Park. He wasn't there when we went to see him, but we were told that he would be back in an hour. We decided to wait but Baljit returned two hours later. We introduced ourselves and informed him of Avneesh's death. He was visibly distraught and shaken up. We spoke a lot about his family, childhood, and college days; however, it is what he told us about Avneesh's new job that piqued our interest."

"What was that?"

"Avneesh had indeed left his previous job and had found a new job with much better pay and prospects. His family's financial situation was not that great, and with a kid, he wanted to get a better-paying job. Although he was coy about sharing where he was joining, Baljit guessed that it was one of the security agencies."

"What made him guess that?"

"It's because Avneesh had told him earlier that a government security agency had set up a recruitment office in Old

Delhi and was hiring personnel to fill their ranks as entry-level agents."

"Did he mention which agency or arm of the government?"

"No, but he did say that Avneesh had told him that he was working on something that was of national importance."

"National importance? What could that be?"

"Avneesh didn't divulge any more details to Baljit. All he knew was that Avneesh was proud of what he was doing and expecting some sort of promotion or reward that would make his family proud of him too."

"It's odd that he didn't tell Baljit or his family what he was working on."

"Yes, ma'am. Then a week and a half ago, everything changed."

"What do you mean, changed?"

"Avneesh suddenly told Baljit that he was leaving for Dehradun. The last time they met Avneesh seemed extremely unhappy, sad, and angry. He kept saying that he had been duped and betrayed. He told Baljit that he would tell him everything once he returned from his trip. He told Baljit that he regretted taking up the new job and also said that he would be uncovering a big conspiracy. He kept saying that unless he made things right, he would never forgive himself. Baljit was very worried about him but seeing him in that state decided not to press things further till he returned from his trip."

"Hmm. Of course, now Avneesh is dead so we don't know what he would have told Baljit."

"That's right, ma'am. Baljit regrets not finding out what was worrying him."

"Where did he travel to in Dehradun? Do we know?"

"Well, we do have the other numbers in Avneesh's notebook. We dialed them one by one. All but one led to public phone booths. The one that didn't, belongs to a tool factory in Dehradun. They had never heard of Avneesh. When we asked them about Rajeev Lekhi, they quickly hung up. We tried to reach them again, but they refused to speak to us."

"Interesting," Nitya said, trying to get a grasp of everything.

"I think ma'am, given what we know, we can piece together a few things. There are still a number of unanswered questions, but some things are definitely clear."

"Tell me what you are thinking, Shiv," Nitya asked thoughtfully.

"Let's recap what we know so far starting with Avneesh's notebook, the numbers in it, the flier that had an ad for a recruitment drive, his family, the people in Haus Khaz, and of course his friend, Baljit. I think Avneesh was recruited by a company or agency involved in some unlawful activity. My feeling is that Avneesh joined the organization thinking that it was a legitimate government agency. He was secretive because he bought into the idea that the project he was working on was something that was of national importance and could not be made public just yet. At the same time, he got duped into believing that once it was completed, he would be getting a promotion or reward. However, something didn't seem right to him. He probably found out the truth and when that happened, he felt betrayed. He went to Dehradun to confirm his suspicions and would have probably revealed the truth upon his return. Meanwhile, his employers also found out that Avneesh had uncovered the truth about their activities, and once that happened, it was over for him."

"That part makes sense. I guess that's why he kept telling Baljit that he was duped and betrayed," Nitya said, nodding in agreement.

"Yes."

"That still doesn't explain why his body was whisked away in the middle of the night and why he was cremated in such a hurry."

"I do have a theory on that, ma'am."

"Let's hear it."

"Avneesh told Baljit that he was going to Dehradun. He probably went there to get some evidence of the conspiracy. Maybe he was carrying some paperwork as proof. Perhaps the people he was working for found out and couldn't risk leaving him at the hospital with that evidence. They needed to take his body away and get rid of the evidence."

"Yes, that is possible, but then why not just take the evidence and dump his body somewhere?"

"Because that would raise a lot of questions and would lead to an official investigation. On the other hand, if it was something that happened during the riots and he was cremated in the presence of his family, things would look normal."

"Right. That is possible of course."

"One more thing, ma'am."

"What's that?"

"I am convinced that all this would not have been possible without some help from within the police department or the security agencies."

"Yes, I agree. There definitely is someone or some people among the officials who are part of this," Nitya said.

"Right, ma'am," Shiv said, and paused. For a moment there was silence in the room while they all tried to grasp and replay everything that had been discussed. Finally, Nitya broke the silence as she turned and looked toward Swati who had been uncharacteristically quiet during the entire conversation.

"Do you have anything else to add, Swati?"

"No, ma'am. I think Shiv explained it quite well."

"Anything else, Shiv?"

"Yes, I think we should make a trip to Dehradun to visit this factory. It might give us an idea of what was there in the warehouse. We may get some answers there."

"Yes, I was thinking about that. Let's sleep on it. We will talk again tomorrow. You do know that you have to be in the office for the minister's visit and the inauguration of the new wing."

"Yes, ma'am," said Swati.

"Do we really have to be here, ma'am? Seems like a waste of time. I'd much rather go back to Haus Khaz and see if we can find anything else," said Shiv in a softer tone.

"No, you need to be here. It's not open for discussion. Once the events are over, we can discuss what to do next. Is that understood?"

"Yes, ma'am," Swati said quickly and turned to look at Shiv who still hadn't responded.

"Shiv?" Nitya asked in a slightly raised voice.

"Understood, I will be here," Shiv replied.

"Thank you," Nitya said, smiling. "I have asked for company cars to drop you home. It's late. Get a good night's sleep. Great work both of you. I know I scolded you when you came in, but I am really impressed with what you have done so far."

"Thank you, ma'am," they both said almost in unison. Nitya could see the tired look on their faces, and she suddenly felt bad that she had admonished them for being late. She asked them to wait while she quickly packed up and they all walked out of the office together into the crisp winter night to head home.

* * *

Shankar was at Ghanshyam Das's residence in New Delhi quietly waiting to be called into his study. From the big drawing room, he could see the gardens outside through the large open doors. The sprawling bungalow was one of many in the upscale neighborhood. The area had houses of many prominent ministers. Although Ghanshyam was a junior minister, he was in the home ministry, a department that was considered one of the most important in the cabinet. Shankar had accompanied him earlier that evening to the Trivedi residence where they had met Avneesh's parents and widow. Prior to that, during the minister's visit and tour of Old

Delhi, Shankar had made sure that he took him to the Old Delhi Railway Station to speak to the officers and constables there, and also to the scene of the crime where Avneesh's body had been found. The minister had returned to his residence in the evening and had asked Shankar to come by at around 10:00 p.m. for a meeting. It wasn't unusual for ministers to call meetings late at night, especially when it was for matters related to crime.

Shankar didn't know who would be at the meeting, but he knew the minister well enough to know that he would be rounding up key people from various departments investigating Avneesh's death. He wasn't wrong. When Ghanshyam's secretary ushered Shankar into the minister's study, the police commissioner, the home secretary, and a senior official from the CBI were already present. They introduced themselves, and after exchanging a few pleasantries got down to business. The minister had already apprised them of his conversations with Shankar. From the stoic expression on the faces of the other senior officers in the room, Shankar was unable to gauge whether they were pleased or annoyed with his meddling in their investigation. However, it was the minister who had called the meeting, so they had to lend him an ear, at least for now. They sat around a big table with the minister leading most of the conversation.

"Shankar, I have already told everyone about our conversation earlier today. I am sure everyone here wants to get to the bottom of this," Ghanshyam said, as he looked around the table. "Is there anything you would like to ask Shankar?"

"Yes," said the CBI official, "as you know, Shankar, we are leading this investigation with help from the police and the home ministry, of course. We have followed up on Avneesh's death as well and at this point the investigation is ongoing."

"Understood, sir," Shankar said, and just as he was about to continue, he was interrupted by the minister.

"Well, I am the one who called this meeting. What triggered it was not Shankar's discussion with me this morning. Rather, it was my visit to the family of the victim, who as you all know is from my constituency in Old Delhi. I understand that they have already lodged an FIR that prompted Shankar to start looking into this. I was alarmed by what the family said about what happened to Avneesh. They still haven't received any details from the police or the hospital. As you can imagine, I was shocked to hear this. I also came to know that they have spoken about their concerns to the press. Can you imagine if we see headlines in the paper on how this family has been treated? I want Shankar to be part of the investigation. The death happened in his jurisdiction and the victim's family is also from the same area," the minister said.

"Absolutely sir," replied the CBI officer in a much softer and agreeable tone.

It was then the police commissioner's turn to speak. "Shankar, during your investigation, did you have any reason to believe that Avneesh was involved with a gang or in any nefarious activities?"

"That is certainly possible, sir, and I still need time to ascertain his whereabouts. At this point, as I am sure the minister may have told you already, my theory is that he was killed in Dehradun, brought back to Delhi, and then his body dumped near the station."

"Yes, we heard that," said the commissioner, "and then his body was taken away from the hospital in the middle of the night for cremation."

"Yes, sir. The motive is unclear. What is clear, though, is that the people who took him away impersonated either the police or a government agency. They were in a hurry to perform his last rites and destroy any evidence in his possession."

"So, we heard," said the commissioner.

It was now the CBI official's turn to speak.

"I think we need to first find out who is involved in all of this. I agree with Shankar that someone on the inside is involved. Obviously, it's a gang and we need to nab at least one of the members."

"We know at least one of them, sir," Shankar said, and immediately the others turned to look at him.

The minister seemed surprised. "Shankar?"

"The night Avneesh's body was taken away from the hospital, there was a police presence there, but they were called away to Old Delhi. The call was made from the control room via the police radio. Whoever made the call to divert them is certainly worth looking into," Shankar said and paused.

"How do you know that it wasn't a genuine call?"

"During the course of my investigation at the railway station, I spoke to the officers and constables there. One of them directed me to the members of the team that had arrived from the hospital. I spoke to one of the members of the team to know what was said over the radio. He told me that the instruction was for them to head from the hospital to the railway station because of a sudden disturbance in the area. There was no such incident at that time in the area. The force at the station had not requested any further help. I was near the station at that time and most of the rioting had subsided well before that. Whoever placed that call created the diversion so that Avneesh's body could be removed from the hospital. We have the transcripts of all the communications from that night. We know approximately the time he was taken away and should be able to trace who sent that message."

There was a long pause. Shankar could make out that any misgivings anyone might have had about him meddling in the investigation had now disappeared. He also knew that if indeed people from their departments were involved, it would lead to an embarrassing scandal. Time was of the essence, and he could sense that they wanted to find out the truth as soon as possible. Finally, the commissioner turned to the minister.

"Sir, I will take the lead in getting to the bottom of this. We have the transcripts and the recordings from that night. There were several people in the control room. Things were chaotic, but I am sure there are plenty of people who can recall when this message to the hospital was relayed. Pardon my expression, sir, but if there is a traitor in our uniform, we must nail him right away."

"Yes," the minister agreed and then continued with a raised voice, "we must nail the bastard and throw the book at him."

"I wouldn't advise that, sir. At least, not right away," Shankar said softly, and immediately everyone turned their gaze toward him.

"Why the hell not?" the CBI officer asked angrily.

"I think the prudent thing to do would be to identify the person and place him under surveillance. I believe there are multiple people involved here. He may have been given an order by one of his superiors to relay that message. It is possible that he may not be the only one involved in the department. It is clear from what happened that night that there is a dangerous gang involved. As I am sure the minister may have told you, I believe the riots themselves were a diversion to ensure that a convoy of trucks carrying some unknown cargo could leave Delhi that night without being inspected. Forces from all areas in the city, including the checkpoints that usually check and inspect cargo, were sent to Old Delhi to deal with the riots. I feel that at this point we should follow this person, and when the time comes, nab as many of the gang members as possible."

"What was in the cargo you think, Shankar? Drugs? Illegal arms?" the minister asked.

"It's hard to say, sir, but if we keep an eye on him rather than nabbing him right away, we may be able to find out a lot more," Shankar replied.

"We can always arrest him and interrogate him," said the CBI official.

"Yes, sir, we could, but chances are he won't divulge much in fear that the gang might harm his family."

"True," the commissioner agreed.

This was followed by another long pause during which Shankar could see that everyone was trying to absorb what he had said and the implications for their own respective departments. He was aware that these men were territorial and getting them to cooperate was going to be a challenge. Ghanshyam was probably thinking along the same lines. His suspicions were confirmed when the minister finally spoke.

"Gentlemen, given where we are now, I suggest that we share everything that we have on the investigations with Shankar. I want him actively involved in this, and please give him all the support that he needs."

"We can keep you apprised of the progress, sir," the CBI officer said.

"Sure, that will be fine, but I want to hear from Shankar, too, on the ongoing investigation," said the minister, turning to Shankar. "Please keep me updated on the progress. My secretary will give you my direct line. I want a progress report at the end of the day, every day."

"Yes, sir," Shankar replied.

"I think that will be all gentlemen," the minister said, getting up. Immediately, the rest of the group were on their feet too. Before leaving the room, the minister turned and looked at all of them and said, "needless to say, this stays in this room and we involve only a handful of people as required for the surveillance and investigation. Is that understood?"

"Yes, sir," they all replied. Shankar saw the CBI officer and the home secretary departing quickly. Before leaving they turned and shook hands with Shankar and the commissioner. They now seemed more receptive to him being a part of the investigation. The minister hadn't left them with much of a choice.

The commissioner and Shankar slowly walked together toward the gates where their cars were parked. Shankar could see that the commissioner was quiet and seemed immersed in thought. The expression on the commissioner's face was one of concern.

"You know, Shankar, I am so angry that one of ours is involved in all of this. These bad apples bring shame to the entire force. I agree with the minister on one thing—when we nab him, I hope he gets locked up for a long time, forever, if you ask me. Absolutely disgusting."

"Yes, sir."

"I must say, Shankar, you have done a marvelous job with the investigation so far."

"Thank you, sir."

Before getting into his car, he turned to Shankar. "So, the family spoke to the minister and made the request themselves?"

"Yes, sir."

"And they spoke to the press too?"

"That's what it seems like, sir."

"My God. What's the world coming to? Soon people will be calling radio stations to tell them about their personal problems. We are living in a strange world."

"Right, sir."

As the commissioner's car left, Shankar turned to walk toward where Motiram had parked his jeep. For the first time, in many days, he had a smile on his face.

Spectacle

Weekends at *The New India Courier* were usually quiet. The senior management typically allowed their staff to come in late and leave early. Everyone was usually relaxed and laid back, but not this Saturday. The minister was expected at any moment. The entire staff was present, and many of them were in the large conference room near the new wing that was going to be inaugurated. The parking lot was mostly empty. The cars that were normally parked there were now scattered across all the streets in and around the building to make way for the minister and his entourage. There was of course the matter of security. Though there was no perceived threat to Ghanshyam Das, he traveled with his fair share of security personnel. It was not only a matter of security, but also a status symbol. A larger entourage gave the impression that a minister wielded power and authority. Ghanshyam, for his part, could have done without all of this, but he had been reminded by other senior ministers in the cabinet that perceptions mattered. Each event was an opportunity to project an image of power and significance. The junior minister was still on the learning curve and had decided to pay heed to his boss's advice.

When his entourage arrived at the paper's office, Ghanshyam took his time getting out of his car. He was greeted by Prakash and Manoj. There were the customary garlands and bouquets. In the reception area, many people from the senior staff greeted him. Manoj and Prakash then took him to their office for an elaborate array of snacks and tea. This was followed by a tour of the existing offices, and then they proceeded to the new wing. There was a ribbon across the main entrance to the new offices. Several photographers had been lined up. Ghanshyam Das took his time posing for them and then cut the ribbon. After a few handshakes, he was ushered into the conference room and onto the dais. He was greeted with a round of applause. His speech was short and articulate. It was evident that he had read up on the history of the paper. He thanked the owners and the management team for giving him an opportunity to come and meet them. The politician in him made some subtle remarks about how the government and his party always stood for the freedom of the press. He narrated a personal story of how the press had treated him kindly when he first entered politics and was not a well-known figure. He finished his speech by saying how the fourth estate and the freedom that is accorded to them is critical in a democracy like India. After he thanked the audience, there was another round of applause, and then he was led to a smaller but more elegant conference room to have another round of tea with the senior staff.

During his interactions, Ghanshyam casually inquired about the riots, its aftermath, and the victims. He was careful not to specifically broach the subject of Avneesh's death. Nitya was in the group of journalists when he brought it up. She couldn't make out whether it was a deliberate ploy by the minister to find out how the paper was covering the story and understand what they knew. She kept quiet. She knew that Ghanshyam might be a different kind of politician, but he was still a politician and had a reputation of being a wily one. Once most of the other journalists had moved on, Manoj took the minister aside and spoke to him about the riots. He felt he owed the minister some sort of an answer and used the opportunity to brag that the paper was promoting women to senior roles. While talking to Ghanshyam, Manoj called Nitya over.

"Sir, this is Nitya Chaturvedi. She is the newest addition to our senior team."

"Hello, Nitya."

"Hello, sir."

"Nitya is the one leading our stories on the victims of the riots," Manoj said.

"Oh. That's good to know. Terrible business, the riots. It's really sad any time people are killed," the minister said.

He was about to continue when his secretary quickly came up to him and whispered something in his ear. He was late for his next appointment. He excused himself and asked Manoj and Nitya to walk with him back to his car. He was careful not to bring up any specific news item. Nitya was impressed with how deftly the minister was posing his questions. Being the junior home minister, she was sure that he knew what had happened during the riots and the ongoing investigation. Yet, it seemed to Nitya that Ghanshyam wanted to find out how much the paper knew. Once they reached the ground floor, the minister turned around and waved at everyone, and then he started walking toward his car with his secretary and security in front of him and Manoj and Nitya on either side. When they reached the parked car, they could see Shiv, Moina, and Swati drinking tea a few yards away. He greeted them from afar. Manoj quickly waved at them to come over. They left their teacups and immediately went over to shake hands with the minister. Manoj introduced them as journalists on Nitya's team. All of them thanked the minister for visiting, and he chatted with them for a few minutes. They could see that the minister's secretary was getting visibly impatient with this unscheduled delay.

"It's good to see young journalists working on important stories," said the minister.

"Yes, sir," they all said almost in unison.

"Manoj tells me that you are part of Ms. Chaturvedi's team and are covering the stories on the victims."

"Yes, sir," Moina replied. Swati and Shiv nodded in agreement.

"Well, I hope you understand how sensitive riots are in our country and how things written in the newspapers have a direct impact on the public mood and opinion."

"Right sir," Moina replied again on their behalf.

"Plus of course, you have a responsibility to the victims," the minister continued.

"We certainly do, sir," Manoj said, as the driver opened one of the back doors for the minister to get in.

"Then there is the obligation of looking at the national interest and security as well," the minister said to all of them before getting into the car.

"Well, it's a good thing, sir, that we still live in a country where politicians don't get to say what should be written in the papers," Shiv said softly. Everyone turned toward him in shock.

For a moment, there seemed to be a tinge of anger in the minister's expression but that quickly gave way to a big smile.

Manoj glared at Shiv angrily, almost as if he could reach across and tear him apart. Even if the minister had been offended by the comment, he was smart enough to hide it well. His smile pacified Manoj momentarily. Once again, they all thanked the minister, and he got into his car. When he drove away, Manoj turned to Shiv.

"What the hell was that Shiv?" Manoj shouted while everyone else was quiet. They knew that Shiv's comment was not going to go unnoticed.

"Sir, it's clear to me that he suspects that we may write something that may be damaging to his ministry or the government."

"He was our guest. This was not the time to offend him. Good thing he didn't get angry."

"Why should he? I didn't say anything to offend him, sir. I just made a comment with regards to the freedom of the press. He was touting that upstairs during his speech. Why should he be offended now?" asked Shiv in a firm but polite tone.

"I don't get you, Shiv," Manoj said, continuing, "you have a knack of saying the wrong thing at the wrong time." A few people had now gathered in the parking lot and were observing the exchange. It was apparent from Manoj's volume that he was not happy with Shiv. Nitya decided to step in.

"I think we should head upstairs, sir," Nitya said.

"Yes, can you please meet me in my office," Manoj said, turning to Nitya.

"Yes, sir."

They all slowly started heading back to their respective floors. Nitya followed Manoj into his office. There were a few people waiting for him. He asked them to wait outside for a few minutes, and once they were inside, Manoj told Nitya, "Shiv's comment was uncalled for."

"Yes, sir. It could have been worded better. Although I don't think he said or did anything wrong."

"You really believe that?"

"Yes. I mean it was quite apparent that the minister was fishing for information. He knows where the police and CBI are at in terms of the investigation, and he wanted to know what we know. The moment you told him that my team was looking into the victims, he was suddenly interested in them and didn't talk about anything else. Don't you think that's strange, sir?"

"Yes, it is. I shouldn't have mentioned it."

"No harm done. Now we know that they are worried about what the press might publish. That tells me they may have something to hide."

"Yes, true. That's possible. Anyway, I want to talk to you about Shiv."

"What about him, sir?"

"You saw what happened downstairs. This fellow seems to talk his mouth off. Absolutely no respect. He just doesn't know what to say and when. You'd think he would be smart enough to keep quiet. How is he doing his job by the way?"

"He is doing it well, sir."

"Hmm."

"Sir, I don't know what has happened in the past with others, but he has been part of my team for a few days, and I can tell you, he is good. Yes, he may not always say the right thing, but he is intelligent."

"Alright. Well, I may not agree with you there, but it's good to see that you are defending your team. That makes you a good leader. Right, then, we are meeting you this evening at the Gymkhana Club. I hope you haven't forgotten."

"No, sir. I will be there. Thank you."

Once Nitya left the room, her colleagues who were waiting outside started to make their way into Manoj's room. Swati, Moina, and Suresh were waiting for her in her office. She had called them to discuss the first drafts of their articles. She spent the next hour going over their drafts and offering her comments. When she finished, and they were about to leave, she said to all of them, "when you get downstairs, can you please send Shiv to my office?"

They looked at each other and then at Nitya. After a brief pause, Suresh said, "I know what happened, ma'am. It wasn't Shiv's fault."

Before Nitya could say anything, Swati jumped in. "It really wasn't, ma'am."

Nitya turned to Moina. "Do you have anything to add, Moina?"

"I agree with them, ma'am. I mean he could have just said nothing but, what he said was right, and he didn't really say anything personal for the minister to get offended."

Nitya looked at all of them. She recalled the time when Suresh and Swati had misgivings about Shiv joining the team. Now, they were defending him. She spoke in a calm and reassuring voice.

"Shiv's not in trouble. At least, not with me. If you must know, I need him in my office to talk about his article. That's all."

"We will send him right up," Moina said happily, as they all turned and left the room.

When Shiv reached Nitya's office, she was on the phone with Kavita. He waited outside although Nitya gestured him to sit. Nitya took down the details of Kavita's arrival and promised to pick her up at the station. The conversation with Kavita left her feeling worried. It wasn't one of their usual lighthearted chats that she was used to. Things seemed serious, and although she didn't say anything over the phone, Nitya could make out that Kavita was sad. As soon as Nitya hung up, Shiv came into the room. He had his notepad with him and a large, folded paper that looked like a map of some sort.

"Ma'am, I am sorry about what happened earlier with the minister."

"That's alright. He is a politician. He should have a thick skin, don't you think?"

"Yes, still, I think Manoj wasn't happy with the way I behaved, and it may have got you into some trouble too, since you are my boss."

"Never mind that. I want to talk to you about your story. We need to have something fairly quickly."

"Yes, ma'am. I wanted to talk to you about one other thing related to the case."

"What?"

"I had a chance to talk to the rest of the team on their assignments. They have already done a fair amount of research on the victims assigned to them. They have conducted interviews with relatives and friends and have started writing their first drafts. "

"Yes, I know. I have read some of them. What about it?"

"The victims are all from Old Delhi."

"That's not surprising. The riots happened there. They were probably caught in the crossfire. Most of their deaths were either from stabbing or gunshots. I have read the details. They worked in different places and were found in different parts of the walled city."

"Right, ma'am," Shiv said, and he carefully unfolded the map that he had been carrying on Nitya's large desk. It was a map of Old Delhi that had been marked with some red and blue circles and one black circle.

"What am I looking at?" Nitya asked pointing to the circles.

"The black circle is the rented office of the fake government agency that was on a recruitment drive in the area. The blue circles are the addresses of all the victims of the riots. The red circles are the locations where, according to the police, the victims were found."

Nitya carefully looked at all the color-coded markings. It was evident that all the blue markings were within three or four streets of the black circle. The red markings were all over the map, stretching from one end of Old Delhi to the other in all directions.

"Alright, this tells me that most of the victims lived close to where this fake recruitment office was. That may be odd but not necessarily too strange given that Old Delhi is such a congested area. I mean, I've heard from everyone that you could be living a street or two apart for decades in this area and still be complete strangers."

"That's true, ma'am. I live there and I see new faces every day even though they may be living a street or block away."

"And the red circles show that they were probably killed in different areas or at least were found there."

"Yes, ma'am, but there's one other thing," Shiv said as he carefully folded the map and started leafing through his notebook.

"What's that Shiv?"

"In the past riots or, for that matter, in any riot, the victims were from different backgrounds, ethnicities, age groups, and genders."

"True."

"Let's look at all the victims here. They are all men between twenty-five and thirty years of age living within three or four streets of each other. They are all from different backgrounds and have very little in common except for their age and where they lived."

Nitya leaned back on her chair. She could see that Shiv was giving her the time to absorb all this and form her own opinion. There was something strange about this and Shiv was right. The odds of all the victims being from the same area and in the same age group were rather low. She had seen the reports but had not made the connection until Shiv showed her the map. She turned and looked directly at Shiv.

"What's on your mind? You obviously have a theory on this."

"Yes, ma'am."

"What is it?"

"It's just a theory at this point. I need to go back to Old Delhi and check some of this out with the families of the other victims. I think there is a connection between the victims and this fake recruitment office."

"Yes, but the other victims were working in different places. The rest of the team must have told you that. They interviewed their families and colleagues from work too. Unlike Avneesh no one had left their jobs to move to a new one in the recent past."

"That's right, ma'am. My theory is that all the others may have gone for an interview at this office. They didn't leave their jobs, nor did they get duped into joining this gang, unlike Avneesh. Some of them may have found out that it was a fake advertisement and may have gone to the police."

"We are not sure if they did."

"We didn't ask. What I want to do is go to the families of these victims, show them the flier that Madhavi found in

Avneesh's diary, and ask them if they know anything about it. Perhaps some of the victims may have told their families that they had been there for an interview."

"Yes, it's worth a shot, I guess, but you know these families are grieving. They have already told us a lot. Going back to them repeatedly might seem like pestering."

"Maybe I can start with their friends. I don't need to go to all of them, just two or three to see if there's a connection."

"Hmm, alright. You can pursue this, but I want you to take Swati with you, and please be sensitive to the victims' families."

"I will, ma'am."

"Right," Nitya said with a degree of finality, expecting Shiv to take the hint and leave. But there was something else on his mind.

"There are two other things, ma'am."

"What is it?"

"Is it possible to check with Mr. Sen about this office and whether there were any complaints by the residents?"

"Yes, I was thinking about that. I can ask him about it. I will let you know."

"What else?"

"From what we know so far, at least from Avneesh's friend, Baljit, is that Avneesh went to Dehradun to find out something that he was going to reveal. It's possible that he did uncover something and was killed before he could share it."

"Yes, you might be right."

"If the answer lies in Dehradun, then we must go there. We already know the number of this industrial plant or factory. We can get the address and check it out."

"Yes. Let's get moving on what you want to do in Old Delhi, and then we can talk about Dehradun on Monday."

"Sure."

"Off you go then, and remember what I said—be nice and show some sensitivity while talking to the families or friends of the victims. You are quite capable of it. I know it and I have seen it," Nitya said with a smile.

"I will, ma'am. Thank you," Shiv said. Then he gathered his folded map and notebook and left the room.

* * *

In Old Delhi, Shankar was looking at a huge stack of papers on his desk. They were copies of the files from the various investigating agencies and the home ministry. The minister's intervention had helped, and the various departments had sent him all the materials, but it also meant that he had to sift through a big pile of files of various shapes and sizes.

Thankfully, they were in order and seemed organized. He had been looking at them for nearly three hours now. The investigation, for the most part, had proceeded quickly. A big map that he had pinned on the wall showed the addresses of all the victims and where they were found. It was quite evident that all the victims lived within a few blocks of each other. There was no indication in the files whether they knew one another. The files on almost all the victims were fairly complete. The one exception was Avneesh Trivedi. Officers from the Chandni Chowk Police Station and the CBI had interviewed the family and had inquired about Avneesh's employers, colleagues, friends, and any other contacts for a clue on why he was killed. Shankar wondered why he wasn't asked to investigate Avneesh's death. After all, he lived in an area that was under his jurisdiction in Kotwali and not Chandni Chowk. He took meticulous notes in his notepad of all the key findings, the investigating officers, and their contact numbers.

Then he turned his attention to the files from the home ministry that contained the transcripts of all the radio messages that were sent and received through the police channel. He looked through them carefully. Then he finally found the name of the person who had relayed the instructions to the hospital before Avneesh's body was whisked away—Mukesh Sanghvi. Shankar couldn't recall whether he had ever seen or spoken to Mukesh before. The CBI had already placed him under round-the-clock surveillance. Shankar was confident that the CBI would do their job efficiently, and if indeed Mukesh was the rogue officer and was in any way involved or connected to those who had instigated the riots, he would certainly be apprehended.

After another hour or so, he finished reading through most of the files. He couldn't help but think that something was missing. The victims didn't seem to be connected in any way. However, the fact that they were all from the same area and belonged to the same age group made him suspect that there was a missing piece. He couldn't find it in Avneesh's file. The one common link among the victims was that most had been looking for a better job. A few family members and friends knew that they had gone for some interviews, but there were no details. That was not surprising. Most victims came from lower middle-class families and were constantly looking for better opportunities. What was surprising, though, were the handwritten notes in some of the files suggesting that the victims had gone for interviews for some government jobs at a recruitment office in the area. Shankar had been stationed in Old Delhi long enough to know that there were only a handful of government buildings in the area, and he hadn't heard of any recruitment drives. The investigating officers hadn't followed up on this piece of the puzzle. There was nothing to go on—the families hadn't provided any details, nor was there anything to suggest that it had led to the untimely deaths of the victims.

Shankar took out a telephone directory from one of the drawers in his desk. He started calling all the government offices in Old Delhi one by one to see if any of them had posted any notices for recruitment drives in the area. None of them had. After finishing all the calls, he leaned back in his chair, folded his hands, and tried to think of the missing piece of the puzzle. Suddenly, his gaze fell upon a colored flier that was lodged precariously between a thick set of papers in one of the files. Shankar had disregarded it as a flier for some advertisement, but this one was different. It was an ad for a job in an unnamed government agency. He looked at it carefully and immediately spotted a few things that made him suspicious. Although it had the emblem of the Government of India, it was short on details. He decided to call the three numbers on the flier and two were unreachable. The one number that was reachable was from a small public phone booth, one of the many hundreds that were cropping up in the city, in offices and shops, and even in little lanes and corner stores. Most Indians didn't have a phone at home and even the ones that did had to wait for months to get a connection. These phone booths were a godsend to those who worked in the city with families in other parts of India. Shankar spoke briefly with the owner of the shop which housed the booth and could sense that there were many people waiting in line to make calls. He noted the address. The investigating officers had also tried to follow up on it. But when they had found that the number was of a public phone in a shop, they had simply put a question mark next to the ad and disregarded it.

Shankar went over the details in the file where he found the flier. From the notes in the interviews conducted by the investigating officers, it seemed that the victim had gone for an interview at the address mentioned on the flier but then never heard back from them. The officers had paid a visit to the address, but that had led nowhere. The owner had leased out the location to some tenants who had paid him in cash for a few weeks of rent. One day, the tenants had mysteriously disappeared. The owner hadn't thought much of it. They had given him his asking price without bargaining and there were no arrears. It wasn't uncommon in this part of town to rent out small offices or shops for cash payments.

It was almost late afternoon and Shankar decided to pay the owner a visit to see if he could provide more details. From the files, he found that the owner worked in another shop in Connaught Place during the weekend. Shankar decided to head there but make a few stops along the way.

One was to the telephone exchange to get details of the two fake phone numbers and see who they were registered against, if at all anyone. The second was to the family of the victim in whose file he had found the flier. Finally, he wanted to check in with the shop owner he had just spoken to. The shop was also in Connaught Place. Shankar got up, stretched his legs, and headed toward the door to call out for Motiram. When he reached the door, the phone started ringing. He wondered whether to ignore it or pick it up. He knew it could be Rohini, and he also knew he wouldn't be able to keep his promise of being back home early that evening. His relationship with Rohini had been getting worse. She was either constantly worried about Shankar being tied up at work or thinking of how her life would have been if she had stayed back with her parents where she grew up. The arguments and quarrels had become more frequent, and for Shankar, the long hours at work seemed blissful. He gently picked up the receiver. It wasn't Rohini on the other end. It was Nitya.

"Hello, Shankar. How are you?"

"Fine, Nitya. This is a bit of a surprise."

"Yes, well it's not entirely a social call."

"Oh, that sounds ominous. What did I do now for the press to report me?"

"Oh no, nothing about you," Nitya said defensively without getting the joke. "If you are in a hurry, we can chat later."

"What's this about?"

"It's about the story on the victims of the riots. We are planning on running something next week, but we still have some missing pieces."

"You know I cannot talk to the press about an ongoing police investigation."

"I understand that. The questions are mostly about what we have already uncovered. Obviously, I am not asking you to verify whether it's accurate, but I do want to run something by you, purely off the record. It is important."

There was a pause on the other end of the line. Nitya could sense that Shankar was thinking about the request, and she was well aware of his misgivings about the press. After a few seconds, Shankar offered a guarded response.

"Nitya, I really shouldn't be talking to anyone in the press till the investigations are completed. We can speak off the record. If you are fine with that, we can meet. I prefer doing this in person rather than on the phone."

"I agree. I can come by the police station …" Nitya replied before Shankar cut her off.

"That won't be necessary. I am heading to Connaught Place in a few hours and can meet you in a coffee shop there."

"Sure, that would be fine," Nitya replied.

It was better this way. She didn't want Shankar showing up in uniform at her work. That would certainly set some tongues wagging among her colleagues. They agreed on a time and a place for their meeting. After she hung up, Nitya looked at her watch. There was still plenty of time to finish some paperwork, meet Shankar at the café, and then head to the Gymkhana Club for the evening dinner with her colleagues. Although she tried to focus on all the drafts that her team had left on her desk, her mind was preoccupied with only Avneesh's story. She read and reread all the details that Shiv, Swati, and Rakesh had compiled. Unlike the other victims, there were many unanswered questions. From Shankar's guarded response, it was clear that she wouldn't get much out of him. It didn't help, of course, that Shankar had become wary of the press because of what they had written about him in the past. She couldn't blame him for that. She read through the drafts on her desk and quickly marked up some changes. She was happy to see that the research that her team had done was quite comprehensive. She made a mental note to talk to some of them about their use of language, specifically when describing the victims. Once she was happy with the changes, she headed downstairs to leave the marked-up copies on their respective desks. Moina was on the phone but the others had left for the day. Moina hung up as soon as she saw Nitya. Nitya handed over her draft.

"Anyone else around?"

"They have all left, ma'am."

"Alright, we will talk about this on Monday," Nitya said, pointing to the draft.

"Sure."

"Tell me something … it seems that the victim you were working on went for an interview recently with a recruitment agency in the area, right?"

"Yes, ma'am. That's what we learned from one of his friends, but nothing beyond that. It seems he went for an interview but then never heard back from them. There was really nothing more to go on."

"Is there anything to suggest that the victims knew one another?"

"Shiv asked me that. In fact, he checked with all of us. But that doesn't seem to be the case."

"Hmm."

"Did we miss anything, ma'am?"

"Oh, no. Not at all. I am happy with what all of you have done. The details I have seen in the files and the drafts are quite impressive. It's just that there are some missing links for the victim Shiv has been working on."

"He looked over all our files and he said he will visit some families tomorrow."

"Yes. It's not because any of you missed anything. It's mainly because we are trying to connect the dots in this victim's story. Something's not adding up."

"Avneesh, right?"

"Yes."

"Shiv seems to believe that he was duped into joining a gang and then was killed while trying to uncover the truth. I am sure he told you, ma'am."

"Yes, he did. There's some logic in that deduction."

"He is a good researcher, ma'am," Moina said in earnest. That made Nitya smile. It was good to see members of her team backing each other, and she knew that Moina and Shiv were close.

"That he is, and I know that. Don't worry, he is not in any trouble," Nitya said as she turned to leave.

"Do you need us for anything on Sunday?"

"Yes, I need you and the rest of the team to take a break and get some rest. All this will still be here when we are back on Monday morning."

"Thank you, ma'am. Have a good evening."

"You too," Nitya said, looking at her watch. It was almost time for her to meet Shankar at the café. She went back to her office to grab her coat and purse, and then headed down two flights of stairs, past the reception, and into the large parking lot. Tilak saw her leave the building and immediately headed toward the car, but she stopped him. She told him she would walk to the café as it was nearby and then on returning would head to the club for dinner. She asked him to get some snacks and tea and then started walking the few blocks to the coffee shop. The evening breeze was chilly, but it felt good to be outside. A Saturday evening meant more pedestrians in the area than usual. The restaurants and coffee shops were filling up and she could see the café from afar.

Nitya was also looking forward to her meeting with Shankar. They enjoyed each other's company, and she considered him to be a good friend. She knew he was preoccupied with the events in Old Delhi, and she knew about the tension in his marriage as well. As she opened the door to the café, she immediately spotted Shankar waving at her from the far end. He was not in uniform. After exchanging pleasantries, she took a seat and selected some snacks and tea from the menu. Shankar quickly hailed a waiter, placed the order, and then they jumped into the conversation about the riots. It was Nitya who broached the subject first.

"I know this is off the record, and I know you cannot comment on an ongoing investigation, but I am going to put my cards on the table and tell you what's irking me."

"Sure," Shankar said, leaning back into the comfortable chair.

"From what we have learned so far, it seems that there could be a link between the victims and an agency masquerading as a government security agency that had set up a recruitment office in the area."

Shankar was surprised. How did Nitya know this already? It had taken him and the other investigative agencies some time to come to that conclusion. He chose his words carefully while replying.

"Maybe there is a connection. I am impressed with how much you have learned. I must say, I am surprised and impressed."

"Well, it's not all me. It's mostly Shiv. You remember Shiv, don't you?"

"Yes, of course. The one who doesn't fit in."

"Yes, I shouldn't have said that about him. He is actually pretty good and has done some good work researching about Avneesh Trivedi."

"So, you think there is a link between Avneesh and the other victims through this fake agency?"

"Yes," Nitya replied.

"Impressive."

"There's more. It seems there's reason to believe, based on interviews with his family and friends, that he may have joined this agency thinking that he was doing something important for the country. Once he realized his mistake, he went to Dehradun to find some evidence. We are not sure what happened there or whether he uncovered anything. He most likely did. And we think his employers found out about it, and he might have been killed because of it."

Nitya paused to take a sip of water, and she could see that Shankar was listening intently. After a minute he leaned forward and started speaking softly.

"I cannot corroborate your theory, Nitya. Again, this is off the record, but I think you are on the right track."

"I am happy to hear that. There must be a gang involved in all of this. Or else it doesn't make sense. Another thing, and I don't want you to answer this if it gets you into trouble, it seems that someone from the police or the CBI or the government is involved."

"Why do you say that?"

"Because it's a cover-up from all sides. The family wasn't given any details about Avneesh's death. Avneesh's poor parents were taken away in a hurry in the middle of the night to the crematorium to perform his last rites. In a country where the government machinery seems to move at a snail's pace, all this happened at an alarming speed. Don't you think?"

Shankar looked at her and shrugged his shoulders. Nitya knew that there was an element of truth in what she had just said. The tea and snacks arrived, and they paused for a couple of minutes to take a sip and help themselves to the pastries they had ordered.

Finally, Shankar said, "Nitya, I want you and your team to be very careful while investigating this."

"What do you mean?" Nitya asked, taking another sip from her cup.

"It's quite obvious that you are dealing with a dangerous gang here. They are possibly involved in multiple crimes and have accomplices and members everywhere."

"Are you trying to tell me that it was the gang that was involved in the riots as well? How dangerous are they? I would like to know that for sure, Shankar. I have a young team probing this. Are they in any danger?"

"I am not sure. But please ask them to be careful. I don't have all the answers myself, but it's quite apparent that we are dealing with a well-connected, well-organized group of people who will not hesitate to take the law into their own hands. I am not trying to scare you. Nor am I trying to dissuade you from your investigation. You and your team have done good work. Just please be careful."

Shankar's tone worried Nitya. She knew that he was genuinely concerned about their safety and was not just trying to ward off the press. Although Shankar didn't say it explicitly, Nitya got the feeling that he was convinced that the riots were started by the same gang and were somewhat different from the communal disturbances in the past. Then their conversation shifted to their time in Callipur, Bollywood movies, and finally, their own lives. Nitya told Shankar that Kavita would be visiting her.

"How is Vikram?"

"Oh, he is growing up fast. Thankfully, he likes his school and has settled in quite nicely."

"That's good, and Rohini?"

"I am afraid I can't say the same about her," Shankar said softly. He seemed sad. Nitya sensed it right away and leaned forward.

"Is she alright?"

"Yes, she is alright, but it hasn't been easy for her. My job keeps me away from home for long hours. Vikram's at school. Rohini's having a hard time finding something to keep her occupied. She is bored and hasn't really made any friends."

"Oh. Wasn't she a teacher? Doesn't she want to go back and teach, maybe?"

"Yes. She has applied to some schools in the area, but the hours don't suit her. She wants to be home when Vikram gets back from school. He is still young."

"It must be hard."

"It's not easy being the wife of a police officer who is away from morning till almost nine or ten every night. I can't say that I blame her. My job, the whole situation with me working so far away in Old Delhi, and her being new to the city hasn't really helped. I think she wants to move back to Mussoorie to be with her parents."

"Oh," Nitya said softly, unsure of what to say next.

"I did see this coming."

"Maybe a few days home with her parents won't hurt."

"Yes, I have given this some thought, and she has done it a few times before. I mean Mussoorie is a few hours away and she visits her folks often, but I think that makes matters worse. She sees how things could be better for her back in her hometown and she yearns for the life that she left behind."

"I am sure she will settle in," Nitya said in an understanding tone.

"I am not so sure anymore. I know she has applied to some teaching positions in the school she used to work at in

Mussoorie. She hasn't told me yet, but I got to know from one of her relatives who accidentally revealed it during a conversation."

"So, she still hasn't told you?"

"No."

"Does she know that you know?"

"No."

Nitya sighed. She didn't know what to say. They finished their tea and pastries in silence and then it was time for both to leave.

"Shankar, I hope things work out with you and Rohini. I have met her a few times. I know she is a good girl, and she cares about you. I just hope you give her some time and are able to take some time off work to sort things out. I am in no position to give advice, but I think that's the best I can think of."

"Thank you, Nitya. Honestly, I don't know how things stand between us. We don't talk much anymore. When she is away visiting her parents, she seems happier, and I feel less guilty about coming home late at night. It's also a relief from the arguments and quarrels that we seem to constantly be getting into. I feel that it's not easy on Vikram and that's what worries me the most."

"I really don't know what to say, Shankar."

"Oh, I am not looking for an answer. I am just airing out an aspect of my life that's been a disappointment to one of my friends," Shankar said and smiled.

"Disappointments? Obviously, you haven't spoken to my mom lately. Your troubles will seem miles away," Nitya said in jest, and they both laughed.

"Well, this has been great, but I really need to head home. We are expecting some guests for dinner, and it won't look good if the host is late."

"I won't keep you," Nitya said quickly and then added, "there is one other thing that I wanted to talk to you about." Shankar waved at the waiter for the bill and then turned to Nitya.

"What is it?"

"This has been on my mind for quite some time. It's about the articles that we wrote in the aftermath of the labor union strike and protests near India Gate."

"What about them?"

"The entire press got after the police about their high-handed tactics and use of force to quell the disturbance. You were one of the officers in charge that day and ended up bearing the brunt of the criticism levied at the police."

"I know. It was just bad luck, I think. I mean we tried our best to maintain calm. It got to a point where we had to resort to some force, and then there was some retaliation from one section of the protestors and things just got out of hand."

"Yes, but the press, including me, focused on only one side of the story."

"Well, that's understandable. I mean most of the injured were among the protestors. Honestly, I have played out the events of that day over and over in my head. I can't think of anything that we could have done differently."

"I understand, Shankar. What I am trying to say is that I feel that we didn't give you a fair shake when it came to the reporting of the incident and in the subsequent articles. They were all one-sided, leaning toward the protestors and blaming the police. I feel that you were made a scapegoat and that must have contributed to your transfer to Old Delhi," Nitya said. The waiter had come over with the check. Despite Nitya's protests, Shankar graciously decided to pay it.

After the waiter left, Shankar paused for a bit before responding.

"Nitya, if it makes you feel any better, I have never blamed the press, or you for what happened to me. As I said, it was just bad luck."

"That may well be the case, but I can't help but think that a fair and more balanced reporting may have resulted in a different outcome for you."

"I don't know about that. I mean if there was anyone who should have had my back, it would be my superiors. There's no point rehashing the past. Please don't feel responsible for anything that happened to me as a result of your reporting. I am glad we live in a country where the press has the freedom to be adversarial when needed. Yes, things may sometimes get out of hand and seem unfair, but it's better this way than the other extreme where the government controls what should be written."

"Still an idealist, I see," Nitya said, as she slowly started to get up to leave.

"Always," Shankar said with a smile, and got up.

They exited the café and chatted outside for a while. The clear winter sky was now dark. It was a fair bit chillier than when they had first arrived. Shankar walked Nitya back to her office building and then turned back to look for Motiram to take him home. As she saw Shankar slowly walking away, Nitya was convinced that they were on the right track on Avneesh's story. She was also worried about what Shankar had told her about the gang. She decided to tell her team on Monday to finish their stories quickly and refrain from probing or investigating things on their own. Also, instead of sending Swati and Shiv to Dehradun, she decided that she would accompany Shiv and take Tilak along. Nitya found Tilak dozing in the car in the empty parking lot outside the office building. He quickly woke up and after she got in, they headed toward Gymkhana Club.

* * *

Delhi's Gymkhana Club was a relic from another era. It was one of the oldest clubs in India, founded well before independence by the British. Over the years it had been deliberately slow in its modernization efforts and still retained some of its colonial hangover. The clientele had changed, and the club was now a popular hangout of the rich, famous, and well-connected. Nitya had only gone at the behest of Manoj. Being the newest member of the senior management team at *The New India Courier*, she was expected to be present during each quarterly get-together and other festive occasions. It was common for people to arrive fashionably late and that suited Nitya just fine. She didn't want to spend too much time at the club. The stories on the victims were still on her mind and one of the things she wanted to talk to Manoj about was the trip to Dehradun.

When Nitya reached the club, she walked through the grounds and headed straight to one of the majestic rooms that had been booked for the evening for the cocktail and buffet dinner. Delhi was still in the middle of a cold spell in January. She engaged in some small talk with the rest of the senior management team. Harry Singh was in his element, and with a few drinks under his belt, his voice was booming across the room, loud and clear, over and above all the others. Nitya quickly helped herself to some food. Then she slowly walked over toward Manoj. He was standing in the corner talking to a few others. When he saw her, he excused himself and pointed toward the door leading to a common hall outside the room. Once outside, they could see some other patrons in the large common area, but they were well out of earshot.

"Is there something on your mind, Nitya?"

"Yes, sir. It's about the story on one of the victims, Avneesh Trivedi. I had spoken to you earlier about him."

"What about it?"

"His death seems to be more of a mystery compared to the others."

"How so?"

Nitya proceeded to tell Manoj everything that they had learned about Avneesh, including her chat with Shankar. Manoj listened to her carefully without interrupting and she could sense that he was paying attention to every word she was saying. When she finished, she could see that he was trying to process everything. After a while, she decided to break the silence.

"What do you think, sir?"

"So, you really think that there is a rogue police officer or an official from one of the security agencies involved in all of this?"

"That's what it is pointing to."

"Hmm. No wonder Ghanshyam was worried about what we are going to write."

"He is the junior home minister. I am sure he knows much more than he is letting on publicly."

"Yes, of course."

"Are you fine with us making the trip to Dehradun?"

"You think that's where the answers are?"

"Some of them."

"Then it's fine. Go right ahead. I will leave it up to you to decide when you want to go and for how long."

"Thank you, sir."

"Will you be going alone? I hope not. After what we know, you should be careful."

"I am taking Tilak and Shiv with me."

"Shiv? Is that a good idea?"

"Yes, sir. Most of what we have uncovered in this case is because of him."

"Really?"

"Yes, he is good at what he does."

"Hmm. Well, I will take your word for it, for now. Go ahead and make the arrangements and please keep me posted on what's happening."

"Right, sir. If you don't mind, I will call it a day and head home."

"Yes, it's getting late, I know. Well, thanks for coming. I will see you in the office on Monday."

"Good night, sir."

"Good night," Manoj said, and turned to head back to the room to join the rest of the group. Some of them had already left. A few were smoking on the lawn outside. Nitya looked at her watch and sighed. It was nearly 10:00 p.m. and she was exhausted. She said her goodbyes and then headed toward the exit.

As she exited the building, she could see others in different areas of the sprawling lawn and gardens. There was a pathway leading to the gates. Nitya pulled her blazer tightly around her to fend off the Delhi winter chill. Halfway across the lawn, she was suddenly confronted by Vijay and another gentleman whom she hadn't seen before. Vijay was completely intoxicated. He was talking loudly, and his eyes were bloodshot. He could barely stand. Nitya could sense that the other guests in the club were looking at him. When he saw Nitya he stopped, pointed at her, and lunged toward her. Nitya took a step back. He was so intoxicated that Nitya was unsure what he would do next. Then he stood a few feet away from her, blocking her path, and started yelling at the top of his voice.

"You know who this one is?" Vijay said pointing at Nitya and turning to his friend who was equally drunk and having a hard time standing still.

"Vijay, please move out of the way. I need to go home," Nitya said sternly. But he completely ignored what she said.

"This one's Nitya," Vijay shouted with his hands waving. "God knows what she had to do to get a promotion and who she had to do it with. I was her thing for a while and now she's moved on."

Nitya was stunned and speechless. A crowd had now gathered and was listening to all this. She was certain that her colleagues were among the crowd, but she froze and was scared to look back. Suddenly, from the other side of the lawn, she heard a soft, unmistakable voice.

"I think you need to take a step back and get out of the way. You are making a fool of yourself. Step aside and let her leave. Now!"

Both Vijay and Nitya turned to see who it was. It was Shiv. He looked very different in informal party attire. Vijay's yelling subsided but he frowned at Shiv and his tone became sarcastic.

"Ah. This one's Nitya's latest. How is it going with him, then?"

"Enough of this nonsense," Shiv said, as he moved closer to Nitya to guide her away from Vijay.

"What's going on here?" asked a booming voice from behind. It was Harry Singh.

"It's Vijay, sir," Shiv said looking at Harry and pointing to Vijay. "He is making a fool of himself."

Vijay and his friend had slumped to the ground. They were coughing and were about to throw up.

"Unbelievable, what an absolute embarrassment," Harry Singh said, walking up closer to Shiv and Nitya. Some waiters were trying to help Vijay and his friend get on their feet and guide them to some sofas in the garden. Nitya, Shiv, and Harry Singh left them there and continued on the path leading to the club gates. Once they were outside, Harry bid them good night. Nitya was still shaken by what had happened, but she was happy to see Shiv and Harry. Shiv had a worried look on his face.

"What are you doing at the club, Shiv? I didn't expect to see you here."

"Oh, I am here for a friend's birthday, ma'am."

"I am sorry you had to see all that," Nitya said slightly embarrassed by what Vijay had blurted out. She knew that Shiv had probably guessed already that she had an affair with Vijay. After all, it was common gossip in the office.

"You have nothing to be sorry for. He is the one who should be sorry for his utterly disgusting behavior. An absolute disgrace," Shiv said softly, looking directly at her.

"Thank you for stepping in. I really didn't know what to say or do for a split second there."

"You did nothing wrong, ma'am."

"Anyway, are you heading back inside to your friend's party? Do you want me to drop you home?"

"No, ma'am. Thanks for the offer. I have my bike and I will stay here for a bit and then go home."

"Alright, good night, Shiv, and thank you, again. I will see you on Monday."

"Good night, ma'am."

As Tilak drove her back home, the events of the evening played out in her head. She knew that she had done nothing wrong, but she was still inexplicably embarrassed about what had happened. She wondered which of her colleagues had heard Vijay's outburst and how they would judge her. Then her thoughts shifted to Shiv. She wondered what he was doing at the club. For someone who lived in Old Delhi, having friends who went to the Gymkhana Club was not common, but then she remembered that Shiv went to college in Delhi, and that meant he had a circle of friends from all backgrounds. As the car sped through the leafy neighborhoods of New Delhi and headed toward her apartment building, she thought of the trip to Dehradun. Kavita would be arriving from Bombay in a few days. Nitya had promised to take her sister out while she was in town. That meant she would either have to go to Dehradun and come back in the middle of the week before she arrived or wait until Kavita went back to Bombay. However, little did she know that the events on Monday would force her to decide.

Journey

Monday morning was abuzz with activity at Shankar's police station. The commissioner was expected at any time. The officers and constables were ensuring that the station looked spick-and-span. Shankar had arrived early not only for the commissioner's expected visit, but also to look through some more files that had been sent over by the home ministry and the CBI. He had had an eventful Sunday following up on the investigations on all the victims. At the behest of Ghanshyam Das, the lead officers from the other agencies were now completely cooperating with him. It had become abundantly clear that the riots were staged to divert police to the area so that a convoy of trucks could be moved from the city to other states without any inspection. The CBI had expanded their active surveillance to more than one officer and outside elements who had been assisting them. No arrests had been made just yet. The consensus was that they needed to apprehend as many of the gang as possible along with the cargo. Shankar's assessment was that the cargo was either illegal arms and ammunitions or drugs. The more he thought about it, the more he leaned toward arms and ammunitions.

Once he finished reading and rereading the files on his desk, he turned to a box on his table where the daily mail was kept. As always, there were several letters of inquiries, complaints, suggestions from citizens on what the police should be doing but weren't, and requests from business owners in the area asking for more patrols. He disregarded most of the items in the stack, but his eyes fell on a thick envelope. What caught his eye was the name of the sender. It was Avneesh Trivedi. It was addressed to the "Head of the Kotwali Police Station." Since Shankar was the most senior officer, the envelope had landed on his desk. He looked at the postmark and the date. It was mailed a few days ago from Dehradun. He quickly opened the envelope and found two sheets of paper. One was a hastily written note stating that Avneesh had unearthed a conspiracy, that his life was in danger, and that he was writing to let the police know that there was a hideout of a criminal gang in Dehradun and that there was a convoy expected to leave around midnight from that address on a certain date. The date mentioned was that of tonight. The second paper was a hand-drawn map and the address. There was nothing else. Shankar could make out from both the notes that they were written in a hurry. Avneesh had feared for his life and probably suspected that there was a chance that he wouldn't be able to make it back to Delhi from Dehradun. Shankar reread the letter, looked at the postmark, and immediately called his constable and told him to ask Motiram to bring the car around. He phoned his contact in the CBI who was overseeing the surveillance of the rogue officer and had a long conversation with him. Then he placed a call to the police station in Dehradun. Soon he heard a commotion outside. The commissioner had arrived. Shankar met him and let him know that he had cracked the case and would be apprehending the suspects in a day or two.

* * *

When Nitya walked into her office building the same morning, she was surprised to see Madhavi waiting for her in the reception area. Madhavi quickly walked up to her and after exchanging some greetings, accompanied Nitya to her office. They stopped by the canteen and Nitya asked them to bring them some tea. Once they were both settled in, Nitya could see that Madhavi had a worried look on her face and was clutching on tightly to an envelope.

After taking a sip of the tea, she asked Nitya, "is Shiv here?"

"No, he isn't. He is following up on something at the moment and will be coming in later. Is there something I can help you with?"

"Yes, I know he is looking into what happened to Avneesh."

"Yes, he is, but I am aware of everything that he has been working on. Is there something you want to share?"

Madhavi looked at the letter she was clutching and slowly placed it on the table in front of Nitya. Nitya picked up the envelope. It was a bit crumpled due to the force with which Madhavi had been holding on to it. She opened it gently to see a handmade map with an address in Dehradun and a hastily written note by Avneesh that stated that he was returning with evidence of a big conspiracy that he had uncovered. Nitya reread the note. Then she looked at Madhavi who had a sullen expression on her face. Before Nitya could say anything, Madhavi started speaking.

"I think Avneesh had found out something that put his life in danger, and that killed him."

"Perhaps. The letter also mentions that he has sent a copy to the police. Maybe they are aware of it too."

"Yes, but if you read it carefully, you will see that someone in the police is involved too. He says everyone's involved and not to trust anyone."

"Yes, that could well be the case," Nitya nodded in agreement.

"Even if the police got the letter, how do we know they will do anything about it?"

"Well, we will. Whether the police do their job or not, we will find out what's at this address and what's happening at midnight tonight. The place, date, and time are of relevance in finding out what happened, and we will check it out."

"You will have to be careful, ma'am."

"Yes, I am aware of the danger, given what has happened."

"I didn't know what else to do. That's why I brought it here."

"You did the right thing. I will make a copy of this and give it back to you."

"There's no need, ma'am. You can keep it for now and I will take it back later. It's the last letter that he wrote. I would like to keep it. Please hold on to it and keep it safe," Madhavi said, trying to hold back her tears.

"I will," Nitya replied softly.

"I must go back now. I hope this helps," Madhavi said pointing to the letter.

"It certainly will. I think Avneesh may have given us some of the answers we might have been seeking. Don't worry, we will pursue it."

"Thank you, ma'am," Madhavi said, as she got up to leave. Nitya walked her down to the reception and to the main door. The sadness on Madhavi's face was clearly visible, and the letter helped explain the reason.

Once she left, Nitya went outside to the parking lot to find Tilak. He was busy chatting with other drivers but as soon as he saw her, he quickly walked up to her.

"Tilak, we will be leaving for Dehradun today. Make sure the tank is full."

"Yes, ma'am."

"I want you to go to my apartment and pick up a bag from there. My maid will be home. I will call her and let her know that you will be going over to pick it up."

"Yes, ma'am."

"Do you have a change of clothes in your car? We may have to stay in Dehradun overnight."

"I do. I am all set."

"Thank you, please pick up my bag from home and be ready to leave in a couple of hours."

"Sure, ma'am."

Nitya then headed back to her desk. Before taking the stairs, she stopped at the reception and instructed them to let Shiv know to come straight to her office. Once she was back at her office, she placed a call to her apartment and instructed the maid to pack a small bag. Then she started looking through all the notes on Avneesh's story, recalling everything that Shiv had told her. She made some notes, called Manoj to let him know that she was leaving for Dehradun, and instructed one of the secretaries to book them a place to stay for the night. They were quick to find a place and gave her the details. At the newspaper, they usually had a list that they could work off, and Dehradun being a popular tourist destination, there was no shortage of places to stay. She tried to get through to Shankar but couldn't. She was told that he had left his station in a hurry, and they didn't know when he would be back. When Shiv arrived, she quickly told him about Madhavi's visit and handed him the letter.

"Wow! So, this is it," Shiv said excitedly. "Something big is going down tonight at this address in Dehradun. We need to be there."

"Yes, we will be. What else can you decipher?"

"Avneesh knew he was in danger. This letter is written rather hastily, and he was carrying back something with him,

I think more evidence of the gang involvement. That's what killed him."

"Right."

"Did Madhavi say anything else? This letter suggests that a copy of some sort was sent to the police. Did they contact her? Does she know where it was sent?"

"No, unfortunately, she didn't have any other details."

"We could contact the police, ma'am, but it seems one or more of them might be involved too. Perhaps we can try Mr. Sen?"

"I tried calling him, but he is not at the station."

"Then we must leave now. Dehradun is a good six hours away. This is happening tonight, and we don't have much time."

"Right. I want you to go and get a change of clothes and pack a small bag with what you need. Then we can leave. You can take the car once Tilak is back. It will be faster that way."

"No need, I have a change of clothes here."

"In the office?"

"I play badminton at a place nearby and I keep a spare set of clothes here. Don't worry, ma'am, I won't and don't smell bad."

"I didn't say you did," Nitya said with a smile. "Alright, give me fifteen minutes and I will be ready."

"Do you want me to ask someone downstairs to book some rooms for us?"

"That's taken care of."

"I doubt we will have much time there. I mean it looks like we will have to stake out this place tonight, and I am not sure what we will find."

"That's true."

"What about informing the police in Dehradun?"

"I was thinking about that. The thing is we don't know what we will find. We should find this place and see what happens at the designated time. If it's something fishy, we will inform the local police and have them check it out."

"Yes, ma'am. We can't go barging in and asking questions. That might tip them off."

"And put us in danger too, and I don't want that. Right now, we are just going to see if anything happens at the location at the time indicated in Avneesh's letter."

"Right."

"Alright, off you go then. I will meet you in the parking lot in a few minutes."

"Sure," Shiv said, and headed downstairs to his desk.

When Nitya reached the parking lot, she saw Shiv standing outside engaged in conversation with Tilak. She couldn't make out what they were talking about, but it seemed like an animated discussion. They stopped on seeing her, and Tilak quickly opened the trunk of the Ambassador. Nitya put her handbag with some folders inside. Tilak had picked up her bag, and there were two other bags that she presumed belonged to Tilak and Shiv along with a camera bag.

"Good, you are taking a camera."

"Yes, ma'am. Just in case."

Once they were settled in the back and Tilak started driving, Nitya turned to Shiv.

"What was that all about?"

"What, ma'am?"

"Your argument with Tilak."

"I wasn't arguing."

"Yes, he was ma'am," Tilak replied from the front before Nitya could respond.

"What was he saying?" Nitya asked.

"He was saying that he wanted to drive part of the way in case I got tired, and I told him no."

"Good for you, Tilak," Nitya replied, "I am happy with that answer."

"It would be only in case he grew tired, ma'am. It's a long drive," Shiv said softly.

"And a very nice gesture," Tilak replied with a smile. "But honestly, I think I am fine. If I am tired, I will let you know."

"We have plenty of time, Tilak. Let's not rush, and we can stop somewhere along the way," Nitya said.

"Sure, ma'am," Tilak replied, as the car slowly started leaving Connaught Place and picked up speed on one of the grand avenues crisscrossing the city.

Nitya and Shiv spent the next few minutes looking outside at the landmarks and monuments in the grand capital. Slowly the neighborhoods changed and with it the volume of cars and people. Luckily for them, there wasn't much traffic on the roads leaving Delhi. Since Dehradun was a popular tourist destination, the highways were good and had a number of roadside stops for taking a break or enjoying a meal. As the car sped past the borders of Delhi and headed north toward Dehradun, Nitya started asking Shiv more about himself, something she had done with everyone else in the team except for him.

"You know when you became a part of my team, we didn't have a one-on-one meeting with each other. I had one with all the others on the team except you and then things got busy because of the riots."

"That's right."

"We are going to be in the car for a few hours now, so here's our chance. I certainly would like to know more about you. It goes both ways. You can ask me questions or share any concerns that you may have."

"Certainly, ma'am. What would you like to know?"

"I saw on your file that you are from Bangalore. Have you always lived there before moving to Delhi?"

"Yes, born and brought up there. I moved to Delhi for college."

"Delhi University?"

"Yes, ma'am."

"Didn't you want to stay in Bangalore?"

"The program was better here, and I really wanted to have some time away from home," Shiv said softly, and Nitya didn't want to press him further.

"How do you find Delhi in comparison to Bangalore?"

"Lots of similarities in terms of the urban lifestyle, but some stark differences too."

"Like?"

"The pace is much faster in this city. Also, this is a bit more cosmopolitan."

"True."

"Less family here, at least for me, which means more anonymity and less interference."

"Right," Nitya agreed, as her experience was the same.

"I became more independent after staying away from home. I guess that would have happened anywhere. I come from a large family and things can get complicated."

"What do your folks do, if you don't mind me asking?"

"A family business, ma'am. It's my father really. My mother passed away a few years ago when I was still young."

"Oh, I am sorry to hear that."

"My father runs the business with my siblings. I have an elder sister and brother."

"So, you are the youngest?"

"Yes."

"And didn't you want to join the family business?"

"It's complicated," said Shiv as the car stopped. There was a big procession crossing the street. They were now near the outskirts of Delhi. Nitya figured that Shiv's story was similar to the one playing out in thousands of family-run businesses in the country. Not everyone in the younger generation wanted to take over and run the family business. In many cases, the business was either too small for everyone in the next generation to make a decent living out of it or just not that interesting. From Shiv's responses, it sounded like it was a bit of both.

"So, you decided to pursue a career in journalism?" Nitya asked as the car started moving.

"I tried to involve myself in the family business, but my father is not an easy taskmaster. He wants things his own way and gets upset and loses his temper if his orders are not followed. He usually takes all the decisions."

"Hmm."

"It was fine when my mother was alive. Then things became difficult. He started spending more and more time at work. When we tried to help, he just wanted us to agree with him on everything. My siblings are a good bit older than me, and they manage to put up with him, but I couldn't. My mother was the glue and after she died, things went downhill."

"And journalism? Why pursue a career in that? Were you always interested in it?"

"Before marriage, my mother was a journalist at a small regional paper in Bangalore. After getting married, she stopped working. Bringing up three kids with my father always busy at work was a full-time job."

Nitya sighed. She knew this was again something that was being played out across the nation. A lot of women were forced to give up their careers to be homemakers.

"It was your mother that sparked your interest in writing?"

"Yes, ma'am. She encouraged all of us to read and write outside of the regular school curriculum. She coaxed me into writing for the school paper. I stopped for a while when she passed away and then picked it up again when I entered college."

"How was college?"

"A lot of fun."

"I can imagine. Staying away from home for the first time, making friends in a different city, no family nearby to complain about late nights," Nitya said with a smile.

"Yes."

"I am guessing that's why you decided to stay back in Delhi after graduating and not look for work in Bangalore."

"Not quite, ma'am."

"Oh."

"I stayed back for a girl."

"Really?"

"Yes, ma'am. We met during the first year of college. We thought we'd end up together, but it didn't work out that way."

"Family issues again? We don't have to talk about this."

"No, it's alright. Family issues, yes, but not from my side, more on her side. She knew that they wouldn't accept me. We come from different backgrounds with very little in common. They wanted her to get married to someone from a similar background. She ended up marrying the son of a family friend."

"Yeah, well, it's more common than you think. Did she at least tell her family about you?"

"Yes, she did after we had been going out for more than two years. They came down hard on her. She wanted to break up, but we still carried on knowing well that it wouldn't last, and that her parents would never agree."

"What about your father and your siblings?"

"I'd have made them come around."

"Even your father?"

"Well, I am already out of his sphere of influence as they say. We don't really talk much and when we do, we end up arguing."

"It's different for girls you know, much harder."

"I don't know but yes, I agree, and I can only imagine. I know what she went through when she told her parents about me. Yet, we went on hoping that things would change."

"These things happen, Shiv. You were in love. You thought it would work out."

"Yes."

"Well, as you say, now she is married."

"Yes, ma'am, and I really didn't stay in touch after that."

"Rightly so. Has it been a few years now?"

"Yes, ma'am."

"I am sure you will move on."

"Right. Well, not all love stories are meant to last. Some are short, but that doesn't mean they are bereft of love or incredible affection while they last."

"A poet, I see," Nitya said with a smile on her face.

"Far from it. I am not into poetry like you are."

"How did you figure that out?"

"From your notebook, ma'am. It's not hard to make out that you are a Robert Frost fan. You also have quotes from Tagore, Blake, and Plath. They are all written in your handwriting, which means you are into poetry, and they mean a lot to you."

"Yes, they do. I always liked poetry of all kinds and different languages. You do have a keen eye to notice these things. Are you into poetry?"

"Oh, not at all."

"And yet you know about all these poets. I mean Frost and Tagore I can understand, but not many people know about Blake and far less about Plath."

"I have read some of their poems. Frost was required reading in school."

"Ah yes, 'The Road Not Taken.' Is that still in the curriculum?"

"Yes, that's the only one from Frost that I know of and have read, and it's a good one."

"Yes, one of the best. So, tell me, what do you think it's about?"

"The poem?"

"Yes."

"When I first read it, I thought it was about regret. Then I read it again and thought it was about taking chances and success. Now, I am not sure. I don't think it's either. It's not that straightforward."

"It isn't. So, what was your conclusion?"

"I don't know, ma'am. I haven't figured it out yet. I think the poem means different things depending on which stage of life you read it. As in any other form of art, it means different things to different people."

"Different interpretations."

"Yes, ma'am."

"You are probably right. I have been reading it for years and know it verbatim, but I am still not always certain what it's about and that's the beauty of it, I guess," Nitya said as she turned to look out the window. By now they had left Delhi and were speeding along on the highway. There were only a few cars on the road and Tilak was driving at a good speed. Nitya and Shiv marveled at the landscape. There were mostly corn and sugarcane fields, and they could see some farmers working on their crops. The bright sun and the blue skies made the view very pretty. They were crossing a flat area and could see the tree line behind the farms. They knew that the landscape would change as they got closer to Dehradun. It was still far away, and they continued to enjoy the ride and the surroundings as the car weaved its way through the fields on either side. Behind the tree line, they could see some thatched roofs and dusty roads. It reminded Nitya of the surrounding areas of her hometown, Callipur. The villages looked similar, but the surroundings were different. Callipur had more paddy fields of rice. The ones they were crossing were mostly wheat, sugarcane, and corn. They weren't green but had a whole slew of colors that made them look like an unfinished painting.

After a few minutes, they resumed their conversation. Nitya found Shiv easy to talk to. He spoke fondly of his college days, at times mentioning his failed relationship in passing, sometimes with a touch of melancholy, but always with fondness. No conversation was complete without Bollywood or cricket. This was no different. Nitya also told Shiv about her time in Callipur and her passion for the new genre of movies that was slowly taking hold in India under the banner of art films or indie movies.

"Do you like them?"

"You mean art films, ma'am?"

"Yes."

"Not really. I like movies with heroes and villains. I want to know exactly who they are with lots of drama, music, and action."

"Really? Well, the art films are more about realism, of a life that is plausible and realistic."

"Why would I want that in a movie?"

"What do you mean?"

"Ma'am, I get to experience real life every day while I go about my daily chores. Why would I want that when I go to the cinema? I want to see something unrealistic, extraordinary, fantastical, adventurous, or something thrilling."

"Really, Shiv. I mean I guess you could and should enjoy both as long as they are good."

"I agree, but honestly I really don't have the urge to pay good money and spend time in a theater to get a dose of reality."

"Yes, I can see that."

"Most of my friends are like you, ma'am. They like this artsy stuff because it's kind of different. I really don't get it."

"Yes, I wonder why that is. You know, I am starting to get worried about you. Well, I am glad you keep good company," Nitya said teasingly.

"You mean, my friends?"

"Yes."

"Yes, they are alright," Shiv said, and they both had a good laugh.

Nitya quickly asked Tilak if he needed a break. He stopped at a roadside *dhaba* to get some refreshments. Nitya stayed in the car while Shiv and Tilak got down to get some water, tea, and biscuits. Once they were back near the car, Nitya got down and stretched her legs, and they all took a few minutes and finished their tea. The rest area was full of cars and people enjoying a break or a meal or both. Once they were back in the car and on the highway heading to Dehradun, Nitya and Shiv started talking about the case and the reason for their trip.

"You know, there's one thing I don't quite get about our victim, Avneesh."

"What's that, ma'am?"

"We met his family, and they are all decent, law-abiding people. You also met his friend and I read your report on all the interactions with his colleagues as well. I don't get why someone like him would get involved in this sort of thing. He had a good job, and it seems everyone liked him there. So why all this?"

"I don't know, ma'am. He probably wanted to elevate his status, get a better job, do more for his family."

"Still, he could have just continued and done well for himself at his previous workplace."

"He wanted to make things better. There could be many reasons for that. He was newly married, in love, had a young child, was taking care of his parents. I can see why he would want a better opportunity."

"That's true," Nitya nodded in agreement.

"There's nothing so far to suggest that he did anything wrong himself. I mean everything we know points to the fact that he was duped into joining this gang and then once he realized what they were up to, he tried to make things right. We are not sure if he tried contacting the police before this letter was sent. Maybe he wanted evidence before engaging them lest they suspect him of being a member of the same gang. Who knows? It would have been good if we could have spoken to Mr. Sen about this one more time."

"Yes, I don't know what's going on with Shankar either. I know he is investigating the case. Obviously, the police are not going to tell the press too many details about an ongoing investigation."

"Last time we spoke, it seemed you had a lot of faith in Mr. Sen."

"Yes, I do. I just wish that he would let me in a bit more on what they know. I understand why he can't though."

"Didn't you want to press him further, ma'am?"

"It's a bit complicated."

"How so?"

"It's a long story."

"If only we were stuck in a car on a long journey with hours to kill till our destination," Shiv said, and Nitya smiled.

"Alright, I guess you have earned it," Nitya said, and she told Shiv what had happened with Shankar during the labor strike, how the press, including her, had reported the police's heavy-handedness and how that, in part, had led Shankar to fall out of favor within the senior ranks of his own department. She told Shiv that Shankar had repeatedly tried to get a transfer out of Old Delhi with no luck.

"Do you somehow feel guilty about what happened to Mr. Sen?"

"Yes, a bit."

"Have you spoken to him about it?"

"I did, and he doesn't blame me or the press at all, but then again that's how he is. I know him. Even if he did, he wouldn't come out and tell me."

"He likes you," Shiv said and smiled.

"Yes, and I like him too, but not in the way that you are inferring," Nitya said sternly.

"I didn't infer anything."

"Right, and let's keep it that way."

"I am surprised to hear that he was heavy-handed though."

"What do you mean?"

"When I met Shankar in Old Delhi while taking pictures, it wasn't the first time that we had met or the first time that I had seen him."

"Really? I thought that was the first time you had met."

"That's when we spoke for the first time, but I had seen him a few years ago in my final year of college. There was a student protest at Delhi University. It's quite common as you know, ma'am. Students like to protest about many things and this one was on campus. The students had surrounded the administration building and were not letting any of the staff in or out. It was quite a peaceful protest, and things were going smoothly."

"And Shankar was there?"

"Yes, the principal of our college had requested police presence. Shankar, along with other officers and constables from different police stations was sent there to keep the calm."

"You were one of the students protesting?"

"No, ma'am. I was in the library, which is in the same building, and we were stuck inside. There is a large open balcony on the second floor, and we could see the students protesting in front of the building, giving speeches, and shouting slogans. We could also see the police in front of the protesting students and in front of the entrance to our building."

"Hmm. I am guessing things ended like they usually do by the end of the day with students dispersing and going back home or to their hostels?"

"Not quite. You see, toward late afternoon there was some sort of verbal argument between a few protestors and some constables. I am not sure what really happened or who started it, but within a few minutes, a small section of the students became very rowdy and started abusing the police. They picked up the mic and hurled profanities at the police. Suddenly, a bottle was thrown toward the officers and constables, and this understandably agitated them. A few constables and some officers were really angry by this time and were looking for a reason to rough up the protestors. The bottle that was thrown at them gave them the justification they needed."

"Oh my God. Was there a fight? I don't recall seeing this in the papers. I mean, we did mention these protests in passing but if a fight broke out on campus, it would have been news and I would have remembered it."

"Yes, you would have, and you are right, ma'am, things would have escalated quickly with tempers flaring on both sides had it not been for Shankar. He quickly brought his jeep between the protestors and the police and with great difficulty convinced his own team not to turn violent. I could see him pleading with both sides not to resort to violence. We could see clearly that he was having a hard time, but after a few minutes, he took the mic and urged everyone to stay calm."

"Nothing happened after that?"

"Well, some of the verbal abuses continued, but there was no physical violence. I could see that the policemen were itching for a fight and some students were disappointed too. In the end, cooler heads prevailed and by evening everyone had dispersed."

"Wow, that must have been something."

"I remember Shankar from that incident. That's why I was surprised when you said he resorted to excessive physical force in quelling the labor strike. Maybe he had no other choice, or it could be that he was trying to prevent things from getting worse."

"Yes, it could be. Somehow, I think, we got that wrong in the papers. We certainly didn't cover both sides of the story."

The landscape slowly changed as the car moved along toward their destination. Things outside were becoming greener, the fields were being replaced with wooded areas and small hamlets, and the land wasn't all flat anymore. After an hour or so they could see some hills on the horizon and the roads had gained altitude.

Located in the foothills of the Himalayas, Dehradun was known for its boarding schools, government academies, and places of worship. The national parks, mountains, and historical sites in and around the city made it a popular tourist destination. Nitya asked Tilak if he needed another break, but he said that he could wait until they reached Dehradun. That suited Nitya and Shiv as well. Every now and then they would talk about the case. Nitya found Shiv to be good company. She hadn't seen this side of him before. He was well-read, and although she didn't agree with many of his viewpoints, she was pleased that he was open to dissenting views and easy to get along with. Once they reached the outskirts of Dehradun, Nitya turned to Shiv.

"Been here before?"

"Yes, ma'am."

"Visiting?"

"Yes, as a tourist with family and friends. How about you, ma'am?"

"Yes, many, many times. Love the place."

"Yes, it's a beautiful town, lots to see."

"Pity we won't have time to do all that."

"Ma'am, I was wondering, since we are getting close to the town now, can we please go to the railway station first?"

"Yes, sure. Any particular reason?"

"The envelope."

"Sorry?"

"The one that had Avneesh's letter."

"What about it?"

"The postmark on it was from the post office at the railway station. If you look closely, you can see it."

"Oh, so you think it may have been mailed from there?"

"That's what I think. It looks like Avneesh was in a hurry and mailed the letter from the station."

"True, but what good would a visit to the station do?"

"Maybe someone saw him at the post office. I still have his photograph and we can ask around. I know it may not be much, but it's worth a shot. We still have a few hours before our stakeout, ma'am."

"Sure, why not? Tilak, please take us to the railway station first," Nitya said.

"Sure, ma'am," Tilak replied.

As the car entered the town, the difference with a big metropolis like Delhi was all too visible. The streets, though busy, did not have many cars. There were hardly any high-rise buildings. The sparsely populated yet lively streets and avenues were lined with hotels and guesthouses for tourists. There were signs on the roads for many of the known landmarks and schools that the town was famous for. As the car veered onto the street leading to the railway station, they could see that things were getting busier. The station itself was established by the British, but the building had been renovated and expanded. Compared to stations in other cities, it was small, and entertained relatively fewer trains. That meant that during off-hours the station and its platforms were not that crowded. When Tilak parked his car next to the main entrance to the station, they could see that it wasn't a busy time. A few travelers with their suitcases lined the benches in the waiting area while some others were chatting at tea stalls on the nearest platform.

The post office was easy to find. It was a small office between the waiting room and a large canteen with a window facing the platform. There were no visitors present at this time. When they reached the counter, they saw an old gentleman reading a newspaper with his feet on his desk. It was clear that he wasn't expecting any clients at this time. When he saw Nitya and Shiv, he quickly got up and walked up to them and addressed them through the little window on the counter.

"Can I help you with anything?"

"Yes, it's actually someone and not something," Nitya said. She hoped that he would be more forthcoming if she was the one conversing with him rather than Shiv. She was right. There weren't many instances for the old man to engage in a conversation with a smartly dressed attractive tourist.

"Someone?" the old man asked.

"Yes," Nitya said, handing him Avneesh's photograph. The old man went back to his desk to pick up his glasses, and then looked at the picture.

When he returned to the counter, he said, "Oh yes, this fellow again. I remember him. He was very strange."

"How so?"

"Well, it was because of the way he was behaving," the old man replied, handing the photograph back to Nitya. "He was in a hurry. He asked for two envelopes and when I gave them to him, he took them quickly, stuffed some papers inside both, and then quickly sealed them, wrote the addresses, and handed them back to me. He was in a tearing hurry. So much so that he handed me some money for the postage stamps, pleaded with me to ensure that the letters are mailed, and then left without taking his change."

"There must be so many people buying things at this post office. Why do you remember him?"

"Like I said, the fellow was very odd and in a hurry. I was about to close my counter and the office and leave for the day when he arrived. The letters seemed important to him, and I mailed them to the addresses. He never came back to collect his change."

"Was there anything else? I mean any other thing that was 'odd' as you say?"

"Well, come to think of it, he kept looking back. There was no one standing behind him, and I don't know why he kept looking back."

"Was someone following him?"

"I can't say. I didn't pay much heed to it. I thought he may have been worried about missing his train, but there wasn't a train for at least another half hour. I even told him that, but he just left the letters, gave me money, and disappeared. Very strange fellow."

"Was this next train for Delhi?"

"Old Delhi, yes," the old man replied lost in thought.

Shiv and Nitya looked at one another. They were convinced that someone was following Avneesh when he arrived at the station.

"Sir, you have been most helpful. Just one more question, when ma'am showed you the picture of this man, you said 'this fellow again.' Is there any reason for that?" Shiv asked.

"Ah, yes. It's because there was a police officer here earlier today asking the same questions."

Nitya turned to Shiv and said, "Shankar. I am sure it's him. Remember the letter says that a copy was sent to a police station in Old Delhi. That must have reached his desk."

"Perhaps," Shiv replied, as they both turned to look at the old man. They thanked him for his help and then slowly walked back to the exit to find Tilak and the car.

Shiv stopped on the way to pick up a few snacks at the tea stall just outside the entrance. Nitya was walking ahead of him and had already reached the car. She gave the address of the guesthouse to Tilak. Their next stop was going to be the address on the letter that Avneesh had mentioned. They had decided to locate it and slowly drive past it. They didn't want to arouse any suspicions. Any attempt to approach the residents at the address could jeopardize what Avneesh had mentioned could be happening later that night. It could also be potentially dangerous given what this gang had already done during the riots. When Shiv got back, he handed the bag of snacks to Tilak. Tilak thanked him profusely. He had also got three cups of tea in small disposable earthen cups, a common sight at railway stations throughout the country. They decided to take a break, have their tea, and then continue.

While sipping tea, Shiv asked Nitya, "ma'am, do you think we should try calling Shankar again when we reach the guesthouse?"

"Yes, but if he is here, then we won't be able to reach him."

"Maybe his station can give you a local contact number?"

"I am wary of doing that. You see, if someone inside the police department is involved, Shankar may not have told everyone there about this investigation."

"True, I guess it rules out involving the local police here as well."

"Yes, for now, but as we discussed earlier, if we see something fishy tonight during our stakeout, then we drive to the nearest police station right away, report it, and have them take a look."

"Yes, that makes sense."

"Shiv, I don't want you to do anything foolish tonight. We stay in the car at a safe distance. We don't engage anyone at this address, and if things look bad, the police will have to deal with them. Is that understood?"

"Yes, ma'am."

"Good," Nitya said, finishing her tea, and walked over to the nearest trash can to throw her cup.

Shiv and Tilak did the same, and soon they were on their way from the station to the address Avneesh had mentioned in his letter. It happened to be on the other side of town. While Tilak made his way through the neighborhoods, both

Nitya and Shiv looked out the window. They rolled up their windows to keep out the cool evening breeze. The address was in a remote part of town in an industrial area in the outskirts of the city. The street was lined with what seemed to be warehouses and factories belonging to different companies. Tilak slowly drove past each of them. They were all separated by fences and boundary walls and were all gated compounds with a small path or road leading up to the building.

Once they reached the address, Tilak slowed down so that Nitya and Shiv could catch a glimpse of the compound. There was a big iron gate that was shut. On each side were two small makeshift huts that looked like guardhouses. They could see a few private security guards in uniform chatting with one another. Behind the gates was a path lined with trees on either side leading up to a building that looked like a large factory. It looked run-down and they could see two trucks parked on one side. There wasn't much more that was visible to them. When Tilak drove past the compound, they saw that the surrounding area looked similar. They saw a small makeshift tea stall and Shiv asked Nitya if Tilak or he could go and ask some of the customers about the building. Since that could arouse suspicion, they decided against it.

They noticed a small lane past the gates on the opposite side of the road. It seemed to be leading to a residential neighborhood a bit further out. When Tilak turned into the lane, he stopped momentarily, so that they could look around. The gate to the compound was visible. The main road was well-lit, but the lane wasn't. It could serve as a good vantage point for a stakeout. Any activity near the gate would be clearly visible, while at the same time, it would be difficult for anyone from the gates to see the lane due to poor lighting. They decided to make this their stakeout location for later that night. Nitya instructed Tilak to take them to the guesthouse that had been booked for them.

The guesthouse was in a lively part of town in a touristy area. It was an old summer house of one of the princely estates that had been converted into a guesthouse for travelers seeking long-term stays. Nitya and Shiv were the exceptions since they were staying only for one night or rather for a few hours. Their paper had a deal with the establishment. *The New India Courier*, like all businesses, had negotiated rates with some hotel and guesthouse chains all over India. As soon as they reached the guesthouse, Nitya instructed Tilak to eat something and get some rest for a few hours. They would be leaving around 10:00 p.m. That would also give Nitya and Shiv plenty of time to freshen up and get some dinner. Nitya headed to her room with a copy of the daily paper. She saw Shiv talking to the receptionist after he had checked in. She didn't catch the conversation, but she overheard something about a typewriter. She was too tired to turn around and ask. She headed to her room. She had asked Shiv to meet her at the lobby around nine for a quick dinner. There was no shortage of restaurants in the area.

After a shower and nap, Nitya decided to spend some time reading. Once she finished reading the paper, she started with one of the books she had bought along but hadn't had the time to start before. After half an hour, she glanced at her watch. It was time for dinner. Shiv was already there in the lobby, talking to one of the employees in the guesthouse. He stopped as soon as he saw Nitya and then walked up to her.

"There's a restaurant just outside the guest house on the opposite side of the road. We can go there if you want, ma'am."

"Sure. Is that what he suggested?" Nitya asked, looking toward the gentleman Shiv was talking to.

"Yes."

"What kind of restaurant?"

"Mostly Indian fast food, if that's fine with you."

"Yes, I am fine with that. Maybe we should check with Tilak?"

"I already did. He has had his dinner and said he is going to meet us here at ten."

"That's good. Alright, let's go. We will have to make this quick."

"Yes, ma'am."

The restaurant was almost full, mostly with tourists from nearby hotels. The service was quick, and the food seemed better than usual, probably because they were both hungry. They ate in silence, and Shiv quickly ordered some ice cream for Nitya and himself. It amused Nitya that he didn't even ask her whether she wanted one or which flavor she liked. He just went ahead and got her the same one that he got for himself. They spoke briefly about their experiences at *The New India Courier*. Nitya was careful not to ask him about his arguments with other journalists. She knew that Shiv had had several run-ins with senior reporters. She could sense that he was careful not to complain about anyone. In fact, she was surprised that he had a good opinion of most people, even some who had given him a bad rap.

In the limited time she had spent with him, she could understand why Shiv got into spats. He was prone to saying the wrong thing at the wrong time. He could come across as arrogant and his off-the-cuff remarks could easily be misunderstood. At the same time, he had the makings of a good reporter. After they finished their meal, they headed back to the guesthouse. It had started drizzling and the skies that were clear until evening suddenly looked ominous. Once they reached the lobby, Shiv turned to Nitya.

"I have to go to the room and pick up the camera."

"Sure," Nitya said.

While waiting for Shiv, Nitya looked at a large map on the wall behind one of the counters in the lobby. She could spot the location of the guesthouse. Then she looked at the main avenues that were clearly marked and the local police station that was a few blocks away from the railway station that they had visited earlier in the day. Then she started looking for the road where the warehouse was located.

"Anything interesting, ma'am?" Shiv asked, surprising Nitya who quickly turned around.

"Yes, take a look at this," Nitya said pointing to the road.

"That's where we are going."

"Yes. What do you think?"

Shiv surveyed the map carefully before replying. "It seems to be far away from the police station and near highways leaving the town."

"That's right."

"From Avneesh's letter, it seems that something will either be arriving or leaving this location tonight. At least that's my guess."

"Yes, we did see a couple of trucks, but we can't really be sure until we see what's going on."

"Right, ma'am."

Nitya headed toward the reception and informed them that they would be back late. The receptionist told her that there would be some guards at the front gate, even late at night and that it would be open. Tilak seemed well-rested, and they were soon on their way to their stakeout location. The city looked completely different at night. The main streets were filled with cars, but the side lanes and the neighboring streets were mostly empty. Although the main avenues criss-crossing the town were well-lit, the smaller streets and lanes were completely dark. The rain had picked up and they could see some lightning further up. The visibility was still good, but they knew it would be a challenge if it started raining more heavily.

Once they reached their destination, they slowly drove past the compound. The main street was well-illuminated and was not very busy. The lights inside the compound were switched off and they couldn't see anything past the gate as their car slowly drove by. The number of guards at the gate had increased. The tea stall across the compound was now closed. They slowly turned into the lane and then, after a mile or so, Tilak did a U-turn and headed back toward the intersection. He parked the car behind some hedges from where they could get a clear view of the gates. The lane was completely dark. They waited in silence, listening to the rain falling on the roof of the car. The cold night made it easier to wait. At the same time, it was difficult to wait in complete silence and in the dark. They could see some pedestrians and cyclists on the road and the occasional lorry or car. No one seemed to be entering the lane, and that was a good sign. The incessant rain was making it harder to stay focused on the gate, which was a few hundred yards away. A noise behind them made Shiv look back down the lane leading to the residential area to see if there was anyone there. The lane where they had parked their car was a narrow dirt road, and it didn't seem like it was used much, especially at this hour. They could see some shadows through the rain and assumed that they were pedestrians on their way home. They were wrong.

Revelation

Nitya could sense that Tilak was getting restless, and he hinted that he wanted to step outside, but she stopped him. She could also see that Shiv was fidgety and was constantly looking back through the rear window, and that bothered her. He whispered to Nitya that there was someone a few yards behind the car. She looked back and could see some shadows. It didn't seem like they were approaching the car. She told him to ignore it, but he couldn't. The rain had subsided, and they now had a clearer view of the gates. It was nearly eleven, and they kept their gaze focused on the activity outside the compound.

Suddenly, they were startled by a gentle tapping on Nitya's window. Someone with a flashlight was standing outside in a raincoat and a cap. He turned the small flashlight on his own face. It was Shankar. He gestured to Nitya to slowly roll down her window. Then he whispered and told her to ask Tilak to move the car toward another small path a few hundred yards away, without switching on the headlights. He said he would explain later. Nitya asked Tilak to comply. Then Shankar quickly disappeared behind the hedges. Tilak deftly moved the car back onto the lane and then onto the small path that was almost invisible to passersby. He was guided by another man in a raincoat who was carrying a small flashlight.

Tilak parked the car on one side of the narrow path. The man who was giving him directions told them he was with Shankar and politely asked them to step out. He then led them on the grassy path toward what looked like a makeshift hut and a tent. It seemed completely dark from the outside. He pointed to the large tent. Once they made their way inside, they saw many policemen waiting in complete silence. There was only one small lantern at the far end of the tent. The gentleman who had ushered them in told them to sit on one of the empty wooden benches and informed them that Shankar would come to talk to them soon. After a few minutes, Shankar entered the tent. He briefly spoke to another officer in whispers and nodded to the policemen who were sitting inside. It seemed to be some sort of a cue that they had been waiting for. They all were immediately on their feet with their rifles ready and quietly exited the tent leaving only Shankar, Nitya, Shiv, and Tilak inside.

"What's going on?" Nitya asked Shankar. He looked at all of them before replying. Shiv and Tilak had moved to the side of the tent that was near the exit. Nitya and Shankar were sitting toward the center. It was evident that Nitya wanted some answers.

"I am guessing you are here because you received one of these?" Shankar said, reaching into his pocket and bringing out the letter that he had received from Avneesh.

"Yes, Avneesh's wife got one and shared it with us. She gave it to me earlier today," Nitya replied.

"Well, it seems Avneesh sent one to the police, too, and luckily it landed on my desk at the right time. Had it been a day later, we would have missed all this," Shankar said pointing outside the tent.

"What's all this supposed to be?"

"We are here for the same reason you are. We have multiple officers and constables in and around the compound and have been surveilling the area since morning. I am sorry, Nitya, but I couldn't have you park your car in the lane and risk exposure as that would have botched up our investigation."

"We were out of sight, and I am going to head back there unless you tell me what you think is going on here tonight," Nitya said sternly, somewhat peeved at Shankar's assertion.

"I am sorry. That didn't come out right," Shankar said apologetically. Nitya could see that he was genuinely sorry.

"That's alright, but why aren't we outside? We have done a lot of work up until this point and would like to know what's happening tonight."

"Alright, what do you know so far? I will try to explain the rest. I can't tell you everything about the investigation, but you do have a right to know what will happen here tonight."

Nitya turned to Shiv, who was trying to peek outside the tent to see if he could make out any sort of activity. When he turned back at Nitya, he took her cue and slowly explained to Shankar everything that they had learned about Avneesh. Shankar listened to him without interrupting. When he finished, Shankar slowly reached into one of the files he was carrying and took out a piece of paper. He then turned to both Nitya and Shiv.

"What you have learned so far about Avneesh is fairly accurate. As I mentioned, I cannot tell you everything about the ongoing investigation. What I can tell you is that he was killed because of what he had uncovered about the gang, which he had been duped into joining. He was heading back with some evidence. Unfortunately, we don't know what that was, as he was killed, his remains cremated, and most likely all evidence destroyed."

Nitya was still agitated because Shankar had brought them here and because they were unable to see what was happening near the compound.

"Shankar, you still haven't answered my question. What is it that you are expecting here? If you won't give me all the details, then we may as well be outside trying to figure out what's happening near the gate."

"Yes, Nitya we will take you close to the compound as soon as there is any movement. I don't think you realize how much of a danger you are in. We are dealing with a deadly gang. They have killed before and will not hesitate to do it again. I promise you that as soon as there is movement near the gate, we will go there, and you can be present when we nab them."

"What are you expecting?" Nitya asked.

"Here's what I can tell you. We have placed several people under surveillance in many locations in Delhi and Dehradun as part of this investigation. Some of them may be directly connected to Avneesh's death. Others are part of a much larger plot, the details of which we are still trying to figure out."

"So, you are expecting people to show up at this time?"

"Either that or a convoy of trucks might be leaving this location with cargo that they want to hide, which they received from Delhi a few days back."

"From Haus Khaz, sir?" Shiv asked.

"Yes," Shankar nodded.

"And what's in this cargo?" Nitya asked.

"Initially we thought it might be drugs. Now it seems that it is probably illegal arms and ammunitions that are being sent to insurgents in the northern states, most likely Kashmir, but I am not sure. We will only come to know when we have nabbed and interrogated them," Shankar replied.

"If you know or suspect anyone, why don't you raid the premises? You seem to have enough to justify that," Nitya said.

"Yes, that we do. However, I think if we wait, we will see some people arriving here or leaving from here. Some of them may be the masterminds behind this. I want to cast as wide a net as possible and catch as many people as possible."

"And you want to catch the people within your force who may have gone rogue, sir?" Shiv asked softly.

"Yes," Shankar replied. He looked at Shiv and said, "it's impressive what you have managed to figure out so far. I have had the advantage of the police force, surveillance, and research done by the police and other agencies. You have done well alone. And you are right. We had to keep things close to our chest and involve as few people as possible. The CBI has these rogue elements under surveillance, and you might actually see them tonight."

"So, you won't stop us from reporting any of this? Not that I'd agree, but …" Nitya said, and Shankar interrupted her right away.

"My reason for moving you from the stakeout location was to ensure that the people inside the compound don't get suspicious and of course, to ensure your safety. You will get to see what happens tonight and it is definitely not my intention to tell you what to write. That really isn't my job," Shankar said, stepping toward the exit of the tent and taking a peek outside. He glanced at his watch. It was now close to midnight. A constable came in and whispered something in his ear.

"I am happy to hear that, Shankar," Nitya said sounding relieved. "For a moment, I thought you would do everything to stop us from seeing what's happening and put a lid on this entire thing under the guise and pretense of national security."

Nitya wasn't sure whether Shankar heard all that she said. Another constable came in and whispered something in Shankar's ear and left in a hurry. Shankar turned to Tilak, Nitya, and Shiv.

"There is movement at the gate. It seems it is opening, and a few trucks are getting ready to leave," Shankar said. "I will be getting into my jeep and following them along with other police vehicles. We have people manning different checkpoints in the city. You can follow us, and then once we nab them, you can report it. As I said before, you can report what you see and of course, what you have learned about Avneesh."

Shiv quickly grabbed his notebook and camera. Tilak got up and Shankar told him to slowly make his way and to wait in the car. After a couple of minutes, there was a flurry of activities. A constable came in again and whispered something to Shankar. He quickly left the tent and asked Nitya and Shiv to follow him. As soon as they got out, they saw several police jeeps and vans parked near the tent and hut. These had not been visible in the dark when they first came in. Now the lights were on. There was a huge roar of all the police vehicles hitting their ignition. Shankar had already disappeared into one of the jeeps in the front and it was already on its way. A constable came and told Nitya that they could follow the police convoy in their car, but from a safe distance. Tilak was ready, so they quickly got in their car, and were on their way. They could see the jeeps with their sirens ahead of them. There was also a police van in front of them.

Nitya marveled at the speed with which the police started the chase. Shankar had told them that there were other officers stationed at checkpoints that would intercept the trucks. The roads were nearly empty at this hour. The noise of the trucks and police vehicles with the sirens was deafening. Tilak was having a hard time keeping up. Nitya and Shiv were on the edge of their seats, holding on tightly to protect themselves from any sudden bumps along the way. The chase did not last long. After a few miles, the trucks were completely surrounded by police vehicles. The police guided them to an open area on the side of one of the highways to a field that was used as a makeshift truck stop. Tilak parked his car behind a police van. A constable quickly came up to them and told them to wait inside the car till police had secured the area and apprehended everyone. It didn't take long. After fifteen minutes, they were told that they could go and meet Shankar.

Nitya and Shiv slowly stepped out of the car and walked toward the front of the row of vehicles and trucks. Some constables were already inside inspecting the cargo and some were in the process of unloading the trucks. There were big wooden crates and lots of boxes. The police had formed a circle in the middle of the field, and inside it were all the gang members in handcuffs. During the chase, some trucks had driven off the road and fallen into a ditch. Shankar and the other officers were busy taking an inventory of the cargo. Some constables had started roughing up the members of the gang and questioning them. After a few minutes, Shankar walked up to Nitya and Shiv.

"This went off better than expected. I wish all our stakeouts and chases ended this way," Shankar said, and for the first time, he was smiling.

"All good then?" Nitya asked.

"Yes, for now. We were right. We caught some of the leaders too. It was worth the wait."

"Where are they?"

"Over there," Shankar said, pointing to the circle where all of them were now on their knees with their hands tied behind them.

"Did you get the rogue officer who the CBI had placed under surveillance?"

"Yes, he is here too."

Shiv quickly stepped up and asked, "can I take some pictures of the cargo and the men who were apprehended?"

"Yes, it should be fine now," Shankar said, as Shiv quickly walked over with his camera and started taking pictures. Nitya turned to Shankar.

"So, what's in the cargo?"

"Illegal arms and ammunition."

"And who is the rogue element that you captured?"

"You will see his photograph. You may have seen him before. He is the one in the middle of the circle crying profusely," Shankar said pointing again to the suspects huddled in the field. Nitya could not see their faces clearly from afar. She could make out that they were all sullen and silent. There was a man in the middle who was visibly shaken and crying. It was a chilly night, but he was sweating profusely. From this distance, she couldn't recognize the face, but it wouldn't take long for them to find the identity of the person.

"Avneesh might have been carrying back details about the cargo," Nitya said.

"That would be my guess. He probably had files and other details that he had taken from the warehouse. I don't think he realized that he was being followed. I think he had a hunch when he got to the station, so he quickly mailed the letters to his wife and to us and planned to travel to Delhi with the rest of the evidence. He was most likely killed near the railway station in Dehradun."

"Do you know what happened after that?"

"I can guess, and this is totally off the record. I think the people who killed him put his body in a large rice bag and dumped it in the cargo compartment of the train leaving for Old Delhi."

"He was killed before any of the other victims. Then that's what the missing postmortem report would have said."

"Yes, that's what the doctor at the hospital in Delhi told me. I also suspect that the people who killed him didn't know that he had evidence on him. That's why when the train reached Delhi, they tried to quickly burn and dump his body. They botched that up and weren't sure whether all the evidence had been destroyed. That's why they returned to the hospital to take his body away."

"The police must have been in on it or else they wouldn't have been able to take his body out of the hospital or even take his family to the crematorium at night in the middle of the riot."

"That's right. I can't be entirely sure, but I think that's what happened. There are still a few holes, and I will be able to get to the bottom of it once we have been able to question everyone."

"So, I can't quote you on all this yet?"

"Not at the moment, but that's what I think happened. Tell me something. I wanted to ask you when we were in the tent but didn't get a chance. When you got this letter, why didn't you go to the police here or in Delhi?"

"Well, for one, we didn't know what this was all about. I tried calling you at your station in Kotwali, but you had left, and no one was telling us when you'd be back. When we got here, we didn't want to involve the local police. From what we know, it's clear that maybe one or even a few people in the force may have gone rogue. That's why we didn't want to risk asking too many questions because we didn't know whom we could trust."

"Well, all I can say is that you did the right thing. We have reason to believe that Avneesh tried to engage the police here when he came to know what was going on, but he didn't get much help. It is possible that it might have been an oversight or that someone here is involved as well. The personnel that we used for the operation tonight are all from out of state. So that should tell you something."

"And his letter connected the dots as far as the gang and cargo were concerned."

"Yes, Avneesh's letter helped us with all the missing details that we needed to unravel this conspiracy and of course, to some extent solve his own murder. It gives us the motive. Now, we are only missing some details that I'm sure we will be able to get once we start questioning these people."

"His family has a right to know what happened to him."

"They will. I will visit them in a few days and explain what happened. I am sure you and Shiv plan to visit them, too, right?"

"Yes, we will, tomorrow. We will write about what went down here and what we know about what happened to Avneesh. It will be in the papers the day after. Are you going to make all this public just yet?"

"No. I still have to question these people. We also must find out where the trucks were headed and inform the local police there to carry out some raids. We are not making any press releases just yet. Maybe later in the week. But that doesn't mean that I am stopping you from writing about what happened here tonight or what you and Shiv have learned about Avneesh so far."

"Yes, his story needs to be told. His family needs to know. What happened to him was tragic and horrific. The way they murdered him and tried to dispose of him is sickening."

"Yes, it makes me very angry too," Shankar said.

"I am guessing you won't be going back to Delhi today," Nitya said.

"No, I will be here for a couple of days," Shankar said, as they saw Shiv talking to some constables. He was out of earshot. Shankar continued, "I want to thank you for heeding my advice to move the car. I had no intention of stopping you from doing what you came here to do. I hope you know that."

"I know, Shankar. I agreed because it was you. Nasty business, all this. I am so glad you nabbed them."

"And to think they almost got away with it," Shankar said solemnly.

"Well, they didn't know they were up against an intelligent police officer and a pesky young reporter who question everything," Nitya said with a smile.

"Thank you, I am sure any other officer would have done the same."

"I am not so sure."

"And by the pesky young fellow, you mean Shiv?"

"Yes."

"What happened? I am guessing you changed your mind about him."

"Yes, I have. He is a strange one, much like you," Nitya said with a smile.

"Well, I must get going now. Are you staying the night in Dehradun?"

"Unfortunately, I can't. We will have to drive back to Delhi in a few hours. You know we are in a competitive business. We need to get the story out as soon as possible before any other papers do. Plus, my sister is arriving from Bombay tomorrow. I have to be there to receive her."

"Alright, I will leave you to it then. Good night Nitya. We will catch up in Delhi. Have a safe trip back."

"Good night, Shankar, and thank you," Nitya said as they shook hands. Shankar walked back to where the rest of the officers were. He stopped briefly to have a chat with Shiv. Nitya saw them shaking hands. Shiv walked up to Nitya, excited. He had already finished a few rolls on his camera and was making sure everything was neatly packed away.

"Are we done here, ma'am?"

"I think so. Did you take all the photos you needed?"

"Yes, ma'am. You won't believe the cache of arms that they retrieved from the trucks. There were hand grenades, rifles …" Shiv wanted to ramble on, but Nitya raised her arm to stop him.

"We have a long journey back and you can tell me all about it then," she said with a smile.

"Yes, ma'am."

They got back into the car and headed back to the guesthouse. Nitya quickly told Shiv what Shankar had told her off the records. They could print what they had learned tonight from the raid and any related information. They already had a good story on Avneesh and they had more than enough to write the truth about how brave he was. Nitya told Tilak and Shiv that they would be heading back to Delhi in an hour. It was already 2:00 a.m. They freshened up at the guesthouse, packed their belongings, and got ready to leave.

Nitya called Manoj at home and let him know what had happened. He was still awake and was thrilled to hear all the details. This had the potential of being very good for the paper both in terms of business and reputation. Time was of the essence. Nitya enquired whether Manoj would want something ready for today's paper, but Manoj decided against it. He told her to work on the articles on the raid and on Avneesh so that they could be reviewed and printed the following day. After speaking about their plans for the next day, Nitya headed to the lobby to checkout. Shiv had already checked out and was chatting with Tilak near the car. Nitya told Shiv about her call with Manoj.

"I will give you all the details during our drive back."

"Sure, ma'am."

"There's something else. He told me that the office had called him at home to let him know that your brother had called from Bangalore and was trying to reach you."

"Oh," Shiv said with a worried look on his face. "Did he say what it was about?"

"No. He only had the message that your brother is trying to reach you."

"Hmm," Shiv said softly.

"Do you want to call him from the guesthouse?" Nitya asked. She could see Shiv was wrestling to decide what to do.

"No, it's fine, ma'am," he said composing himself. "I will call him when I reach Delhi. In any case, I can't do anything from here."

"Are you sure?"

"Yes, ma'am."

Once they were both settled in, Nitya told Shiv about her conversation with Manoj. The drafts had to be ready in the morning for the senior team to review and for Manoj's approval. They also had to visit the Trivedi residence not only to tell them what happened to Avneesh, but also to see if they were fine with what they were going to publish about him. They didn't foresee too many objections. Avneesh had been duped into joining the gang assuming that he was joining a security agency involved in fighting insurgents. When he joined, he was convinced that he was doing something important for the security of the country. Once he realized that he had been cheated, he tried to do the right thing by contacting the local police. That didn't work and made things worse. Then he collected evidence and tried to bring it back to Delhi to expose the gang, and in the process, he got killed.

The car was speeding along smoothly on the near-empty highways since it was late at night and the roads were empty. They were already in the outskirts of the city and could see the fading lights of the houses far on the horizon. After Nitya and Shiv reviewed what had happened, Shiv opened a folder and handed over a few pages to her.

"What's this?"

"I had them bring a typewriter to my room, and I typed up a very rough first draft."

"Wow, that was fast work."

"Thank you, ma'am," Shiv replied, pleased with himself.

It was difficult to read in the dark, but Nitya still made the effort to read portions of it. She promised to look as soon as there was some daylight. The day's events had left them both exhausted. They hadn't had a moment to rest. The cold air and the drive made them sleepy. They leaned against the windows on their sides and dozed off. When Nitya woke up, the horizon was showing signs of daylight. She picked up Shiv's report again. It was well-written for a first draft. She knew he wrote well. Though it wasn't concise, and required some editing, it had all the relevant details. She quickly marked up some changes she wanted in it and edited some of the sentences. Shiv had included everyone in the credits section at the end. That pleased Nitya immensely. She reread the report, marked up a few more things, and then placed it back in the folder.

She glanced sideways at Shiv. He was fast asleep with his head against the window. She softly asked Tilak if he needed a break, but he said he would need one only once they were in the outskirts of Delhi. She tried to take another nap but couldn't. After an hour or so, it was dawn, and the beautiful morning made the landscape outside look like a painting. They had left the foothills of the Himalayas far behind and gone were the forests and parks. Now they were traveling through the plains with farms on either side of the road. Nitya could see the farmers slowly making their way to their fields on their tractors through the dusty roads. The sun was trying to make its presence felt on the horizon. In another hour everything was brighter, and they were in the outskirts of Delhi. Shiv had woken up and was discussing the changes that needed to be made to the article.

They stopped at a rest area with a few small roadside eateries and food stalls and decided to stretch their legs and get some tea. Nitya headed to one of the stalls that was selling newspapers and bought a couple of national dailies. Tilak and Shiv bought snacks and tea. When they returned to the car, Nitya handed Shiv a paper. They finished their tea and were back on the road again. When they reached Delhi, Nitya decided to get dropped off at home first and instructed Tilak to drop Shiv home after. They planned to get to the office in a couple of hours. It would give Tilak some time to rest as well. Nitya had already decided to let him off early, right after picking up Kavita. Despite his protests, she had insisted that he take the next day off.

In the car, Nitya and Shiv caught up with the daily news. Shiv scanned the headlines while Nitya read through one of the inside pages. Nitya noticed that Shiv's eyes were fixed on an article on the front page of his paper. He seemed serious and solemn. She gently turned to the front page to see what had caught Shiv's eye. It was a small news article in the top right corner. The daily that Nitya had picked up usually kept this section for late-breaking news items, just headlines with small snippets included at the last minute, without too many details. Usually, that meant any late-breaking news about law-and-order situations, sports results from other time zones, important deaths, or news of events that had just broken at the time of printing.

The article was about Sanjay Hegde, a well-known industrialist, who had passed away of a heart attack in the middle of the night. Hegde Enterprises was not among the largest but belonged to one of the most well-known business families in India. Although most of their businesses were in the south, they were expanding to the other regions. Nitya had read a few articles on their business interests and how they were trying to diversify from their traditional textile business into other areas such as food, mining, and hotels. She wondered why this article had brought about this strange expression on Shiv's face. She read it again and then looked at Shiv. He had tears in his eyes.

"Shiv, what's going on?"

"Ma'am ...," he said pointing to the article in the paper. "Sanjay Hegde was my father. I am Shiv Kumar Hegde."

"Oh my God, I am so sorry, Shiv," Nitya said, shocked and trying to comfort him.

"I am sorry, I haven't told anyone."

"That's alright. You don't have anything to apologize for. Do you want me to take you home now? I can make arrangements for you to be in Bangalore."

"That's alright, ma'am. Can you please drop me off at an address in Jor Bagh? It's in central Delhi and should be on the way."

"Absolutely. Are you sure we can't help you more?"

"I am sure, ma'am, thank you," Shiv said, as he gave Tilak the address.

Nitya felt extremely sorry and helpless at the same time. She was also surprised to hear that Shiv belonged to the Hegde family. In another half hour, the car slowly turned onto a beautiful leafy street in Jor Bagh, one of the most upscale localities in New Delhi. The address was that of a guesthouse belonging to Hegde Enterprises. As they turned toward the building, they could see the majestic gates. There were many cars parked inside and outside. The gates were closed, and when Tilak tried to enter, some security guards immediately came over to inspect the car. Shiv rolled down his window, and they recognized him right away. They didn't ask any more questions and quickly opened the gate. Tilak drove past the lawns on either side to a large bungalow. There were quite a few people outside. Once Shiv stepped out of the car, they all rushed to him. He greeted all of them and slowly walked inside. An elderly gentleman escorted Nitya and Tilak inside and asked them to sit in a beautifully decorated drawing-room. Another gentleman brought them some refreshments. There were many people in the room, and they all seemed to be waiting. A few minutes later, Shiv came in. He walked past the other guests toward Nitya. He seemed more composed now and looked different somehow.

"As you can understand, ma'am, I have to head to Bangalore right away. The folks here have already made the arrangements."

"Of course, Shiv, I understand. Take all the time you need, and please accept my condolences."

"Thank you, ma'am. I don't think I will be able to come back to the paper," Shiv said softly. Nitya could sense the sadness in his voice. She understood. With his father's death, the responsibility of running the enterprise would be thrust on him and his siblings. Coming back to work at *The New India Courier* seemed far-fetched. Shiv slowly walked Nitya and Tilak back to the car. He asked the gentlemen who seemed to have formed a coterie around him to stay inside. Nitya noticed that Shiv suddenly looked older. But despite his sadness, he still managed a smile.

"I want to thank you both for everything."

There was nothing to more say. Nitya felt a sudden urge to give him a hug. She probably would have had it not been for the probing eyes of all the people behind Shiv. So, they shook hands instead. Tilak turned the car around and left through the gates. Nitya turned to look back and saw Shiv give her a final wave and then slowly walk back to the group of people waiting for him inside.

* * *

After the eventful trip to Dehradun, Nitya was exhausted when she reached her apartment. She wondered how she would break the news about Shiv to the rest of her team and her colleagues. She called the railway station to find out when Kavita's train would be arriving. She had plenty of time to shower and take a short nap before heading to work. She decided to drop by the Trivedi residence after her meeting with Manoj. Avneesh's family had a right to know what had happened to him and she wanted to give them a gist of what the paper was going to print the next day. She had dozed off, but her nap was interrupted by the arrival of her part-time help. Nitya gave her instructions on what she wanted prepared and ready for the evening. Tilak had also taken some time to freshen up and get a quick breakfast. On the way to the office, Nitya informed him that she would be going to Old Delhi and then to the railway station to pick up Kavita. It would be a short day and she would let him go early to get some sleep after an exhausting two days.

By the time she arrived at work, Manoj had already briefed her team about what Nitya had told him over the phone. They were excited to get a first-hand account from her. She relayed everything about her trip to Dehradun. They all knew that the article appearing the next day would be an exclusive that had uncovered the conspiracy behind not only Avneesh's murder but also the riots themselves. Nitya reminded them to be tight-lipped about it until the article was printed the following day. Her team was only too happy to comply.

Then she broke the news about Shiv. Her team was shocked not only to hear about Shiv's father's death but also to learn about his background. It was also abundantly clear that there was little chance that Shiv would be returning to the paper. They all decided to send him their condolences, and Nitya promised to get in touch with him in Bangalore and convey their messages. Nitya looked at her watch. There was still some time before her meeting with Manoj. Their article was going to be an important one, an exclusive that would be the talk of the town for a few days. Manoj had decided to assemble the entire senior management team so that Nitya could give them a short update and presentation.

During the next hour, Nitya went over the article that Shiv had written. There was nothing missing. He had provided all the relevant details that would be of interest to the readers. The article focused on the facts and what they had discovered during their investigation. It was careful not to portray the police or security agencies in a negative light. At the same time, it clearly mentioned the involvement of rogue elements within those agencies and the attempt to cover up the murder of Avneesh Trivedi. It also lauded the investigative efforts of the police officers in finding out the truth. After making some cosmetic changes to the draft, she asked one of the secretaries to type up a few copies. Once they were ready, she took them to the conference room and handed them out.

As she outlined what they had uncovered, she could see the admiration on the faces of most of her colleagues. She answered all their questions. Manoj was happy to see the work that her team had done. The entire management team was ecstatic that the article would be an "exclusive" and all the other papers, in their reporting, would have to refer to it. After their meeting with the senior management team, Manoj asked her to join him in his office for a quick chat. Once they were in his office, he looked over the article one more time and marked a few minor changes. He had a smile on his face. He was visibly impressed. He handed the article back to Nitya and gave his enthusiastic nod of approval to send it to the printing press for the next morning's paper. He was also surprised to hear about Shiv. It seemed Shiv had applied for the job like everyone else and hadn't used any family connections or influence. Manoj was convinced that if Shiv indeed took up a position in the family enterprise, he was unlikely to return. Before leaving, Manoj informed Nitya that after the publication of the article the following day, he would be personally thanking the rest of her team for doing a great job on the project that they had been assigned. It was now time for Nitya to head over to Old Delhi and meet the Trivedis.

* * *

The drive to Old Delhi seemed different this time around. Nitya finally had some answers for the victim's family. As Tilak veered the car into the narrow lanes of the walled city, she could see the hustle and bustle of the crowds. She asked him to stop at a convenient location and decided to walk the rest of the short distance to the Trivedi residence. As she walked through the congested lanes, she recalled her many conversations with Shankar about this part of town. Old Delhi was a great place to visit and appealing to outsiders who came for short trips. But those who lived and worked there would probably move in a heartbeat if they had the means to do so. She hoped that cracking the case and uncovering the conspiracy would help Shankar in his career and that he would finally be able to get transferred out of this part of town to a better location.

Once she reached the Trivedi house, she gently knocked on the old wooden door. After a few minutes, Avneesh's mother opened the door and let her in. Once she made her way inside to the small courtyard where the rest of the family was gathered, they quickly got her a chair and offered her some tea. Apart from Avneesh's parents, his sister and Madhavi were there too.

After exchanging a few pleasantries, Nitya explained what she had learned about Avneesh. She didn't leave anything out. Her captive audience gave her all the time that she needed and didn't interrupt her during her monologue. She could see the shifting emotions in the expressions on their faces as she recited the chain of events. There was fear, anger, shame, and pride, and then just sadness. Once Nitya finished, they all had a lot of questions for her. She answered them patiently. They thanked her profusely and informed her that Shankar had sent over Avneesh's death certificate and a copy of the report from the hospital. Once they finished their tea, Nitya brought out a copy of the article that was going to be published the next day and handed it over to Madhavi. She started reading it aloud, and once she had finished, she could see Avneesh's parents crying. They had no objections to the article being published. His sister informed Nitya that she was going to take her parents to a nearby temple for a puja, but Madhavi would stay back. Nitya could sense that Madhavi wanted to speak with her in private. Before leaving, Avneesh's parents and sister hugged Nitya and thanked her again. While the answers of what happened to Avneesh had certainly helped, it could never take away their sadness of losing him.

Once they left, Nitya was alone with Madhavi. She was also in an emotional state but gradually recovered some of her composure. Nitya sat across from her quietly until Madhavi spoke.

"What you did today, ma'am, really helped us. We were completely in the dark about what had happened. Now we know, and tomorrow everyone else will know."

"Yes, they will," Nitya said softly in an understanding tone.

"The policeman who visited us was nice too. He helped us get the death certificate and report from the hospital and that will help with a lot of the formalities."

"You mean, Shankar?"

"Yes, ma'am."

"Yes, he is a good officer. You shouldn't hesitate to contact him if you need help. Or me for that matter if I can assist in any way."

"You already have, ma'am."

"I am glad you feel that way. I wish I could take all the credit, but it wasn't really me. It was mostly Shiv; you know the one who was working this case with me."

"I know," Madhavi said softly with tears in her eyes. "Where is Shiv? He didn't come with you."

"No, actually he couldn't. I am sure he wanted to come, but …"

"But his father passed away. I read in the newspaper," Madhavi said before Nitya could finish her sentence. Nitya was stunned.

"So, you know Shiv?" Nitya asked, still shocked.

"Yes, ma'am. I know him. I don't know if he ever told you, but we were in college together. We were close friends, and we were in love. Knowing him, he probably wouldn't have told you unless you asked."

"He didn't," Nitya said softly. Suddenly, a lot of things made sense to Nitya - the promise that Shiv had made to the family to get to the truth, the ease with which Madhavi spoke to Shiv, and her desire to reach out to him each time she wanted to convey new information. Nitya could see that Madhavi was having a hard time keeping back her tears.

"I didn't do right by him. We wanted to be together. I knew my family would not agree, but I still couldn't let him go. When I broke it off, I know he was heartbroken. There wasn't much that I could do. Life took us in different directions. I moved on with my life and was happy with Avneesh, but it did bother me that I didn't do right by him."

"I understand. It is more complicated for girls. For what it's worth, Shiv doesn't blame you for anything. He didn't mention you by name but when he talked about his past, he spoke of you fondly and with affection."

"That somehow makes it worse, doesn't it?"

"Yes, perhaps."

"I hadn't seen him since we broke up and then that day, he walked in with you and I couldn't say anything. Neither could he."

"I understand."

"I guess he is not going to be back."

"It's unlikely that he will come back at the paper."

"I wish I could tell him how sorry I am for the way things turned out between us and how thankful I am for his role in finding out on what happened to Avneesh. For that, he deserves my gratitude. There isn't much else that I can give," Madhavi said in tears.

Nitya gently got up and moved her chair close to Madhavi and hugged her. She could only imagine how difficult it had been for Madhavi and the range of emotions that she was going through. She had a tough life ahead of her. She had to take care of Avneesh's family and raise her son. Life hadn't been fair to her, and Nitya couldn't help but feel for this young girl. After a few minutes, Madhavi composed herself. Nitya said to her, "if I hear from Shiv, I will let him know how thankful you are."

"Please also convey my condolences."

"I will."

Madhavi then pointed to the article that would be printed the following morning and said, "this will certainly help us. Hopefully, it will mean some sort of closure for my in-laws as well. They are good people, you know."

"You will reach out to me if you need help, won't you?" Nitya asked.

"I will, ma'am," Madhavi replied, now much calmer. "I have a lot on my plate, but I have help too. My parents are nearby, and so is my sister. My sister-in-law will be moving back to Delhi, and she is very helpful."

"That's good. Well, I must leave now. My sister is coming from Bombay. I must get to the station on time. Otherwise, I won't hear the end of it. You know how younger sisters are."

"Oh, I know, ma'am," Madhavi said, managing a smile.

"There is one more thing that I want to tell you. In the aftermath of this article, you will most likely get a few calls from other reporters. If you think things are getting out of hand or they are infringing on your privacy in any way, as I know some of our kind sometimes do, please don't hesitate to contact me. I can certainly help and so can Shankar."

"I understand, ma'am. Thank you, for everything."

Nitya got up, gave Madhavi a slight hug, and slowly walked toward the door leading into the lane. Once outside, she stopped and turned back. Madhavi was still standing in the doorway. She smiled and waved at her, and Nitya waved back. Once in the car, she checked her watch and asked Tilak to hurry. It was time to pick up Kavita from the station. She couldn't help but think of Madhavi and Shiv and how things had turned out for them.

When she reached the station, she quickly checked the board for the platform where Kavita's train would be arriving. She headed over to the platform and waited on one of the benches near a tea stall. The train arrived after a few minutes. Nitya quickly made her way to the middle of the platform to make sure she could spot Kavita when she alighted. She didn't have to wait long. Kavita spotted her first and waved at her from one end of the train. As Nitya made her way through the crowd of passengers, she could see her sister more clearly. Kavita looked older. *Probably because she is in a saree*, Nitya thought. But her face looked older. Her vivaciousness had been replaced by a certain sadness. Nitya quickly made her way through the crowd to Kavita. She saw all the luggage that Kavita had brought with her – a large trunk, three big suitcases, and a small bag. It was quite clear that Kavita was not visiting Nitya only for a few days. She was moving in with her for some time to come. As the sisters hugged, Kavita started crying inconsolably.

* * *

A series of articles were published on the riots in *The New India Courier*. They were the only ones to expose the truth about the conspiracy behind the murder of Avneesh Trivedi. The articles also laid bare the facts around the deaths of all the other victims and how the recent riots had been different from past ones. It also praised the police and Shankar's team. The involvement of rogue elements within the police and other investigative agencies had been a bombshell. It had led to the transfer of a number of high-ranking officials. The ongoing investigation had uncovered other criminals who had infiltrated the various organizations. Shankar's profile had improved. The transfer that he had requested and had been looking forward to finally came through.

Shankar's new role was a mixed blessing. It was a better profile but also a lot more responsibility and work. Ghanshyam Das had taken much of the credit for the decisions that led to the investigation of various agencies of the government. He was instrumental in ensuring that Shankar was in charge of the task force that was looking into the ongoing investigations in different parts of the ministry and other agencies. That had an immediate impact on Shankar's profile and workload. All the other agencies were only too keen to work with him and provide all the assistance he needed. It also meant overseeing a larger organization and even less time for his family. His transfer from the rundown, riot-prone Kotwali Police Station in Old Delhi to a spacious new office in a plush neighborhood in New Delhi hadn't resulted in any extra time for himself or his family. Rohini and Vikram decided to move back to Mussoorie to live with Shankar's in-laws. Vikram got enrolled in one of the schools there and Rohini planned to go back to being a teacher at the same school.

A few weeks after the article was published, Nitya received a neatly typed letter from the office of the new vice-president of Hegde Enterprises. It was addressed to the HR department at *The New India Courier* with a copy to Nitya. It was a formal resignation letter from Shiv Kumar Hegde. It also contained a nicely worded apology because Shiv was unable to serve out the notice period of one month. In lieu of it, there was a check for a month's salary made out to the paper. Also attached was a handwritten letter to Nitya. Shiv thanked Nitya personally for the opportunity that she had given him. He also mentioned kind words of appreciation for the rest of the team and sent cards for each of them. He mentioned that he had tried to call Nitya a few times but had been unsuccessful in getting through to her. This was mainly because Nitya had been busy at meetings and with Kavita.

As Nitya had guessed, Kavita's marriage had fallen apart. She had decided to move to Delhi to stay with Nitya rather than go home and be with her parents. Kavita was afraid that her mother would constantly be pressuring her to make things right with her husband, and she wasn't ready for that. In fact, from what Nitya could gather, the marriage was well past any sort of reconciliation.

Nitya had tried calling Shiv at the Hegde Enterprises number in Bangalore a couple of times but each time he had been busy, either tending to family obligations or in meetings. She later read in the papers that Shiv had left for an extended trip to the U.S. to pursue some business interests and was not scheduled to return for at least a few weeks.

* * *

By the end of March, the chill of the Delhi winter had subsided, and it started to get warmer. A lot had happened since the publication of the articles. It had propelled the reputation of the paper. The circulation had increased and so had the ad revenues. *The New India Courier* was quickly becoming a paper of repute and its increasing national presence meant that the management team had to be expanded. That worked out well for Nitya. Her team received a lot of accolades and nominations for awards. The paper's expansion meant that Nitya could hire more people on her team. That meant more work for her and more assignments from Manoj. It was a good problem to have and a challenge that Nitya was looking forward to.

Kavita had settled in well with her sister. Initially, she was extremely sad. It had been hard for her to come to terms with her failed marriage. But with Nitya's help, she had gradually come around. The sisters had broken the news to their parents. As expected, their mother's initial reaction was one of shock and disbelief. Eventually, it had given way to understanding and affection. Their parents visited Delhi for a long weekend and although their mother hadn't come to terms with Kavita's failed marriage, she understood that Kavita was unhappy and couldn't continue in the relationship any longer. Nitya was pleasantly surprised by her mother's show of affection and her understanding. Both sisters promised to visit their parents over the summer.

Kavita kept herself busy. She had found a part-time job in one of the new stores in Connaught Place near Nitya's office. That suited her well. Every now and then they could go out for a quick coffee and lunch in one of the many establishments in the area. At Nitya's insistence, Kavita enrolled herself in a course on hotel management at a nearby institute. Kavita had pursued hotel management before marriage but had given up midway after moving to Bombay. Nitya thought it best for her to pick up where she had left off.

Work and Kavita kept Nitya busy. She was enjoying her new role and liked having her sister around. She had also found some time to make some inroads in her social life. She met a professor at one of the many cultural functions she had to attend. One of her classmates from college had introduced him to her. They had gone out on a few dates and things looked promising. After what had happened with Vijay at work, Nitya was wary of getting involved with anyone from work or even from her own industry. The professor was closer to her age—in his late thirties—and had lived abroad after completing his PhD. He had been married to a foreigner before, but it hadn't worked out. Word was that after a messy divorce, he had decided to move back to India and had accepted a teaching position in one of the prestigious universities in Delhi. Their initial interactions had been pleasant, and Nitya enjoyed his company. His profile didn't check off many of the boxes that matchmakers in India or even her parents would approve of. She wondered if that's what made him more appealing. Most people who went abroad to study or work didn't move back to India in their thirties. Then there was of course the divorce. Urban India was slowly changing its mindset but marrying a foreigner and getting divorced was still frowned upon among the conservatives. Nitya was happy to move things slowly and sensed that the professor had the same mindset. She hadn't told her parents about him and had sworn Kavita into secrecy. Kavita was more than happy to oblige under the condition that her sister told her all the gory details of her love life.

When Nitya walked into the office on the Monday in the last week of March, she decided to quickly meet her team at their desks before heading upstairs to her office. They were all busy working away and some were on their phones. With new members joining the team, the floor looked busier than usual.

She quickly handed out some files that she had reviewed. Just before heading upstairs, she saw Swati and Moina waving at her. They were still on their phones, but Swati quickly hung up and turned to her.

"You have someone waiting in your office," she said with a smile. Nitya could see Moina smiling as well, although she was still on the phone. Before Nitya could ask who, Swati's phone started ringing and she had to take the call.

As she slowly headed upstairs, Nitya wondered who it could be. She had asked Kavita to meet her at work for coffee, but it was still early for her. The people at work had become accustomed to seeing her around. She wondered why Swati and Moina were smiling secretively and almost mischievously. She wondered if it was Shankar or the professor, but they would have warned her before coming and wouldn't spring such a surprise on her. When she reached her floor, through the open door she could see the back of the person. He was sitting across her desk in a suit. As she slowly walked down the long corridor leading up to her office, she realized it was Shiv. As soon as she entered the room, he got up and turned toward her.

Beaming with his unmistakable smile, he said, "good morning, ma'am."

"Good morning, Shiv. This is a pleasant surprise. Sit, sit, sit," Nitya said, as they both took a seat.

"I hope you don't mind that I came in and was waiting for you here."

"Oh my God, it's so nice to see you. Not at all Shiv. You are always welcome here."

"Thank you, ma'am."

"Well, you do look different in a suit and a bit older, I think."

"Yes, unfortunately, I have to wear a suit more often than I want to."

"Well, it looks good on you. Before we start chatting, would you like a coffee or tea or something?"

"No, ma'am, thank you. I am fine, really."

"So, what brings you to Delhi? I tried reaching you in Bangalore after you left and I know you called a few times, but we kept missing each other. Then I saw that you had left for the U.S. and there was no word when you would be back."

"Yes, that's right. It has been a hectic few weeks since my dad passed away. We were in the middle of many business deals. Right after completing the rituals, we had to get on with all the pending business. That's what kept us busy. I am really sorry. I should have made more of an effort to reach you, ma'am. I just couldn't."

"No, no Shiv, I got all the messages and I know you tried. Don't worry about it at all. I am sure it must have been a difficult and busy time for you after your father passed away."

"Yes, it has been. I just got back from the U.S. and am heading back to Bangalore in a few hours. I thought I'd drop by."

"I am glad you did. Did you meet the rest of the team?"

"Yes, I arrived a bit early and met them downstairs and had a coffee with them."

"That's good. Well, you know your article did rather well. The paper did well because of it and so did we as a team, and I must thank you for it."

"It was our article, ma'am. A lot of us were involved in putting it together."

"That's really nice of you to say, but I know, it was almost all you, Shiv," Nitya said with a smile. "You know you don't have to call me ma'am anymore."

"I think one ought to respect the person and not the position. I wanted to come by to meet the team and especially you to thank you. I know when I joined the team you must have heard a lot of things about me. I can't be sure but there may have been some sort of warning from HR as well, but you put all that aside and let me do my work."

"Yes, I did hear some things about you. But I tried to form my own opinion. What made you think about the HR letter? Not that it matters now," said Nitya with a smile.

"No, it doesn't. When I came to see you in your office the first time, in your old office, you told me that there was something you wanted to talk about. Then we started discussing other things, and then toward the end when I asked you what you wanted to speak to me about, you looked at the drawers in your cabinet before replying that there was nothing. I can only imagine that it must have been a letter of some sort from HR about me. You decided not to hand it over to me."

"You have a keen eye and wonderful memory, Shiv. All I can say is that we were lucky to have you on our team. I didn't have you for too long, only a couple of weeks, but you made a big impact. I must say that although I did get to know you thanks to our trip to Dehradun and the whole business with the riots, I couldn't get to know everything," Nitya said with a smile.

"You mean about my family?"

"Well, you left out the details."

"That's true, ma'am. I wanted to get this job on my own merit. That's why I left some things out. I am not sure if I can make you understand."

"I think I do understand, somewhat."

"Would it have made a difference had you known about my family and background?"

"Perhaps, I can't be sure. Maybe to some people. I'd like to think I'd have treated you the same."

"I think you would have."

"The signs were all there, and I didn't catch on. Paying off people to get information, being at the Gymkhana Club for a friend's birthday, the way you dressed. But what threw me off was that you lived in Old Delhi. It's funny the assumptions we make based on where people live."

"Yes, that's true, ma'am."

"But what really surprised me is when I found out about you and Madhavi."

"I didn't want to tell you. I didn't know how you would take it."

"Oh no, you certainly didn't have to. Have you been in touch with her?"

"No."

"Well, I met her after our trip to Dehradun and spoke to her a few weeks ago. The Trivedi family, especially Madhavi, have thanked you profusely for all the work that you have done in finding out the truth about Avneesh."

"Right."

"Madhavi has found a new job, a well-paying one, in a school where her son can study for free since she is a teacher there. It offers a pension and benefits."

"That's good, ma'am. That family deserves a break."

"You know Shiv, I used to be, and I think I still am an investigative reporter. I found out that the school had approached her to apply for a job. She applied, went through the interview process, and got the job. I also found that the school had received an anonymous donation from a company to hire more teachers and get more resources. It wasn't difficult to trace that the donation came from Hegde Enterprises. Are you telling me you had nothing to do with this? I haven't told any of this to Madhavi, of course. I am assuming you want to keep it that way," Nitya said with a smile.

"Yes, ma'am, I do. Hegde Enterprises is involved in some philanthropic work. I am glad I could help, but I can't take all the credit. I had solicited help from Shankar to get the school to call Madhavi. He made sure that they did and that it worked out for her."

"Well, I will be sure to thank Shankar the next time I see him as well. I am assuming he knows about you now."

"Yes, he does."

"Tell me, when we walked into the Trivedi residence on that January morning, if it hadn't been for Madhavi, would you have pursued the case as diligently?"

"I can't say for sure, but I'd like to think I would have. Maybe I wouldn't have made promises to find the truth and all. I think it's incumbent upon the press to keep digging no matter where it might lead. Don't you think?"

"Yes, certainly. Are you going to keep in touch with Madhavi?"

"No, ma'am. I think we both have different lives, and we both must find our own paths. Hers is definitely more challenging for oh so many reasons."

"Different roads?"

"More like different woods, different worlds."

"True. Are you in charge of the philanthropic arm of Hegde Enterprises?"

"Some of it, yes. I still have to get approval from the board and of course, my brother and sister. So far it has been mostly a formality. It is something I cherish."

"I am glad. Well, you were able to help Madhavi and the school, so that's great. There is no shortage of worthy causes in this country."

"That's true, ma'am. It's not lost on me that I come from an India that is very different from most of the population. I belong to a privileged, connected, and entitled part of this nation. While my failed relationships and at times, bad business decisions may impact me in some ways, it is minuscule compared to the challenges people face every day. It's incumbent upon me to do something for the better and force a change as much as I can."

"Very well said, Shiv. Something tells me that you will be good in business too."

"Oh, you obviously haven't spoken to my brother or sister lately," Shiv said with a laugh. "They'd much rather have me on a steeper learning curve, asking fewer questions, and following their directives."

"Well, they are not going to ask me for my opinion. Now, if they would have, I would have said that having managed you for two weeks I know that you are certainly a pain at times but, there's no one else I'd much rather have on my team. I'd choose you any day and every day."

"That's so nice of you to say, ma'am. Thank you. I did see that your team has grown. That's a good sign for the team and the paper. I am glad things are going well."

"Yes, we had to hire more people. We lost a good journalist a few months ago and he has been hard to replace," Nitya said with a smile. "What's this?" she asked pointing to the brown packet that Shiv had placed on the desk.

"Oh this, well, my trip to the U.S. took me to Vermont. I stayed a few days in an inn at a place called Shaftsbury. I learned from the innkeepers that there is a Robert Frost Museum there.

I didn't know, and perhaps you know better, ma'am, that he lived there in the 1920s and wrote the poems that got him the Pulitzer Prize. He is also buried there. I picked up some postcards and a book signed by him that was part of an auction to raise funds for a nearby college. His estate is now auctioning his signed books and papers to raise money for worthy causes. I managed to get this for you," Shiv said, handing over the packet to Nitya. Nitya was overwhelmed. She opened it carefully. There were a few postcards with pictures of the museum and then a copy of *New Hampshire*, a collection of poems written and signed by Robert Frost.

"Oh my God! This is such a nice gift and so very thoughtful of you. I am sure this cost you an arm and a leg."

"Not really, ma'am. Although I must say that in a place like Shaftsbury, Vermont, they were rather surprised to see an Indian bidding on this."

"It's a lovely gift, Shiv. I'm so touched. Thank you very much," said Nitya with a smile.

"I am glad you like it."

"So, what do they have you working on? What took you to Vermont? It's a bit off the beaten track for businessmen and probably even for tourists from India."

"Yes, it is. I am actually looking into the hospitality part of the business. One of the deals that my father was involved in was merging with some mid-sized budget hotels abroad and bringing the concept to smaller towns and cities in India."

"Sounds like a good idea."

"It is."

"Did it go well?"

"To some extent. I managed to make some contacts and sign a few deals that might help, but maybe not to the extent that my father would have liked had he been alive. So, somewhat successful, I'd say."

"How are things with the rest of the family?"

"It's all well, ma'am. We have always been close, and I think our dad's passing has brought us closer. Don't get me wrong, I often get admonished by my sister, who seems to have taken after my father, except for his temper. We have our differences when it comes to business decisions, but on a personal level, things are fine."

"That's good to know. I am sure you will do well. It has only been a couple of months."

"Yes, it has been a struggle, but I am learning and making mistakes, hopefully not too many."

"You will do fine."

"I am sure eventually things will work out. What I regret, though, is not making things right with my father while he was alive. He was a difficult and complicated man, but now I feel I should have made more of an effort. My brother and sister did."

"People are different."

"True, but life's too short to be bitter all the time. And I learned this the hard way. This trip gave me a chance to be with myself and think about all of that."

"Any other trips planned?"

"Not at the moment, ma'am."

"How about Delhi? Will you be coming here often?"

"Yes, I will be. It is the capital of the country, and as you well know, all businessmen must make regular trips to keep politicians of all stripes happy. I am sure I will be visiting at least once or twice a year," Shiv said, as he slowly got up.

"That's good. At least we can stay in touch."

"I'd like that. Well, I must leave now, ma'am."

"It was lovely seeing you. Do keep in touch."

"I most certainly will."

"And next time, please let me know beforehand so that we can go out with the team for coffee or dinner nearby."

"That would be great," Shiv said.

He stretched out his hand, and Nitya shook it warmly.

"You are a good man, Shiv. I wish you all the best for your future."

"Thank you, ma'am. I hope things go well for you here and wherever your journey takes you."

"Thank you."

Nitya watched Shiv turn and walk toward the end of the corridor. Just before taking the flight of stairs, he looked back and waved at her. After he left, Nitya picked up the book Shiv had left for her and started leafing through the pages. She knew many of the poems by heart. She closed it, put it back on her desk, and then opened the large window behind her desk to let some fresh air in. She looked outside at the leafy park beneath her office. She could see people enjoying the sun, and tourists strolling on the sidewalks.

She thought about Shankar and Shiv. She had grown to like and admire them. They struggled, made mistakes, had regrets, and yet persevered. They were relentless in their pursuit of finding out the truth but managed to stay true to themselves. She wondered if the professor whom she was now interested in had the same qualities. She hoped that he did. It made her smile. As she gazed outside the window and enjoyed the warm breeze on her face, she didn't realize that Kavita had walked in quietly behind her. She was startled when her sister gently tapped her shoulder. Kavita caught her smiling to herself.

"I really, really want to know what you were thinking of that made you smile like that," Kavita said mischievously.

"Ha! Wouldn't you like to know?" Nitya said, grabbed her arm with one hand, picked up her purse with the other, and walked out of the room to get a coffee.

About the Author

Aditya Banerjee grew up in India in the seventies and eighties and moved to Canada in the nineties. He is a graduate of McGill University in Montreal, Canada, and Manipal Institute of Technology in Manipal, India. He has traveled widely and is a history buff. He loves historical fiction and mystery novels. He is also the author of *Broken Dreams: A Callipur Murder Mystery* and *Stolen Legacies*. He lives with his family in Canada.

Made in the USA
Monee, IL
13 October 2021

79953883R00246